P9-CDU-423

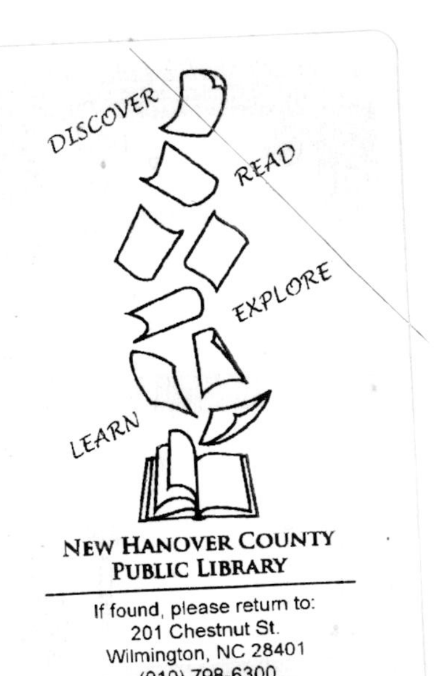
DISCOVER
READ
EXPLORE
LEARN
NEW HANOVER COUNTY
PUBLIC LIBRARY
If found, please return to:
201 Chestnut St.
Wilmington, NC 28401
(910) 798-6300
http://www.nhclibrary.org

HOW WE LEARNED TO LIE

Books by Meredith Miller

Little Wrecks

How We Learned to Lie

HOW WE LEARNED TO LIE

MEREDITH MILLER

HARPER
An Imprint of HarperCollins*Publishers*

This book is a work of fiction. Names, characters, places, and incidents are either the product of the author's imagination or are used fictitiously, and any resemblance to actual persons, living or dead, business establishments, events, or locales is entirely coincidental.

How We Learned to Lie
 For information address HarperCollins Children's Books, a division of HarperCollins Publishers, 195 Broadway, New York, NY 10007.
www.epicreads.com

Library of Congress Control Number: 2018933334
ISBN 978-0-06-247428-5 (trade bdg.)

Typography by Torborg Davern
18 19 20 21 22 PC/LSCH 10 9 8 7 6 5 4 3 2 1

First Edition

For Chrissie V and Ray F, wherever you are

WEEDY SWEETNESS

joan

THE DAY ROBBIE McNamara came and dripped blood on our front stairs, the world was still happening to other people. We were still clueless, hiding in the woods at our end of the harbor, watching the gentle tides. Before the hurricane. Before the disappearing started. Before all the violent surprises.

I was on my way across the street to call Daisy and make him come outside. To go to the McNamaras' from our house, you climb up the wooden staircase outside our front door and cross the road. Through the pine trees and up Daisy's driveway. I've been making that journey every day since I was maybe seven.

Daisy would be in his attic window watching everything, or in his room trying to make his own telephone. If his mother's car was gone, I didn't even have to knock. It was never going to be anyone but me coming through Daisy's door.

You could feel the end of summer coming. Gramps and Arthur had just replaced some rotten boards in the steps, and they stood out all yellow and full of sap against the rest of the weathered staircase. They made a different sound when my sneakers hit them. I crossed the landing halfway up without even checking under the bench to see if Daisy had left me anything. Two steps up from there I ran straight into Robbie McNamara's chest.

His hair was wet, but there was no way he'd just gotten out of the shower because, like I said, his hands had blood on them.

"Joan." He said it like I was what he came for.

His eyes kept pulling away, and he was jumping from one foot to the other and talking in little bursts.

"My brother with you?"

"No, Robbie. I was on my way to your house."

He wasn't going to back up the steps. After a minute I stepped down onto the landing and asked him what happened.

"You see this?" He held out his hands to me. "This isn't mine."

It was getting dark under the trees, and the blood was gray in the yellow street light. It wasn't dripping, but it wasn't dried up, either. Whoever it belonged to was probably still leaking. Robbie's voice was a little proud and a little crazy. He was trembling with fear or excitement, maybe both.

All I could think was *Shit, I have to get him out of here*. What if my dad came home? What if Arthur came bouncing up the stairs two at a time reciting Gramsci to himself, and came across Robbie staring at me with blood all over his hands? I leaned over the railing because I thought I might throw up onto the landing just thinking about it. A twitchy white guy showing up on your front steps covered in blood kind of does that to you.

Honest truth, at the moment I didn't really care what had happened to Robbie McNamara. I just didn't want him, my brother, and somebody's blood all on those stairs at the same time. We all know how that story ends.

The blood had gotten on the sleeves of Robbie's jacket. He had two zits on his forehead and nothing in his pockets. I saw him fish around for cigarettes or keys and look bewildered when he came up with nothing.

"Robbie, I don't understand. Maybe we should go find Daisy, huh?"

"I'm taking care of my family, Joan. I'm the man now."

Oh, God. If Robbie McNamara started thinking he was the one in charge, anything could happen. Half the time, he couldn't muster up enough focus to button his shirt the right way. He was so high he just played with the threads on his jacket and slouched onto anything that was available to hold him up. You had to hit his arm every time you wanted him to join the conversation. If my dad knew him better, I would never have been allowed over Daisy's house at all. Robbie was older than us, but the term *big brother* didn't really apply. We used to have to remind him to eat and take a shower.

"I need to talk to him, Joan. Where is he?"

"I just told you, I thought he was at your house."

"Tell him he needs to look out for my mom for a couple days."

"You're freaking me out a little, Robbie."

"Some people might be kinda mad at me. Tell Daisy don't answer the door."

"Where are you going?"

"I got business, Joan. Help me out, all right? Tell Daisy what I said."

He forgot he was standing on the stairs. When he turned around to leave he twisted his leg against the step behind him and fell sideways.

"Robbie?"

"I gotta go."

"Okay, Robbie. I think you should go inside and wash your hands though, yeah?"

He looked down at the blood and his shoulders jerked.

"Shit. Yeah." And then he bounced up the steps.

I sat down on the bench and tried to stop shaking. I forgot all about Daisy, and it was a few days before I saw him again.

Was I thinking: *This is it; the world changes right here*? Of course not, but it seems like it looking back. Everything rolled on from Robbie's bloody hands to bad angel dust and good biology teachers and people disappearing, and on into a whole string of revelations and consequences. By Christmas, people were leaking out of our lives so fast me and Daisy could hardly keep track. I spent most of last year trying to hold it all together and failing.

However I tell this, it'll just be a slice of everything. The sum total of nothing. The meaning will come from where I decide it starts and ends. So the beginning was Robbie, shaking his bloody hands at me. Me not knowing that soon he would disappear too, gone with his yellow Charger and his Kool 100's and his nervous junkie boredom. That was the moment when everything started breaking apart. I couldn't see it at the time, but it was. I was trying to get to Daisy, and Robbie got in between us, covered in blood. If this was one of my mother's plays, she'd say that was the metaphor that held it together.

Start the story with Robbie's bloody hands, and end it with mine.

Before the leaves fell and came back again, me and Daisy were left trying to figure out how to live in a world chock-full of nasty new information. Which is why I'm on this train right now, taking five million years to get home from Rockaway. Trying to put it all back together in my head. Why Daisy isn't where he's supposed to be and I have to actually think about where to find him.

The A train is still aboveground, but it's dark, and all I can see in the window is the inside of the car. It's just a mirror, throwing orange plastic and fluorescent glare back at me. I'm trying to see through that reflection to what we felt like before everything happened, but all I can see is here and now and no one sitting next to me.

joan

I FIGURE THERE are three things about last summer that need to be remembered, three things that happened before Robbie and his bloody hands. First I got a scalpel, and then I got a microscope, and finally a car crashed into the wall on Jensen Road. Plenty of other things happened too, but those are the ones that go in the story. Looking at the whole thing from both directions, I can see the devastation waiting in those little moments.

It was a hot day in August when me and Daisy went to the abandoned house and there was already somebody there. That house was ours, always empty and waiting in the trees for us. Some family walked away from it during the Depression and never came back. When we were littler we planned imaginary wars and bank heists in there. Once or twice, we snuck out and stayed there all night. We smoked our first cigarettes and drank our first bottle of Rita McNamara's booze in there.

There's a couch in the front room, but all it has is springs with some straw caught between them. Good for torture maybe, but not relaxing. There used to be an art deco floor lamp with two sockets, but we carried it home one night and Daisy rewired it. We got a red and a blue bulb at a head shop in Huntington. I guess later Daisy stuffed the lamp in his aunt's hatchback and took it away with him, because it was there in his room when I visited him today. When we came back from Rockaway Beach in the dark, he turned the bulbs on and we sat in the weird double shadows they made, trying to make sense of everything.

Trying to tell each other this story.

That day last summer, the only light in the abandoned house was a dirty square falling from the window. And there was a stranger with a limp and an old army kit bag. I guess maybe he went to Vietnam, or even some war before that. It was hard to tell how old he was.

The guy was cooking tomatoes and anchovies on a can of Sterno. He waved his fork at us like, *Come on in and have some.* I said no thanks and sat in the doorway. It was one of those days that's so hot you can't even stand your clothes pressing on your skin. I didn't want to be near an open flame.

"Eugene," the guy said. It took us a minute to realize he was introducing himself.

"Hey, I'm Daisy." He could have said Anthony. No matter how many chances Daisy has to shed that nickname, he never seems to take them. "This is my friend Joan."

"Hi." I gave the guy a little wave and offered him a cigarette.

"Eating." He bowed his head at me for thanks. A one-word-at-a-time guy.

We all went quiet. What were we supposed to say? The whole point of the abandoned house was that me and Daisy didn't have to make conversation in there. Not even with each other.

Eugene took his tomatoes and anchovies off the flame and put a forkful in his mouth before he looked up at me.

"You're the one who likes to fish."

Creepy. What was he, watching us through the trees?

"I'm not fishing. I don't eat that stuff."

"She cuts it open so she can look inside. She's weird."

"I'm not weird, Daisy. I'm a scientist. And I only cut up dead stuff."

"I'd change the subject if I were you, Eugene. Unless you want a lecture about the importance of fish guts and hard facts."

The guy didn't laugh. I liked him.

"What d'ya pull out of here?" He waved his fork at the water.

"Bluefish. Clams. Some sea bass. The other day I found a dead spider crab. That was strange, for down at this end."

"It was fucking disgusting. She took its legs off and cut its body open with a kitchen knife. Tell me that's not sick."

"Spider crabs are pelagic. They live in the deep places. How did it get down here?"

Eugene wasn't listening. He was digging around in his kit bag, his arm in there up to the shoulder and his face peering down into the dark. Finally he just dumped everything out onto the floor. There were some boxer shorts, a road atlas, two more cans of tomatoes, his sleeping bag, a bunch of newspapers, and a thermal undershirt. He pushed all that around until he found what he was looking for.

"Better than a kitchen knife." He lifted out something gray and sharp, then loosened up his arms and held his hands down by his hips.

I looked at Daisy to see what he thought, but his eyes were wide and scared, fixed on Eugene's right hand. All the sound drained out of the air around us, and the house settled and slipped another millimeter down the slope. Or maybe I just imagined that.

Then Eugene shook his head and flipped the thing around, holding it out to me by the blade. "It's a scalpel."

So right now I'm thinking, *How did he know?* How did Eugene know that scalpel was what I needed? How much it would change everything? How nine months later that very blade would tell me all the truth about myself I ever needed to know.

"You want me to take it?"

"Yeah. You wanna cut stuff up without butchering it? That's what they designed that thing for. Me, I can get by with a regular knife."

"Uh, thanks." Taking it seemed like the safest response at the time. I didn't feel any kind of premonition. I just put it in the front pocket of my backpack. "Daisy, we gotta go do that thing."

"What thing?"

"For my dad. Come on."

"I have no idea what you're talking about, Joan."

"Well, I gotta go. You coming or what?"

"Oil," Eugene said.

"Excuse me?"

"Clean it with some oil. Use tin foil."

"Oh. Thanks."

We had to jump down from the front door because the steps had rotted away long before. Every time it rained, the space underneath the front room got a little deeper. One day that house will tilt forward and fall down into the water. I pictured Eugene in his sleep, sliding across the floor and out the door, still dreaming of highways and boxcars and women in Minnesota. Or whatever it is guys like him dream about.

It was Mr. Johnson who gave me the microscope. If this was the story of someone else's life, the microscope might even be the reason last summer mattered. The year I saw the tiny world inside the world, looked at water differently, the summer I realized how much of life was invisible. I had revelations, found my vocation, buckled down and got ready to ace the Biology Regents. All those things did happen I guess, but by spring it seemed like I was in some other life, watching them happen to someone else.

Mr. Johnson comes to the church lunch every Saturday and mostly sits at a table by himself. I went there and helped all last year, because Gramps thought it was good for me. Also, it pissed my mom off, which was a bonus. Mr. Johnson was a science teacher from Brooklyn. When he retired, his kids brought him out east and put him in an old folks' home.

He saved up his *National Geographic*s for me, the ones with articles on underwater expeditions. Sometimes when I brought his coffee I'd sit down at his table and we'd talk.

"Tell me something useful, Mr. Johnson," I said to him one day.

He grabbed one of my hands and turned it over, pointed to the veins in my wrists.

"That," he said. "That's useful and it's real. These." He pointed to his own eyes, then his ears. "These are how you get your useful facts. Can't argue with the life that's in front of you, Joan."

Mr. Johnson is the only grown-up I know who actually coughed up when I asked for some real information. He understands about science, about how sometimes facts are all you can trust. No wonder his own kids stashed him somewhere they don't have to deal with him. People hate facts.

So one Saturday in August, he gave me an old microscope and some volumes of the *Encyclopedia of Animal Life*, the ones about fish. He said his kids wouldn't want those things, but he knew I'd appreciate them.

I haven't seen Mr. Johnson in months. He could be dead, for all I know. A nice normal death in his sleep. Sad because I liked him, but natural at least. You breathe out and your heart stops and someone finds you the very next morning, looking peaceful. The way death is supposed to be.

* * *

I was looking through Mr. Johnson's microscope at harbor water on a slide when I heard a car hit the wall on Jensen Road. Somebody had taken the curve too fast. Again. I got up and ran straight over to Daisy's before Gramps or Arthur could catch me and make me stay inside. I was across the road before the sirens started.

We live on a bad curve. There's always been a yellow sign, and after that day they put black-and-white arrows up, too. Every once in a while somebody ignores all that and decides to play chicken with the laws of physics.

The reassuring thing about the laws of physics is that they're immutable. That's why they call them laws. If you get the math right, the outcome is the same every time. No room for metaphors or ambiguity or what Mr. Driscoll calls "poetic excess." Speed, weight, momentum, centripetal force, surface tension, resistance. *Crash.*

Me and Daisy decided to go around into the woods and look over the wall from above. If we went along the road, people would stop us long before we saw anything.

We lifted up some blackberry vines so we could lie down, and stuck our heads out over the top of the wall. The windshield was smashed, and a lady was moaning in the driver's seat while a fireman wedged a crowbar into the door. There was blood all over the steering wheel and some on the dash. It looked like most of it had come out of her nose. I couldn't even see her mouth. There was a jagged piece of bone sticking out of her left arm.

It wasn't like looking at the inside of dead stuff. That lady was all warm blood pumping and breath moaning in and out of her lungs. It was like when you pull a fish out of the water and there's still time to throw it back in. She was going to be fine.

I started memorizing things so I could write them down. I was pretty sure *ulna* was the bone that was sticking out of her arm. I didn't know the name of the membrane that must have ruptured in her nose; I'd have to look it up later. People aren't really as interesting as fish, but how often do you get to see inside one?

Well, if you'd asked me that question twelve months ago, my answer would have been different than it is now.

I looked over to ask Daisy for a pen and he wasn't there. Then I heard him. When I turned all the way around he was standing with one hand on a birch tree, chucking up his breakfast.

I like to know things and Daisy doesn't, basically. The truth makes Daisy cover his eyes and puke. Me, I want to know how the bones inside my own arms work.

So: scalpel, microscope, wall on the curve of Jensen Road with a car crumpled into it. Robbie's bloody hands. Now the props are all in place. Enter my mother, upstage left.

"What's the matter with you, honey? You seem distracted." By which she meant, *Why aren't you paying attention to me? Why aren't I the center of attention?*

"Nothing's the matter with me."

It was the end of summer, a couple of days after Robbie showed up bleeding on our front stairs. Me and my mother were on the back porch looking out over the water, watching the shadows move across the lawns in Carter's Bay. The darkness was rising up and blotting out all the detail. I was trying to memorize the order everything disappeared in. Watching the world go away.

"Well, you could talk to me is all I'm saying."

She was right; I could. I could talk to her all day long. It wouldn't make the slightest bit of difference. Watch.

"It's just that something . . . kind of weird happened. And I haven't seen Daisy in two days."

"Maybe it's time to make new friends. You can't play in the water with Daisy McNamara your whole life." Then the first streak of purple hit the sky and she stood up. "Well, I'll have to drive back now. I've got Morgan's car, and we start rehearsals tomorrow."

My mother manages a theater in the city. None of us can compete with that.

So here is another beginning. To get to it I have to take you two years back. Picture us all at the table: me, my mother, and the house full of men we live with. Gramps was there, and even my dad. It was his day off. Both my brothers were there, too. I guess they made sure Arthur was home for dinner on the night of the big announcement. My mother looked around the table until we all fell silent.

"Something wonderful has happened," she said.

"Your mother has something to tell you." My father smiled

at her. The smile was adoring and sad, like when people look at a crucifix.

"I'm going to manage a theater company!"

Arthur was reading Ralph Ellison under the table, so Gramps wouldn't see the book and tell him off for reading at dinner. He looked up and said, "Mom, that's great."

"Isn't it? We have rented space and a budget for two years. If it works, we'll be able to extend the grant."

Everyone was looking at my mother. That's why they didn't notice the difference between the look on her face and the look on my father's. I was the only one who saw it, but I didn't know what it meant. He looked like there was a lot more inside him than usual.

"It means I'll be away sometimes."

There it was. *I'm leaving you* is what my mother was really saying. It took a couple of months for me to realize what was happening, but after that night she was gone all the time. That was the meaning of my father's sad smile. She didn't love him enough to hang around, not even until we were all the way grown-up.

What I learned that night when my family fell apart is that silence isn't just the lack of sound. It's distance. It's weight. When things get heavy, people back away. The more something matters, the less people want to talk about it.

So two years later I was on the back porch, and my mother was walking away again. I was trying to figure why Robbie McNamara had come and dripped blood in the middle of my life. I thought maybe Daisy was in trouble, and she couldn't even hang around long enough to talk to me about it.

"Can I go with you?"

"Of course not."

"Why?"

"Because of school, as you know perfectly well."

"School doesn't start for another week, Mom. What's the real reason?"

"I have work to do, Joan."

"When is everything going to go back to normal, Mom? When are you gonna be done?"

She lifted her shoulders and let out a breath while she brought them down again, looking me straight in the eye. Her dramatic training never switches off.

"I'm going now, Joanie. I'll see you soon."

Then she kissed the top of my head and walked up the stairs, through the kitchen, and away. I heard her friend Morgan's car start about half a minute later.

My mother pulled away, and I ran up into the woods. I pushed through the trees, tripped on a root in the dark and cursed, then pulled myself up onto the landing in front. Daisy had left a zip-lock baggie under the bench. Inside was a picture of a pod of whales, taken by a diver looking up from below. It looked like it was torn out of a library book. The dick.

In the picture, sunlight speared through the water like the voice of God, making the whales into silhouettes. A baby whale was tucked in between all the grown-ups. On it, Daisy had written, "You don't have to breathe water to live like this. They're mammals!" I looked at that picture and thought of whaling factory boats and the blood on Robbie's hands. I thought of the North Sea turning red and that woman's bone sticking out of her arm while she moaned in the car on Jensen Road. The whole world was full of blood, and I was the only one who wanted to look at it.

I guess Daisy meant the picture to make me feel calm and safe, like my dreams were real. But I just felt suffocated by the blanket people had thrown over my life. I wanted to push it off and start yelling about what was underneath. Right then, standing on our front stairs, I just got mad. I turned 180 degrees, switched from off to on (or vice versa, however you want to see it). Parting of the Red Sea and the Red Sea was me. I wanted to take Eugene's rusty scalpel and open up the world.

The thing is, once your questions stop being the "why is the sky blue?" kind and start to really matter, people panic. You might break the silence everybody's using to glue their lives together. People either gave me a load of pointless advice or tried to make me shut up. Like the truth was just some problem I had. Some phase I was going through. They were all trying to calm me down and shush me. Even Daisy.

I took the whale picture and climbed up to the road through the McNamaras' side yard. That's why no one saw me when Robbie pulled up in his yellow Charger and my brother Andre got out of the back seat. It was the first time I'd seen Robbie since the day he shook his bloody hands at me. He looked normal, except for the part where he had my brother in the car. They weren't exactly best friends. There was some third guy in the front passenger seat, a white guy with stubble and a jean jacket.

"Thanks, Robbie." Andre waved and turned away.

Robbie said something from inside the car that made Andre turn around and go back to the driver's-side window. He gestured at him and Andre leaned into the sound of the car stereo, blasting "Because the Night." I strained my ears, but I couldn't make out what they were saying.

After a minute, Andre straightened up and raised both of his hands. He waved them and shook his head, turned, and walked down our front steps.

Robbie pulled in to his driveway and put the car in park. He left it running while he talked fast and sort of slapped his hands on the steering wheel, nodding at the guy in the passenger seat. I moved into the shadow of one of the McNamaras' pine trees and watched. The other guy took out a wad of cash and passed it over.

Robbie sat right there in his own mother's driveway, counting out those bills on his dashboard where the whole world could see. He didn't even lean down and lay them out on the seat. Daisy's big brother had no sense of caution. He wouldn't have lasted five minutes on a nature documentary. It's a wonder he didn't get himself locked up or killed before he was thirteen.

He folded up the piles of bills and put them inside his jacket, then turned the car off and got out. I took another step back into the shadow and watched Mr. Jean Jacket light a 100. He rolled down the passenger window and let his weird air of thickheaded menace out into the night. I was sure he'd look over and see me, but he just sat there picking at the vinyl on Robbie's dashboard and flicking his ash onto the driveway. We were so close and the night was so still, I wound up inside his cloud of menthol smoke. If I'd whispered, he would have heard me.

Robbie came back and swung his Charger out the end of the driveway onto Jensen Road without stopping to look. His headlights swept the bushes and then disappeared behind the wall, heading out of Highbone toward mid-island.

I moved around to the other side of the pine tree and stayed there, thinking. The bills Robbie had were mostly fives and ones, the kind of cash kids like me and Daisy pay for joints and nickel bags. It was pretty obvious Robbie was trying to run his own business, and he was doing it right in the McNamaras' driveway. That was his idea of taking care of his family. So what did it have to do with Andre?

I stayed there while the menthol smoke and car exhaust faded into the smell of low tide coming up the hill. My heart slowed down and the purple faded out of the sky.

My mother was speeding away down the Parkway, and my brother was popping out of the back seat of Robbie's ridiculous boy-racer car. I couldn't stop my mother, so I concentrated on my brother. Andre is different from me, and we're not even that close, but that didn't mean I was ready to sign him over to Robbie fucking McNamara.

* * *

I went inside Daisy's house without knocking. It was nearly eight o'clock, and Mrs. McNamara was still on the living room couch. I said hello, but she looked right through me. One of her hands was hanging limp and the other one was tracing something invisible on the cushion next to her. She started on the wine at four o'clock, and the pills after dinner. Those dead eyes were supposed to be part of her glamour, I guess. She was supposed to be dreamy, but these days she never sharpened up at all, not even when Daisy needed her to. My mother was making me mad. Daisy's was breaking his heart, and that pissed me off even more.

Daisy was in his room, cutting up some metal with a hacksaw. I took the whale picture out of my pocket and waved it at him.

"You cut this out of a library book, didn't you? You idiot."

He ignored me. "I'm making a blue box."

"I didn't ask what you're making. I asked whether you cut up a library book."

"You didn't ask *yet*, but it's cool. Wait till you see. It can talk to the phones."

"You can talk to a phone without a box, too."

"Yeah, but this will make the phones do stuff. It can make the signals that the switching stations make. I can call anywhere for free!"

"So, it's illegal is what you're saying?"

"You're gonna think it's cool. I promise."

"Your dad's already in jail, Daisy. Your brother is Robbie McNamara. Shouldn't you maybe be the one who doesn't get locked up?"

"I can do this, Joan. This is what I'm good at. Don't worry."

"What's going on with Robbie?"

"What do you mean?"

"I mean he's getting in fights, and I think he's dealing."

"Why are you so interested in what my brother does all of a sudden?"

"Did you see him the other night? He showed up at my house looking for you. He was covered in blood, Daisy. Somebody else's blood."

Daisy went still for a minute and then went back to sawing. I looked at him, waiting it out until he paused again.

"I don't know, Joan. He's Robbie. You know."

I backed away.

"You need a mask. You're inhaling metal dust."

"It's fine. I opened the window."

"That doesn't—okay, never mind. So maybe you don't want to deal with it, but I just saw Andre get out of Robbie's car. What the hell is that about?"

"We're neighbors, Joan. It's not that weird."

"You know those two don't hang out. No one is acting normal lately."

"You're just worked up about school starting. This happens to you every year."

"Daisy, Robbie was in your driveway counting up cash with some creepy guy. What if he gets you and your mom in trouble? More trouble."

"That won't happen."

You could say that was a beginning, too. I'm pretty sure it was the first time Daisy McNamara ever lied to me. It was one of those lies that's so obvious everybody has to either pretend it's true or start fighting.

I went over to the window and leaned out so I could light a cigarette.

"I was thinking—I'm gonna call you Anthony this year, just when we're in school."

"What for?"

"Jesus, what is with the people in your family? Darwin would be amazed that any of you are still breathing. I'm not gonna call you Daisy because I don't want people bursting in and sticking your head in a toilet bowl when you're minding your own business trying to smoke a cigarette in a bathroom stall."

My best friend was the weediest little shit in Highbone. And his mother nicknamed him Daisy. He only survived because two or three people loved him.

"You're exaggerating. And I feel weird when you call me Anthony. Like you're pretending we're not friends."

"That would probably help, too."

Daisy put down his tools and looked up. "Fuck you," he said. His voice had dropped and maybe his eyes were sparkling. I don't know. It was hard to tell in that red-and-blue light.

I turned back around and waved a hand at him and his hacksaw. "All right, show me, then."

Once he started talking about multifrequency signals and A4 switching stations, his voice changed back. It went up an octave and his breath kept running out before his ideas were finished. The end of every sentence was a whisper.

It didn't matter about inward operators and switching systems, but I guess it was comforting. Or maybe just easy. Daisy's sentences all run on and have no borders. One thought just blends into another with him. He's always derailing my logic. Maybe right then it was a relief.

My whole life, when I needed to figure something out, I just ran across the road and let my mind wander while I listened to Daisy.

The year we were ten we tried the thing with paper cups and strings. It only worked when Daisy lay down in the dormer window in his attic and I came all the way up to the bench in the outside stairs. From that distance we could practically hear each other anyway. But I could hear his voice in the cup, too. "Tedium. Telepathy. Transistor. Trunkfish."

"Put away the dictionary, Daisy."

"Come over. *The Great Barrier Reef*'s on TV in five minutes."

Shouting from the window, running across the road to watch TV, seeing the same tide come and go from our bedroom windows. We were never farther away than that in our whole lives. What happens when he's too far away to hear me?

Last year the cracks in our world got so big we couldn't reach across them anymore.

Tonight, I took the subway, because Daisy lives all the way out over the water now. Different water. I went on the shuttle to Broad

Channel and got on the A train back to Penn Station. It took an hour and a half. Now I have twenty minutes until the Huntington train, so I sit down with my back against a brick pillar on the concourse. Penn Station smells like dust trapped in fryer grease. Like hot dogs and rats and diesel. Businessmen keep looking for my crumpled coffee cup, and an old white lady asks me if I'm okay. I just look at her, because I can't answer that.

daisy

THERE ARE THIRTY seconds of my life I would keep. If I had to give everything up, if I was only allowed to hang on to one moment, I know exactly which one it would be. Me and Joan, floating on our backs with the tops of our heads together, breathing in the chemical burn of a stranger's swimming pool. Our arms are stretched up so we can hold hands. We have to stay completely still and fill our lungs with air or we'll start to sink and have to let go. The blinding security light on the back of the house goes out, the stars appear, and we don't need to say anything.

It's all there in that moment. My whole world.

We went pool hopping one last time before school started and everybody drained their pools. Soon we'd have to take our little boat in, scrub the bottom, and put it under Joan's back porch for the winter.

We rowed into a little cove around behind the empty place in the pit where the firemen's fair sets up. There was a field full of gravel between us and all the rich people's houses. A few breeze blocks were still scattered around, and a torn piece of tarp was flapping in the wind from Connecticut. We went in and wedged the boat behind a rock so it wouldn't get pulled out. A bird went fluttering up past us and I jumped.

"Shit! What was that?"

"Night heron," Joan said. "Shh."

We piled in the oars and put our loose change and cigarettes in the coffee tin Arthur had nailed to the crossbeam the year before. I turned out toward the Sound and looked into twenty miles of empty nothing. No boats and no moon, so I couldn't see the waves. Sharp pieces of shale dug into our feet when we scrambled out of the water and up onto the fairground.

We crossed the empty field and slipped through some blue hydrangeas into a backyard on Marine Street. The security light caught us moving and lit up the pool like a baseball field for a night game, but the windows at the back of the house stayed dark. We stripped down to our bathing suits and slid into the blinding glare between us and the stars. The floodlight blotted out the sky, and the water was empty underneath us.

Joan rolled over and her feet slipped under the surface almost without a sound. I watched the ripples where the water closed over her toes and saw her outline blur into the pale blue light. When she touched bottom, I started counting. I got to a hundred and fifty but I didn't panic. She's Joan. I'm used to her doing things that make me hold my breath and pray. It's the same with my mom. And Robbie. Everyone at the school bus stop. Sometimes I think I spent my whole childhood afraid to breathe out.

When I got to two hundred Mississippis, Joan came to the surface next to me and shook the water out of her hair.

"Why does anything live on dry land?" she said. "Why crawl up into a world where you can't breathe and your muscles aren't designed for the specific gravity? Why couldn't we develop brains and keep the gills?"

"Because we're trying to get to the stars."

"We can't live in the stars. We're designed for the exact conditions of this planet. That's how evolution works."

"But we have brains, Joan. Remember what Mr. Kasven said in sixth grade? Thumbs and brains are what make us different. Trying to get to the stars is a side effect of having brains. They make us want things."

"Yeah, like built-in pools full of dead water." She rolled over and exhaled. I watched the bubbles drift up from her mouth and burst around her until she came back up again. "Perfectly clear, completely toxic environment," she said. "Not even a microbe could survive in here. People do this to water on purpose. What the hell?"

I kicked away from her and swam backward to the deep end, using my arms like I was making snow angels.

She got out and climbed up onto the diving board. I lay on

my back while she arced over me into the water, then swam over to one of the pumps. She held her hands out and let it push her toward me.

When she bumped the top of her head against mine, I said, "You want to know where your mother stays in the city?"

"No. I don't know, maybe."

"I can find out."

"What are you, the FBI? You've got enough to worry about at your house, anyway."

"It's not even a thing, Joan. I can do it in five minutes, on the phone."

"Stop moving your arms, Daisy."

We held hands and put our heads together then. We didn't need to think about it; we'd been lying on the water together like that our whole lives. If we did it just right, there was nothing in the world but sky and the little waves at the edges of our vision.

Here comes the moment I will keep. Years from now, when everything is over and I leave my body behind, I will take this one thing with me.

We went still and started counting in whispers. When we got to seventeen, the floodlight went out and the stars came back and captured us. We didn't need to laugh or poke each other or point at the sky. Something carried thoughts between us, but it wasn't sound or language. We didn't need to look in each other's eyes. Was it electricity? Telepathy? Maybe just memory. Habit.

And then Joan's hand in mine felt different. A wave went through me and I could feel all the blood moving inside. My lungs stopped working and then started again with a gasp. There was either something new or something I'd never noticed before. I held perfectly still, because if I moved a finger or said a word I might break the circuit. I might let whatever was traveling between our arms loose. In my body it felt like fear, but I knew that wasn't what it was.

Don't get me wrong. I'm not trying to make this a love story, but it is a story about love. Whatever we had, it was golden. Right then it was still there and still whole, but something was changing inside us. We were about to burn it all and scatter the ashes, like millionaires showing off with hundred-dollar bills.

Now we're broke. Broken.

So I'm looking back from here at that night when I was happy. I think Joan was, too. We were at the top of a curve—the force of the turning earth was about to tip us down. But all I could feel right then was the rising and the rushing and the moving through the starry, watery world.

Then a screen door slammed and a man shouted, "Hey, you!"

We floundered to the edge of the pool and splashed out. I think I yelled "Shit!" which really wasn't helpful. The guy was standing on his back porch in boxers and a pin-striped bathrobe. He was in perfect country club shape, with hair on his chest and a clean-shaven face. We fumbled for our clothes and ran out through the hydrangeas.

He shouted, "I called the police!" after us, but that was probably a lie. If he'd really thought we were dangerous, he wouldn't have stopped for his slippers on his way out to yell at us.

We ran across a stretch of sod and behind a stockade fence, lighting up all the backyard security lights we passed.

"Joan. The boat!"

"We'll go back later." She was leading the way out of the pit. There was only one road up the hill, so she dove into the dark alongside it, waiting to see if anyone was coming.

I fell down next to her, out of breath and missing my shorts. The moon was coming up behind the LILCO stacks, making the stars disappear in the east. It hadn't rained in days, and the dirt was dry and dusty in between the weeds at the roadside. I put on my T-shirt and started to tie my sneakers.

"I can't walk home in my bathing suit, Joan."

"You can so. It's basically shorts, anyway. Come on!" She dashed out onto the road and headed up. "We'll cut through the woods, just in case."

So we went down the ridge behind Main Street, catching our breath and shivering into the air blowing from the harbor. After the pool water dried off me, my legs were covered in yellow dirt from the pit, and my T-shirt was filthy.

Once you pass behind Davis Marine, you can hear the music and the voices from Flannagan's and know when to turn toward Jensen Road. Me and Joan could find our way through Highbone blindfolded and never miss a step.

At the top of the hill we saw the light. Someone had a fire going by the ruined church. Without even thinking, we turned to go around. It would just be some partiers, spending the night getting drunk and stoned in the woods. Probably spooking each other out with stories about the ghosts and witches that were supposed to gather at the church. Whoever it was, we didn't want to run into them in the woods at night.

Someone stood up and walked toward us. I saw the silhouette against the fire, and Joan shoved me behind a tree. Whoever it was, they were stumbling into the dark for a piss. They were just a shadow and the sound of piss hitting the leaves, but while we waited my eyes adjusted to the firelight and I saw the rest of them. Patrick Jervis, Matt McBride, and some guy I'd never seen before sitting there. The shadow, not twenty feet from us, zipped up its jeans and went back.

We headed home through the trees and never gave it a second thought. We were still laughing about the guy in the pit, thinking when we'd go back for the boat and whether someone else would find it first. I followed Joan through the trees and tried not to think about whatever I'd felt in the pool.

Now I'm wondering about what we saw in the woods, of course. Wondering whose face we didn't see that night. Trying to fit it in with everything those kids did later. That might have been the night they first crossed the line. Right then, maybe they were sitting around that fire coaxing each other into a world of chaos and violence. We'll never know.

We climbed to the top of the hill and looked down on Jensen Road.

Imagine it from high up, at night. There is my roof, and then the Harrises', and then the water, sparkling if there's a moon. Carter's

Bay is a stretch of lights across a pool of darkness. There might be the beams of headlights, traveling the road in a circle around the water, the trees lighting up and then disappearing again. You could see the leaves on the slope below Jensen Road because they show up as shadows against the light from Arthur's bedroom. You could see the road between our houses, flat sodium yellow in the summer night.

That was the size of our world. You could take it in with one look. The water came and went, we swam and rowed around in it. We let the screen doors slam behind us while we ran in and out of each other's houses. We lay in the abandoned house and said nothing, blowing smoke into the rafters for whole afternoons at a time. That was enough.

It didn't look any different that night, but all the invisible changes were already working their way to the surface.

daisy

MOST OF LAST summer was like always. I'd spend the whole day with Joan, riffling through things in the abandoned house and watching her unpick the messy guts of bivalves, talking to Arthur, and sitting with the quiet lady who always came to the floating dock at low tide. There was a car crash on Jensen Road, but even that was pretty normal. Every day at sunset, I'd go inside to sit at the dinner table, breathing in lemon Pledge and mothballs, watching my mother drift and sparkle.

The day of the accident was heavy and hot. One look at the wreck made me sick, but Joan just peered down over the wall at the carnage, taking notes. I told her she was a freak, and she said she was a scientist. Then we had to go inside so she could look stuff up in the encyclopedia, on those pages where you can lift up the transparent overlays and see what's inside you. After that, we rowed the boat out and lay in the bottom until we had to go in for dinner.

"Daisy? Robbie? Wash your hands and sit down, you two."

Mom stood behind the table with a white wine spritzer.

"My hands are clean," Robbie said. "I just washed 'em."

"Do it again. Make your mother happy."

I looked through her fingers at the little bubbles in the glass and through the liner at her eyes. Everything about her was shining through the cracks, and it made me happy to see it.

Robbie disappeared for ten minutes. I helped my mother fold napkins and pretend Robbie wasn't taking too long in the bathroom. We lined up silverware while I thought about him in there, leaning against the orange plaid wallpaper with his lighter turned all the way up. Turning powders into liquid, turning the world into something he could handle. I lay the knives on napkins and thought about the chrome fixtures shining in the bathroom.

My mother was really into table settings. She forgot other stuff, but the knives were all to the right of the plates and there were two kinds of glasses, even though me and Robbie only used one. When we finished setting the table, she would stand with her hands on the back of a chair, breathe out, and smile like a president's wife. Quivering with control.

Robbie came back from the bathroom, sat in front of his perfect table setting, and started pouring the salt and pepper out onto the table and playing with it. I guess Mom was high too, but that was legal.

"Can Joan come over and watch TV later?"

"Can Joan watch TV?" Robbie said.

"It's a school night, Daisy."

"School doesn't start for another week and a half, Mom."

"It's not a school night." That was Robbie's way of joining the conversation. He borrowed pieces from us and then gave them straight back.

"Where is that mother of hers all the time, anyway?" Mom said.

"She stays in the city for her work. She writes plays."

"She writes plays," Robbie said. "She famous?"

"I don't think so. Maybe if you're into it you'd know who she is. She's in the city a lot, but they're not divorced."

"Sad, isn't it? Children in an unstable situation like that."

"Dad's in the pen, Mom. Pretty sure that beats the Harrises for instability."

Then I felt guilty because she looked like I'd slapped her. My mother wasn't made for the sharp edges of life. That's what the pills were for, a little bit of padding between her and reality.

She got lost somewhere during the quiche. I looked at her and she was staring out the front door with both hands gripping the edge of the table. Her lips were moving but I couldn't tell what they were saying.

"Robbie?" I said while Mom was distracted. "What happened the other night? You got in a fight?"

"Other night?"

"Joan saw you. She said you were hurt."

"I was just taking care of business, Daisy. Don't worry about it." He picked up his glass and tilted it toward his mouth, then realized there was nothing in it.

Joan was right. He was changing. I knew he was up to something, and I knew him, which means I knew that whatever it was he wouldn't be able to handle it. But whatever was at that dinner table, however fucked-up it was, it was mine. I had to protect it. Even from Joan.

"Not for you to worry about, kiddo," he said, and Mom woke up.

"You and Joan can watch TV until nine. It's a school night. You need to be in bed early."

"It's not a school night, Mom."

"What are you gonna watch?" Robbie was corralling his field of salt and pepper by lifting up the corner of the tablecloth.

"Huh?"

"TV," Robbie said. "What?"

"A *Jacques Cousteau* repeat. We can't watch it at Joan's. Andre always wants to watch *The Waltons*."

"The Waltons," Robbie said.

I laughed out loud. It was just something about Robbie droning "The Waltons" while him and my mom were nodding their separate nods at our kitchen table that had too much silverware, not enough food, and a serious overabundance of opiates. All I could think was, *Wait until I tell Joan*.

Robbie lifted the corner of the tablecloth all the way up and knocked over the empty glass I wasn't using. Mom reached out to set it back up, exactly two inches above the knife I wasn't using either.

I heard Robbie's bedroom door slam while I was loading the dishwasher. Upstairs in my room, the red-and-blue lamp was casting its double shadows onto my bed and my work table. Through the open window I could hear the murmuring of the crowd on the deck behind the Narragansett.

I switched on the overhead light and looked in the mirror, imagining the size of Robbie into the air around me. Would I ever take up that much room in the world? I kept waiting for my body to catch up with his, the way everyone promised it would. I was nearly sixteen, and I only shaved once a month. You could still see all the blue veins through my skin, and my arms were so ridiculous in short sleeves that I mostly wore football shirts. I squinted at my reflection and watched myself disappear into the room behind me.

A strong wind could blow you away, isn't that what people say? I felt like a strong light could erase me. A strong wave could pull my feet out from under me, carry me out into the deep where no one could reach me. I was so pale and insubstantial, any minute something would come along and push me out of the world.

Joan knocked at about seven thirty. We went up and sat in the attic to catch the last of the thick orange sunlight in our eyes. I swung the little round window frame open so we could smoke. Then I did an imitation of Mom and Robbie at dinner and droned out "The Waltons" in Robbie's wasted voice. Joan fell over backward on the attic floorboards and laughed so hard she had to wave her hands around, trying to catch her breath.

That was it, all I wanted. When I hear her laugh, something lets go inside me. My shoulders come down and my breath gets easier.

"Is that lady gonna be okay, Joan?"

"What lady?"

"The one who smashed into the freaking wall! The one who almost died ten feet from us today."

"Yes, you wimp. If you weren't so busy puking you'd know she was fine. She didn't almost die. She could have done that to herself falling off a bicycle."

"It looked bad."

"Everything looks worse to you because you turn your face away and let your imagination take over."

"I know, I know. 'Facts, Daisy. Evidence.' You told me already like four million times."

"And it still hasn't sunk in. You're impervious to logic, man."

"Logic is your job."

"I want to go to the Museum of Natural History," she said. "Wanna come with me?"

"To the city? Yep."

"You're right. I need to see where my mother goes. It might be weird."

"I am with you through all weirdness, Joan Harris. I am the companion of your strange."

"You *are* the strange. Also, I don't exactly know where she stays."

"Ask them." I pointed to her house, sitting bare in between the trees, and thought about the warmth inside. The people at the table, thinking and talking about things that mattered.

"They won't tell me. I think they're afraid I'll run away."

"Why would *you* run away?" I pointed out the window. "Look where you live."

"Yeah, that's my house. Full of nothing but boys and dead people's stuff. Even my mother ran away."

"If it weren't for me, Joan, you wouldn't appreciate the beauty of your life at all. Do you realize that?"

"You spend your spare time playing with pay phones, Daisy. It's not like you're van Gogh or something."

"The telephone system is beautiful, Joan. You just won't let me explain."

She stared out at the darkness leaking onto the driveway from under the trees.

"Okay," she said, "go ahead and tell me one beautiful thing about telephones."

"I explained this to you already! The phones are all connected."

"Well, yeah, Daisy. That's kind of the point."

"No. I mean they can talk to each other, kind of without us. Different beeps make them do stuff. Some guys have figured it all out. The whole world is on an electrical network, just like the nerves in your body. If you know the pattern, you can control it.

We can call Venezuela for free."

"You don't know anyone in Venezuela."

"See? You think I'm the one who doesn't get stuff. You want to know where your mother goes? You can leave that one to me."

"So you keep saying. How the hell are you gonna find out, Secret Agent Man?"

"I could be a secret agent. How would you know?"

"You got the smarts, but you'd never pass the physical."

"Go ahead, make fun of me. You'll see, Harris."

I looked out the window and pretended we were alone in the world. No Robbie and not one mother between us. Nothing but me and Joan and the last of the sunlight, stretching all the way from Newton to Montauk.

We went back down and watched *Jacques Cousteau* on channel thirteen. My mom and Robbie were upstairs behind their separate doors. I made popcorn and got my grandmother's crocheted afghan out of my room. Mom wouldn't let me keep it in the living room because it didn't match. We got under it and watched an octopus change colors while Joan took more notes.

"Okay, that is beautiful," she said. "Happy?"

"Yes."

And I was.

Joan's grandfather called to tell her to come home, and I watched her cross the road and disappear down the wooden stairs. I stood with the front door open, feeling the invisible string between us pull everything tighter inside me again. My breath got shorter and my shoulders tensed up. A little of the brightness leached out of the world, but I was so used to that I barely noticed.

That happens every time Joan walks away from me.

That night, I did see Ray. I don't have to wonder or guess or try to read between my memories to see whether it was him pissing in the dark under the trees. I know. Right after Joan disappeared down her front stairs, Ray came walking around the curve of Jensen Road.

"Hey, Daisy." Then he just stood there in the middle of the driveway.

I can see him, with all his flesh on his bones and the blood pumping under his skin, holding him up. With the water still in his eyes and the breath still moving through his lungs. Whatever it is that makes people alive and real, it was there inside Ray that night, but I didn't even stop to notice it. We never do, do we?

"What's up, Ray?"

"Uh, I came to see your brother. I'm supposed to meet him here."

I leaned in and yelled up for Robbie. He came down the stairs, sliding one shoulder along the wall and pushing his hair out of his eyes. At the front door he turned around and looked up at me.

"Stay inside, man."

I guess I would have told Joan, eventually. It would have come out in the normal course of things that Ray and Robbie were hanging out. If things had stayed whole, if we'd remained who we were and the world made some kind of sense.

But they didn't and we didn't and now I'm in Rockaway, a hundred miles from the only place that will ever feel like home to me. Me and my aunt Regina try to be polite, smiling like seeing each other in the kitchen and on the stairs is normal. Like anything is normal anymore.

daisy

ONE NIGHT AT the end of summer, we rowed out into the harbor, just to get away from the streetlights, the stereos, and the older brothers. Just for some silence. The water rippled up and then lay flat behind us as we went, familiar and then invisible. We were tracing that pattern for the last time, but we didn't know it.

When we pushed the boat out that night, every move we made dovetailed, like it always had. I lay in the bottom and looked at Joan's face against the sky while she rowed us over to Carter's Bay. I looked at her arms rowing and her feet sticking out of her rolled-up jeans. From where I was looking, there was nothing but us, me and Joan and water and sky. I could feel the breeze coming from the harbor mouth, the lights on one side and the darker darkness of the woods past Carter's Bay on the other. The arms of the world closing around us felt warm and safe.

Joan shipped the oars and pulled us in behind a willow root. I looked at her face with the constellations behind it, while she stretched out her arms and blew cigarette smoke at the stars.

"I don't get the bear thing," I said. "Or the archer thing, either. Seven Sisters, okay, it's a metaphor or whatever, but no way that's a bear."

"Symbol," Joan said.

"What?"

"It's not a metaphor; it's a symbol. They're gonna ask you this on the English Regents. Get it straight. You can forget it later. Anyway, the Greeks could see loads more stars, before there were cities full of electricity and neon and crap. Stuff was probably more filled in."

"That's totally a boat. Look. See the prow and the oar sticking out?"

"You gonna take your turn and row us back, or are we going to stay here all night contemplating outer space?"

"It isn't outer space right now, Joan. It's a blanket for dreams. It's a mirror. Look, there we are, reflected in the sky."

She sighed and sat back in that way she does, waiting for me to catch up.

"I'm doing an essential job here," I said. "I'm adding the beauty to this experience."

I lit a cigarette too, then stretched my legs out into the warm small place between us. I thought about the world underneath the boat, the one Joan loved more than this one. The weird grace and the lungs that pumped water instead of air, gills and fins and moving by resistance. Joan reached a hand down and trailed it in the water, resting her head on the side of the boat. Things were jumping and falling back to the harbor with little splashes. We heard the owl that lives over by the quiet lady's house. That was all the noise we needed.

"Okay, all right." I pulled myself up and put the oars in the oarlocks, then took us across and under our own trees.

I rowed around to Main Street and into a place by the floating dock. Joan jumped out and tied us up, and we climbed up to the wooden playground. We looked through the gaps between the pillars, watching Highbone like a TV with the sound turned down at a party. A cop pulled up to the huddle of homeless guys standing around the bench by the harbor, gave them some halfhearted hassle, and went into the Harpoon for his free coffee. Robbie was behind the bandstand, but I was hoping Joan wouldn't notice.

I pointed down at the top of the sewage pipe half full of water, trying to distract her. "A kid got lost in there."

"What?"

"That kid who went missing last May. He walked in there at low tide and nobody knew where he went."

"Daisy, isn't that your brother?"

Robbie was holding both of his hands down and loose, squaring up to some guy in a jean jacket. The other guy was backed against the railing, shouting. The sound didn't carry to us. It was just body language.

"Robbie has a knife!"

"You can't see that from here, Joan."

"You can! He's standing just like that guy."

"What guy?"

"The guy with the scalpel. Eugene. Robbie carries a knife now? What the hell?"

"You know he wouldn't hurt anybody. Get a grip, Joan. He's too high all the time to be threatening."

"So why does he come home with freaking blood on his hands? And who's the little girl?"

The girl was sitting on the grass watching Robbie, with a pocketbook on the ground next to her and a cigarette in her hand. She looked like a kid, but she moved like a grown-up.

"I don't know, Joan. Why are you yelling at me about it? What am I supposed to do?"

"Okay, so you don't care about me or Andre. Fine. What about yourself? Robbie's dealing in your driveway. Also he's totally incompetent, so he's guaranteed to get in major trouble. You'll be in the middle of it."

"I do care about you! And Andre. Guys around here do all kinds of shit. You know that. What do you want me to do, go break it up?"

"No, Daisy. I want you to talk to me. When did you start lying?"

"I'm not lying!" But I was. "I'm sorry he freaked you out Joan, but it was just a bar fight." A lie of omission. Those were the kind we started with.

"He didn't freak me out. You're freaking me out. You're lying, and it scares me, Daisy. At least talk to him," she said. "Or your mother. You need to tell her about it."

"My mother has enough to worry about."

"Your mother should be worrying about *you*, Daisy. But she can't because she's too out of it. She has a problem."

"You don't understand. She's sad. She's sort of . . . breakable."

"So are you! She's the mother. Why are you the one protecting everybody?"

I looked out at the water and away at the stars because I couldn't look at her right then.

"Because I have to." I whispered it at the sky.

"Well, I'm supposed to be your best friend. So let me help."

That was maybe the first time Joan ever came close to saying she cared about me, and I was paralyzed. I didn't answer because I couldn't. I was caught in a trap made out of all the people I loved.

"We both know it isn't *my* mother you're pissed off at. So stop taking it out on me."

I shouldn't have said that. Neither of us should have said any of it.

"Fine!" Joan kicked the sand and ducked out from under the playground. "You don't want to know. You don't want to tell me anything? I'll find out myself."

And she walked away.

Listen, we went home to bed every night. At school we took different classes. But most nights we snuck out again, and in between every class we met in the commons. She walked away from me every day, but she'd never done it on purpose before. Not because she was so fed up she couldn't stand to be next to me. I looked through the pillars in the wooden playground, watching her get smaller and trying to keep on breathing, to stay standing up.

Then some guys blocked my view, walking through the park singing and pushing each other. For a minute I couldn't see Joan, then when I looked again she was sitting next to that ageless girl on the grass.

So, I wasn't really looking at those guys between us. I was trying to see around them to Joan. If I close my eyes right now, I can picture them walking up the path to the bandstand. One of them is Ray Velker, moving under the trees and passing a cigarette to the guy next to him. I can see his crappy haircut and the hole in the ass of his jeans. I can see the skinny arms coming out of his T-shirt sleeves. But I might be making it all up. He might not have been there at all.

Ray Velker keeps appearing in all my pictures of the past. Every time I try to think about last year, about the park or the football field or metal shop class, Ray walks like a ghost through my memories.

The truth is, I don't know if he was there that night, because at the time I wouldn't have noticed one way or the other. I wouldn't have cared. Ray Velker wasn't important until later. Now he's the meaning of us.

* * *

From my new bedroom in Rockaway I can't see the water at all, just two half-deflated gas storage tanks and a bunch of houses exactly like this one. Rockaway is made of straight lines and sky, more windows than trees. At night the world is just squares of yellow light with tunnels of darkness between them. This neighborhood stretches like a giant circuit board from the sea to the channel. It winks back at me with a thousand emotionless eyes.

Right now, Joan is on a train somewhere, moving away from me. I'm trying to piece together the story of how there came to be a hundred miles of Long Island between us. I went away from Highbone one day at low tide, and I'm still waiting for the water to flood in and bring the world back to me.

joan

I LOOKED OVER at Daisy, slouched into a dark corner under the wooden playground. In the street light coming through the gaps, all I could see was one stripe of pale skin. One eye and a wisp of Daisy hair. One earring, which was all he had anyway. I turned my back and walked away.

I wasn't walking away from Daisy; I was trying to get back to him. I was walking away from the sight of him lying to me, pretending he didn't care about what was right in front of us. It scared me and I wanted to fix it, like when they rebreak your arm so they can set the bone right. That was pretty much how it felt, too. Like I told you, Daisy didn't have the stomach for it. It was going to be up to me.

Two years of my mother pretending she hadn't left us, and

now Daisy was lying too. Both of our families were scattered around in broken pieces, and nobody would even look at the mess. I couldn't breathe the air anymore, there was so much deception pressing in on me, so much fury inside. I let the anger hold me up while I put one foot in front of the other and walked away.

By the time I got to the bandstand the shouting had stopped, and Robbie was slouched against the railing next to the other guy. I sat down on the grass by the stranger girl and said hello.

"I'm Joan," I said.

"I thought everybody here was white," she said. Her voice sounded like she came from a house where everybody spoke Spanish. She had blond hair and black eyes.

I pointed at myself and then gave her a little wave. "Here I am. You gonna tell me your name?"

"Teresa." She held out a Marlboro Menthol.

"No, thanks. You a friend of Robbie's?"

"I know him from the Lagoon. He's really nice. The only one who's nice to me."

I guess I was staring. She could have been eighteen from the shape of her, but if she was, she was the tiniest eighteen-year-old I'd ever seen.

"I don't dance!" She laughed. "I clean there, with my cousin."

"You want to take a walk?" I pointed at the rocks along the water. They're full of rats, but at least you can't see Main Street from there.

Teresa held up one foot. She had on four-inch heels.

"How about the pier, then?" I stood and gave her a hand up. "What was Robbie fighting about?"

She walked in those heels like they were sneakers. I'd never seen a woman with balance like that before. My mother thought heels were absurd, but Teresa made them look like the only thing a woman should ever wear. Her toenails were painted electric blue.

"That guy tried to touch me. Robbie said he had to ask first."

"Wow. Robbie McNamara defending your right to your own body. Who'd have thought it?"

She laughed again. Seemed like everything I said was funny to her. "Not ask *me*! Ask him."

"You're going out with Robbie?"

"I don't know. Maybe. He's nice to me. He says we can help each other out."

I couldn't figure out whether Teresa was a ditz or really impressive. She was just this tiny girl who laughed all the time and walked like she was on a tightrope, but she seemed to be looking right through me too. I liked her right away, so of course I wanted to get her away from Robbie.

Maybe it was none of my business. Maybe I should have stopped right there and let her stay in the park with them. Let that creepy little ecosystem behind the bandstand find its own balance.

"You live in this town?" Her steps made little *thunks* on the pier.

"Yep."

She looked around at the boats and the houses in Carter's Bay.

"It's so pretty!"

"Don't be fooled. People here suck."

"You don't like it?" She looked at me like I was an idiot. "Maybe you should try living somewhere else for a while."

"Never happen. Our family has been in our house forever. My gramps says we've been here longer than most of the trees and the white people."

Of course she laughed again, right on cue, then she waved at the houses on Baywater Avenue. "How can you not like it?"

"It used to be cool. It used to be our own little world, at least that part." I pointed at the water. "Lately, everything's upside down and everyone's pretending it isn't."

"You're mad about something!" She said like she'd just turned the channel to a really exciting TV show.

"My best friend is turning into a dick."

I sat down and put my legs under the railing so I could swing them out over the water.

"Why?"

"I don't know. He just is. He's Robbie's little brother."

"Oh! You know Robbie?"

"Mostly I know his little brother. Well, I thought I did until lately. He's supposed to be my best friend."

"Sometimes when you're mad it seems like you lost people, but later you find out you didn't. It might be okay tomorrow, or in a few days, right?"

"Right. I guess. Where do you live?"

"Hicksville. Robbie said if I came down here with him he'd drive me home."

"Look, it's none of my business, but I don't think you should hang around with him."

She leaned against the railing and swung both of her feet out over the water. "You think I'm dumb."

"No! It's just— I've known Robbie my whole life. He's not as nice as you think he is."

"Well, my cousin said he was okay. And I don't have a way to get home. My mother will kill me if I stay out all night. She thinks I'm at work."

I stood up. "Come with me. My brother can give you a ride."

"I don't even know you. How do I know you're not lying about him just to lure me away to your evil den?"

"You don't know this yet, but I am the only person in this town who doesn't lie."

"How old is your brother? Is he cute?"

"I don't know because I'm not a weird pervert. He's smart, though."

"With glasses? Like a Poindexter? I like that—it's sweet."

"Nope. Sorry. Arthur's got twenty-twenty vision. And he's kind of the only cool one in our family. Definitely not a Poindexter."

She snapped her fingers like *aw shucks,* and laughed. Again.

"You coming, or what? He won't mind. He loves driving around. He says cars and trains are America's poetry."

* * *

Arthur did mind, but he was too polite to say so in front of Teresa. I was counting on that. I took her down the Abbates' stairs and around under Arthur's window. He leaned out and said, "Joan. Who's your friend?"

"Hi. I'm Teresa." She swayed back and forth like a Disney princess, I swear. Or maybe she was just trying to balance in the mud on those heels.

"We need a ride, Arthur. Teresa lives in Hicksville, and she doesn't have a way home."

He just stared down from the window, doing a perfect imitation of Gramps's disapproving face.

"It's an emergency. Otherwise I wouldn't ask you. I told Teresa you were way chivalrous."

"You're cool, that's what she said. I'm sorry we're bothering you. I got kind of stuck." No laugh. All of a sudden, Teresa was deadly serious.

When we got to Arthur's car, she jumped straight in the front seat, then scooted over next to Arthur so I could squeeze in. I got in the back.

"Oh, you drive a stick," she said. "Nice!"

We drove the turnpike to Hicksville, stopping at every light. For a while I tried to make conversation, but Arthur wasn't saying much, and Teresa was busy trying to get him to. No one was paying attention to me. The only people out were truckers and kids cruising. All the nice suburbanites were tucked in at home, pretending people like us three didn't exist.

Teresa lived in an apartment building behind Hicksville station. It was a hot night and there were people outside with radios, eating ices. Blondie was competing with Maria Bethânia on two different radios, except I didn't know it was Maria Bethânia until Mrs. Maia told me later. There are all kinds of music in the air of Long Island, traveling the radio waves right through us, and we don't even feel it.

When she got out of the car, Teresa leaned in the back window to say goodbye.

"Thanks for helping me," she said. She looked at me like she knew what I thought and I was wrong about it, but she didn't care. It was just the thing that happened and she'd gone with it, but she would have gone with whatever else, too.

"Now I'll help you," she said. "Don't give up your friend unless you really have to. Hang on to that shit. You never know when you'll need it, right?"

"If you were my friend, I definitely would." We both laughed together then.

Someone shouted something I didn't understand down from the balcony. Teresa raised a hand and stood up. She said thank you to Arthur and went up the outside stairs.

I figured I'd never see her again.

We took the LIE back. Arthur waited until we were pulling up the ramp before he said, "You gonna explain that?"

"She works at the Lagoon."

"Well, yeah, I got that."

"Are you judging the working people, Arthur Harris? I'll tell your sociology professor."

"I'm not judging. But I'm not romanticizing, either."

"For your information she's not a dancer, Mr. Morality."

"I'm not moralizing. Work is work. Everybody is alienated. For women, it's from their own bodies."

"Don't start with your commie shit. She was hanging out with Robbie McNamara. I wanted to get her out of there."

"Joan, you can't rescue every fuck-up you meet. All you'll do is get yourself in trouble."

"How do you know she's a fuck-up? You *are* moralizing, you hypocrite. I like Teresa. I just thought I should let her know what Robbie's like. Something's going on with him, and Daisy won't talk to me about it."

"When Mom says you should make some friends besides Daisy, I don't think this is what she has in mind."

"If Mom wants to tell me what to do, she should try being around more."

"She has work."

"What, all night long? She doesn't work in the city, Arthur. She lives there."

"She does not. The theater is just there. She's doing important things, Joan."

I lay down in the back seat then, exhausted. My brain couldn't contain another pointless conversation. There was nowhere honest to turn anymore. Nowhere clean.

The Expressway is made of cement slabs, not asphalt. Every

few yards there's a seam where they meet and the wheels clomp over it. *Ta dunk, ta dunk, ta dunk,* all the way to the Highbone exit. When I was little, my dad's friend Howard Earle told me that was the sound of horses' hooves. That was what people meant when they said horsepower. That's Howard's version of funny.

I guess I fell asleep, because when Arthur pulled onto Meadowlark Road I nearly slid off the back seat.

"Arthur, does Dad talk to you?"

"What?"

I sat up and put my chin over the front seat.

"Does Dad talk to you?"

"Yeah. He talks to you, too."

"No, I mean *talk* to you. Is he sad? Is she breaking his heart?"

He didn't take his eyes off the road.

"What are you trying to say, Joan?"

"I'm saying it's gotta hurt, Arthur. Being left like that."

"Girl, you have no idea what you're talking about."

"Can't she just come back? When are things gonna go back to normal?"

"You need to stop making assumptions and pay attention. Mom hasn't left."

"Are you serious right now?! I am *the only one* paying any kind of attention. Everyone else is pretending nothing is happening."

"What, you think having a mother with a job is the worst thing that ever happened to anyone? That's a pretty suburban outlook."

"It's not a job, Arthur. It's a whole life. She hardly even lives with us anymore. Why can't everyone stop pretending she does?"

"Enough, now."

And that was it. The wall of silence my family was always building together. The ten-ton weight of nothing. The cement sneakers they put on me so I'd sink into their silence and never be heard from again. I stared into the other cars and wondered what conversations were going on inside them. How much truth were all those average people telling each other?

We pulled up at the light on 25A, and Robbie McNamara turned the corner in front of us. Andre was in his passenger seat.

"Hey, look!"

"You should come out to one of Charshee McIntyre's classes with me one day. She breaks it down. You should meet Professor Von Winbush. You'd like him. He's a science guy, but cool."

"Whatever, Arthur. Why is Andre in Robbie's car?"

He squinted at Robbie's rear window and shrugged. "I didn't see him. Are you sure?"

"Yes, I'm sure! They hang out now, or what?"

Robbie's car disappeared around the corner onto Main Street and Arthur went the back way to Jensen Road. Andre was home when we got there. He said Robbie saw him in Huntington and offered him a ride home.

"Robbie wasn't in Huntington." I narrowed my eyes and tried to see inside him. "He was in the park. I was there!"

"What is your problem, Joan? Why are you interrogating me about the neighbors?" He looked at me like I was the one lying.

"I hate all of you."

I went up to the top of our outside stairs and looked across the road. There was no light in the McNamaras' attic window, but that didn't mean Daisy wasn't up there. He might be looking down at me right then, wanting to know where I'd been with Arthur. Why I'd gone without him. What we were all saying at my house and how we felt. He'd be hanging on for whatever word we were going to say next. Watching my every move and trying to wish himself back into my life.

Daisy took his chance a couple days later when Arthur brought me with him out to his campus at Westbury. I don't know how, but he convinced Arthur to take him, too.

We drove down the LIE into Nassau while I tried to untangle all the silences around me. Even that car was full of lies. Full of Daisy not saying what was happening with Robbie, and Arthur pretending my parents were just fine.

"Daisy," Arthur said like nothing was happening, "what is this book you want?"

"The *Bell System Technical Journal*. It probably won't be there, but it's worth checking. They cleaned it out of the college libraries before the Greenstar trial, even. People say we should check everywhere, though. In case they missed one."

"And you're gonna use it to be grand master of the phone system, eh?"

I stopped listening. The light poles went by at exact intervals and cars slid up and down the ramps, in and out of the right lane. There was a cop by exit 22. I felt Arthur freeze up before I even noticed him, but he already had somebody pulled over. Arthur breathed out and went back to talking to Daisy about phones and corporations.

"Even theft is ideological," he said. "They want you to believe there's no difference between stealing from people and stealing from corporations. What corporations do to us isn't called stealing, even though that's what it is."

"Yeah," Daisy said.

When Arthur expounds on the meaning of the world and what we should all do about it, Daisy's eyes glaze right over. You can see him drinking it up. If he told Daisy to jump off a cliff he would. Most of what Arthur says is true, so you can't even be mad at him for saying it.

When we got to the campus he parked in a space under some trees near Core West. There was a ring-necked pheasant crossing the lawn. When a guy came around the building on a lawn mower, the bird made a panicked bubbling sound and a pathetic attempt at flight. We all climbed out and Arthur shut the driver's-side door.

"Listen." He rested one hand on the roof of the car. "Shirley doesn't know who Mom is."

"What are you, stupid? You said Shirley wants to be an actress. Tell her who Mom is and she'll definitely go out with you."

Arthur just looked at me, drumming his fingers on the top of the car. He was nervous.

"Shit! You really like her!"

"Will you stop it, Joan? Just go find what Daisy wants in the library and then come say hi to everybody."

"You're the one who told me love was a myth created to make us go to work and then go home and make more baby workers. I feel betrayed, man."

"Well, I think I also told you if you're not open to changing your mind you might as well lie down and die. College is supposed to transform your thinking. It's supposed to change you."

"Into what? A railroad mechanic with no dreams and a selfish wife? A sucker with a steady paycheck?"

"Ease up, now. I didn't say anything about love, anyway. I'll tell her. I just want to know why a person's hanging out with me."

Meanwhile, Daisy said nothing. He just stood there with his door open, looking like someone coldcocked him and he forgot to fall down. I guess the idea of Arthur and women hadn't occurred to him.

Arthur went into the commons, and I went with Daisy to check for his weird engineering books in the library. He found one, but all he did was pull it out and put it back again. When we came out, Arthur was sitting with a bunch of his friends on some couches in a little room off the commons.

"This"—Arthur waved an arm around—"is pretty much the Black Student Union leadership." I gave a little wave and he said, "My little sister and her friend." Then he rattled off everyone else's names. One was Shirley, and I liked her, even though I didn't want to. A little girly, but she looked smart. And she looked at Arthur like he mattered.

Daisy was heavily contemplating a poster that said *Egypt is part of Africa* and trying to look like the whole situation wasn't freaking him out. I walked over behind him and said in his ear, "Now you know how I feel every day in Highbone." At least he didn't pretend not to know what I meant.

"I know you're mad at me," he said, "but come to the phone booth?"

There was one out on the wall under the balcony. Daisy made us wait until the clock was at exactly three p.m., then dialed zero and a long-distance number.

"I'd like to reverse the charges," he said to the operator. "My name is Daisy T. J. Westbury."

The charges got refused, and he hung up and smiled at me.

"You're happy someone rejected your call?"

"I was telling him the *Technical Journal* is still here."

"Telling who?"

"I don't know his name."

"He didn't even take your call."

"He's not supposed to. The name is the message."

"You're weird. Where even is that number?"

"Ohio. Listen, I can use the phone to find your mother in the city if you let me."

So Daisy knows a bunch of weirdos like himself, all over the country. If you can call that knowing people. They use fake names, communicate by refusing each other's calls, and draw maps of the phone system. I guess Daisy started one step ahead—he already had a goofy nickname.

As far as flesh-and-blood friends, though, I was pretty much it. Trying to find where my mother stayed was his way of trying to make up with me. I got that.

We went back down the Expressway with the falling sun glaring out of the rearview mirror while Daisy and Arthur had another one of their "Yes, Grasshopper" conversations. Daisy was sucking in Arthur's every word like it was the key to understanding the universe. I looked at the clouds and thought about dinner and maybe going out in the boat. I stared into the other cars and wondered again what conversations were going on inside them. I hoped they mattered more than ours and knew they didn't.

We streaked past something dead lying on the shoulder, but it was behind us before I had time to see what it was. Highways mess with your perspective. When you look ahead, they tunnel inward. The same in the rearview. It's like you could dissolve into some place between the past and the future and get lost there.

joan

NOBODY IN HIGHBONE wanted us for neighbors, of course. Nobody but Daisy. Daisy wanted us for everything. The first time I met him, I was practicing holding my breath in the water. He yanked me out. We were maybe six, and I thought I could learn to live underwater if I practiced. I wanted to travel to someplace without mothers or brothers, someplace where I wasn't always the last person to get told things. I was so little, I still thought you could change the rules. I didn't understand reality at all. People call that innocence, but if you ask me, it's dangerous. Why do people feed kids all that fairy-tale crap about mermaids and learning to fly?

Anyway, I was on a mission, and Daisy interrupted me and made me choke. I think when I came up I hit him. Then I looked at him and the first thing I thought of was jellyfish. He's one of those ridiculously blond people who look like they're made of glass and packed with snow. The blue veins showed through his skin and all his limbs were too skinny and too long, like trailing things that might make sense if he were underwater or in a different kind of atmosphere. Somewhere with less gravity and more grace. His body was built for some other element instead of for air like the rest of us.

Interesting. You wouldn't want to be him, but he was ornamental. When I say ornamental, I mean it in a Museum of Natural History way, not a Metropolitan Museum of Art way. Freaky, but freakily beautiful. But, you know, I think octopuses are beautiful, so . . .

Daisy McNamara was one of the weird things I found by the edge of the water. As far as I was concerned, he belonged under the trees, or out on the harbor bottom. Like a piece of bladder wrack or a misplaced crab. After that first day, he'd be down there whenever I went outside, without a shirt and leaves all in his hair, toes in the mud or scrambling in the branches of our silver beech tree. I didn't really distinguish him from the raccoons and the occasional heron. He was interesting like moon snails are interesting.

Mostly we played in the woods and the water, every day. By the time we were eight, we'd already snuck into the abandoned house and dissected a cherrystone clam together, and he knew enough not to bother me when I was practicing holding my breath in the water. Me and him and the tide, that was the whole shape of the world, and I liked it that way. We told each other what we were scared of and then pretended we weren't. Even then, I was better at that than he was.

So I knew him already, when he showed up one Saturday morning in nothing but his Fruit of the Looms, knocked on the kitchen door, and asked Gramps if he could eat breakfast with us. We were maybe nine.

Gramps stood aside and waved Daisy through the door, then he said, "Andre, get the boy a shirt."

"That's okay, Mr. Jensen. I'm not cold."

"That's as may be, but it's polite to wear a shirt when you're eating at someone else's table."

I wondered if Gramps'd ever met Mrs. McNamara. Her table was always weirdly perfect, but she might be sitting at it wearing just about anything.

Daisy sat there like a naked secret at our breakfast table, making me feel like a bunch of leaves had blown in the door, like something had been tracked in and I should grab a broom to sweep it out again. I just wanted to get him away from my family and back outside where he belonged.

Then he looked up and saw Arthur for the first time, drinking coffee with his chair tilted back. Daisy looked at the two back legs of that chair, gauging the balance and the chances of falling over. You could see the picture of potential disaster pass through his mind, busted head and blood and rushing to the emergency room. You could see him absorbing the fact that Arthur didn't seem worried about of any of that. Daisy got down to idolizing him right away.

"Arthur, put your feet down," Gramps said, and went back to making pancakes.

"Hi, I'm Daisy." He smiled at Arthur and put on the shirt Andre handed him. It was from the laundry basket, but Gramps didn't notice.

"All right, little brother?" Arthur was fourteen. He was already working hard on his cool.

Daisy turned around to Andre and said, "All right, brother?"

Andre just rolled his eyes.

Daisy ate five pancakes and drank a big glass of orange juice. When he was done, his plate was so full of artificial maple syrup I couldn't lift it without slopping some on the table. The feeling of my two lives grinding together was making me flinch, like fingernails on a blackboard. The sound of it was so loud I couldn't hear myself think.

"Can we go out and play?" I only put one hand with crossed fingers behind my back because Andre had told me it was bad luck to cross both.

"You and Daisy clear the table, then you can go."

Gramps wasn't even looking at the glasses he was putting in the dish drainer. He just felt his way with his left hand while he stared across at Carter's Bay, humming to himself.

I took Daisy down the stairs and out the bottom door, straight onto the mud.

"How old is your brother?" Daisy said.

I was looking for clam holes.

"Arthur? He's fourteen. They made a big deal on his first teenage birthday."

"My brother's seventeen. Yours seems older." I could hear the rose-colored glasses in Daisy's voice.

"Everyone's older than us. That doesn't mean they're better."

"Yeah, but Arthur seems cool."

I was never going to keep Daisy out of my house now.

"Can we go back inside?" See.

"I'm looking for clams. It's important. When you dig down where the holes are, you never get to the clams. Are they running away? Are they digging deeper? Did Gramps lie to me about the holes being for clams to breathe?"

"He doesn't seem like a liar."

"I'm getting evidence. You don't go on what people say. Science is evidence. Don't you remember what Mrs. Gandy said when we looked in the microscope?"

After that first breakfast, Daisy started hanging around the edges of our family as much as he could get away with. I told him everything, right from the beginning, because he wouldn't settle for anything less. He asked me where my grandmother was and how long we'd been in the house. He asked why my dad slept in the morning and went to work in the afternoon. He asked me how I combed my hair. He was clueless and pushy, but he wasn't trying to be mean.

* * *

Maybe something snapped between us the night I met Teresa. I don't know. He was being an idiot and I was mad, but neither of us was trying to hurt the other one. Keep that in mind as we go along. Remind yourself: Joan and Daisy were never nasty. Whatever the world threw at them, they weren't asking for it.

daisy

THE FIRST TIME I met Joan I grabbed on to her shirt, and I guess I didn't let go for at least ten years. One summer morning when we were six, I went down through the trees and she was lying facedown in the water, perfectly still. I thought she was dead. The water was up to my knees, but we were only little so maybe it wasn't that deep.

Joan had on overall shorts and a T-shirt that said something I couldn't read yet. Anyway, the front of the T-shirt wasn't showing because Joan was facedown. At first I thought she was looking for something on the bottom, beach glass or green crabs or shiny quarters, but after a few minutes, I started to feel like she'd been still for too long. I don't know how long it was; time is weird when you're six.

Her arms were floating down by her sides. Little circles of her skin and wrinkles of her clothing were dry above the surface, but the water was sinking into the rest of her, making her heavier by the second. Little bubbles of light and shadow hit the bottom all around the shape of her arms and legs. She was so still even the minnows were fooled. They were slipping along her arms and nibbling at her. I thought, *they must tickle.* She should giggle and come up sputtering. I looked to see if her back was rising and falling with breath, but it wasn't and I panicked. Okay that doesn't make sense, but I was six and the main thing I knew about water was that it drowned people.

I didn't know her yet, so I didn't know she practiced. I didn't know the purple spots in her vision and the crushing in her chest were what she was after. I didn't know that she could hold her breath for superhero amounts of time. I didn't know she could walk through water and come up the other side, still burning. I didn't know she was Joan.

So I ran down and grabbed the back of her overalls and started pulling as hard as I could. Well, that made her gasp, probably scared the crap out of her, so then she sucked in water and really started drowning. I put my arm around her neck and pulled her head up and she coughed and spit up a load of water and bile all over my arm.

"Get off me!"

"You were drowning. I had to get you out."

"I wasn't drowning, you stupid. I was going somewhere."

When she said that, all kinds of possibilities flashed in front of me, like maybe the layers of the world weren't as separate as

I thought they were. Maybe she knew the way between them. I decided that first day that Joan had special powers denied to the rest of us. Which is kind of true, but they don't always help her. I only figured that out just this year.

So, that is the series of things I felt when I first met Joan: curiosity, then worry, then panic, my stomach falling away and my lungs bunching up like a fist, my heart trying to push up my throat. Then wonder. Then awe. That was pretty much the recipe for hanging out with Joan. For ten years I woke up every morning ready for all that. Now I wake up every day looking at a strange ceiling and feeling the hole it left inside me. I'm just like Robbie. Jonesing.

She turned into a woman at some point, but I'm pretty sure I'm still not a man. I don't feel like one, even now. I don't feel like anything without Joan or the music from Arthur's window or the ring of lights around the harbor, showing me the shape of my world in the dark.

daisy

THE MORNING AFTER we went to Westbury with Arthur, I went around to Joan's window and chucked some pebbles at the glass. I stood behind a maple tree, so Mr. Jensen wouldn't see me if he came out onto the porch. While I was waiting, the first red leaf spiraled down and landed at my feet. The water was lapping in to lift up all the little boats, including ours.

I heard Joan's feet hit the floor in her room and threw another pebble, in case she was planning to ignore me. She pushed the window up and stuck her head out, then emptied a glass of water onto the leaves.

"Hey."

She looked at me and pulled her head in. I heard the water glass clunk onto the table before she reappeared.

"I know you're still mad at me."

"Her name was Teresa, since you never asked."

"Whose name?"

"The girl your brother was trying to pimp out in the park."

"He was not, Joan. He wouldn't do that."

"He's dangerous, Daisy."

She was wrong. Robbie was never dangerous to anybody but himself. He tried to be, but he couldn't manage it.

"Arthur gave her a ride home. She's nice, Daisy. I liked her."

"You're just saying that because you're mad at me. You never like anybody."

"I like *her*. You would, too. Your brother should leave her alone."

"Get your backpack and come outside. We're gonna take care of this thing with your mother."

"What?"

"Come on. I've been following you around my whole life. It's your turn. Let's go."

She gave me the finger.

"Bring your mom's number. The one you call her at in the city."

She shut the window and I waited. And yes, I held my breath and prayed.

After ten minutes Joan came out the kitchen door and sat down on the steps to put her sneakers on. We took a bus over to Deer Park Avenue so we could catch another one down to Babylon. Joan wouldn't hitchhike.

"Tell me again why we're going all the way to Babylon just to make a phone call?" Joan said.

"You can't do this shit in your own house, Joan."

"You need a pay phone? There's one behind the Narragansett. We could be inside eating popcorn in front of *All My Children* right now."

"So, every time I make an illegal phone call you want me to do it behind the Narragansett? Even Highbone cops would figure that one out eventually. Anyway, you've never watched *All My Children* in your life."

"I was trying to make a point. There's nothing good on in the daytime."

"Exactly. Which is why we're having this adventure."

She rolled her eyes and I smiled to myself. Every once in a while, I won the argument.

I had my blue box in my backpack, but I didn't tell her about it. We stopped at every light between the north shore of Long Island and the south. By the time we got to Babylon I felt like puking.

We stood by the inventory house behind Babylon station and I tried to tell Joan about the computer inside. Robbie used to have a girlfriend who worked there. I went in one time and saw the big stately tape drives, turning behind the glass wall.

"People made a brain, Joan. A big electric brain. People made it and *it thinks.* It's like that Richard Brautigan poem we read in Mr. Driscoll's class, 'All Watched Over by Machines of Loving Grace.'"

"It's capitalism, not poetry, Daisy. Don't get sucked in by that crap."

"Nothing is like poetry until we make poetry out of it."

"Pretty sure that right there is what Arthur calls sophistry."

Then we were starving, so we went into a diner for fries and lemon Cokes. Joan is the one who taught me about lemon Cokes, in the Harpoon when we were maybe ten. This was one of those diners with little juke boxes at the table. We spent a quarter on "Come Together" and "Cherry Bomb," then paid and went outside. I got out my blue box, which was actually red.

"That's what you were making?"

"Yes. I told you. It's an audio oscillator, basically."

"Oh, an audio oscillator. Of course. What is it *for*, McNamara?"

"You think *I* don't listen? It's a blue box. It talks to the phones."

"It's red, Daisy. Are you color-blind? That is cool."

"I'm not color-blind! Blue box is just what it's called. Phones talk to each other with pitch-perfect beeps. Guys used to just whistle or play flutes into the phone, but then AT&T started using multifrequency, two beeps at a time. More, sometimes. You need the box so you can mimic them and make the phones do stuff. The first guy who made one, it was blue."

"See? That's ridiculous. Why can't people just use accurate labels?"

"Did you bring the phone number?"

"Yes. Are you gonna tell me why?"

"Stand behind me so no one can see."

"Okay, Serpico."

"What's their name?"

"Whose name?"

"The people your mother stays with?"

"I can't remember. I don't really care."

"Think! I need a name."

I opened a long-distance line and called a Missouri inward operator, then channeled the voice of the guy who fixes our boiler. I asked for the New York City test board.

"Test board?" I waved my free hand at Joan, telling her to hurry up. "Checking some lines. Need a reverse directory on a Manhattan number." When Joan heard my short-tempered repairman voice, she craned her head around and raised her eyebrows at me.

I put my hand over the mouthpiece and glared at her. "See, I can do shit," I whispered.

"Weird, pointless shit."

"Name!"

The operator asked why I hadn't called some other tech-board something and I braved it out. "Because I'm calling you. It's raining out here, honey. You mind hurrying up?"

Joan opened her mouth, but I put a finger on her lips and gave her a Magic Marker. She wrote NOVAK on the window of the phone booth.

The operator put me through to some kind of internal directory assistance, and that was it.

"She's at 331 Central Park West. Apartment 5B."

I don't think Joan believed it would work. She looked scared and sad, like she didn't really want the information after all.

I looked out the phone booth at the line of cars waiting for the light, stretching past the diner with their windows down and their AM radios barking out into the road. Our eyes slid away from each other in different directions, and I opened the door onto the smell of exhaust and hot tar.

"You're welcome," I said. "Let's go home."

"We really did come to Babylon just to make a phone call."

"Yes. *You're welcome*. Now, when are we going to the city?"

But the days kept getting shorter and Joan kept avoiding our trip to the city.

I went out one Saturday in late September and the smell of mulch blew over me from between the trees. The sun was still shining but the world was starting to die. Soon everything would be sleeping—all the life would be buried under the dirt and the ice. The tide was out that morning, and little pockets of mist hung over the muddy harbor bottom.

The quiet lady was wandering around with a hoe, using it to turn over little clods of mud. She'd bend over and peer down into the holes she made, looking for treasure. Usually she had a metal detector; maybe she'd run out of batteries.

I waved at her and went over to the Narragansett to get two coffees, light with extra sugar. When I came back to the dock, the quiet lady smiled and held out her open palm. There was a rusty ball in it, bigger than a small marble and smaller than a big one. She pushed her hand at me and made an impatient sound with her breath so I'd take it from her. It was heavier than I thought it would be.

Then she raised both her arms and made like she was sighting down a gun barrel.

"Oh," I said. "Musket ball."

She smiled and staggered back, clutching her chest and making choking noises.

"I brought you some coffee."

But she kept playacting until I laughed. Then she smiled and walked over to the floating dock. It was sitting on the mud with just a puddle of water around it. We splashed over and sat on the edge, facing out toward the Sound.

When we were halfway through our coffees, the sun cleared the trees and flooded down onto the glistening mud. I looked over at Joan's window, still closed above her back stairs. I didn't want to knock in case her Dad was sleeping. Mr. Harris doesn't really like me. Mr. Jensen, Joan's grandfather, does like me. I don't know why.

It was Mr. Harris who turned out to be right, of course. I'm the poison, the source of all the lies and the blindness. The violence leaked out of my life into hers and I couldn't stop it. Every lie I told just made it worse. I was the thing weighing Joan down.

At the time, though, I just thought, *I hope Mr. Harris has work today. I can go get Joan as soon as he leaves.* The quiet lady slapped my arm, so I must have said it out loud. We finished our coffee and I went through the woods to the bench on the Harrises' stairs. There was a note. "I went to Hicksville. They think I'm with you. Don't call me," it said.

Everything was different already. It wasn't that Joan had

changed and I didn't know who she was anymore. It was that when she started walking away and leaving me notes like that, I didn't who I was.

When I went up my driveway, Robbie was on the ladder climbing up to the roof. My mother was standing below him in a trench coat and dark glasses, singing Peggy Lee.

"Daisy," she breathed out as soon as she saw me. Her voice was so soft I had to read her lips. They were pink, the exact color of the chiffon scarf she had over her hair.

"Hey, Mom. What's going on?"

"Daisy, make him get down."

The pink was bad on her; she looked better in dark red. Anyway, the leaves were about to change, and soon the world would turn orange and yellow. And she was forty-six years old. Pink was the wrong color. She usually knew stuff like that.

"What are you doing, Robbie?"

He turned around to answer me, then slipped and grabbed the gutter. My mother hid her eyes with one hand and I saw her pink nail polish, the exact same color as the scarf and the lipstick.

"It's fall. I'm cleaning the gutters."

"Robbie, look around. The leaves are still on the trees."

"I'm doing it early. I'm staying on top of shit, Daisy."

If you didn't know him, he would have looked the part. His arms were still strong and his voice carried down into the road, deep and loud enough to scare away the sparrows. Judging us both on looks alone, Robbie was the one you'd trust. The one you'd turn to for protection.

"Daisy, make him get down."

She still had her hand over her eyes. One nail was ruined. She must have brushed it against something while it was still wet. When I was little, she never had a broken nail or a millimeter of brown hair along her scalp. Sometimes she stayed up all night, trying lipstick and touching up her roots, painting her nails and using Nair on her legs. In her bathroom there was one of those frames of round lightbulbs they put all around the mirrors in master bedrooms so housewives can feel like movie stars.

She never wore burnt orange or candy pink. She wore fire-engine red every day and never left a crack for the world to work its way into. She blotted it on tissues and left piles of red paper kisses in the garbage pail. Living with my mother was like having a movie theater in your own house. In my dreams, she materializes out of a beam of dusty light.

Sometimes in those dreams she bends down and brings her face close to me. If she lifts up her sunglasses and I see into the gold circles at the middle of her eyes, I know don't have to wake up. I can just sink through those eyes into the next dream without even trying.

I looked away from the candy-pink smudge of her nail and went over to hold the ladder for Robbie.

"You're freaking Mom out, man. Maybe do this later, okay?"

"I'm done, kid. It's all taken care of. I checked and there's nothing up here."

He fell the last couple feet but I caught him. He was so solid he nearly knocked me over. So full of gravity and strength. How did we come from the same mother?

"That's cool, Robbie. Maybe get some sleep now? Let's go to the deli, Mom."

"I can't go out like this, sweetie. Look at me."

She patted her hands over her scarf and then down her trench coat like she was trying to make sure nothing was falling away. No stuffing coming out of her.

"You look great. Anyway, I'll run in. We all need some breakfast. We could get egg sandwiches and take them to the beach."

She loves egg sandwiches. Loved, I guess. I don't know.

We both went to the deli and I kind of overdid it. I got egg sandwiches and bagels and orange juice and the paper. Two large coffees, light no sugar. They gave us a box.

I opened the back door of the car and put it on the floor. "Beach, James." I was trying to make her laugh.

"I'm a little tired, honey."

"Please, Mom?" I got inside and shut the passenger door.

Mom fell into the driver's seat, then reached over and held a piece of my hair.

"It's turning brown," she said.

"Didn't that happen to Robbie when he got older, too?"

"You won't be my Daisy anymore, without the yellow on top."

She smiled at me like saints smile in paintings. Like they love you but they're keeping it inside. You can't have it.

"If you start calling me Anthony, nobody'll know who you're talking about. Stick with Daisy."

She rested her hand on my cheek for two minutes and looked

at me. I guess she was looking into my eyes, but she hadn't taken the sunglasses off so I couldn't be sure. Then she started the car and headed out Beaton Road toward the Neck. The good beach.

She pulled over on the shoulder and I spread our breakfast out on the warm hood of the car. We tried to open the Arts section so we could count the Ninas in the Hirschfeld drawing, but the wind came up and blew my coffee onto it.

"Mom, what did you want to be when you were little?"

She swept a hand around at the beach and the big gabled house that was the only thing on the Neck. "This, honey. I wanted to be this."

"To live at the beach?"

"To not live in an apartment block in Astoria! Girls then didn't want to *be* things; they wanted to *have* things. I wanted you, Daisy. I wanted to be your mother."

I pulled her out onto the sand. She tried to resist, and when I wouldn't give up, she made me stop so she could take her sandals off. We ran through the sand toward the foamy water, laughing at the sea gulls and the way her scarf tried to blow away. In the bright windy sunshine, all that pink was okay.

"See? The fresh air is good for you."

"You're good for me," she said. "What would I do without you?"

She was out of breath but smiling. Her cheeks were pink too, and she waved her hands around like all of a sudden she could think straight; she had things to say. Right then, I thought I was saving her.

We got home and fell onto the couch with the rest of the paper, smelling like ozone and salt, with wind-burned skin and watering eyes. I was so happy.

Joan had run away to Hicksville and I didn't know why, but my mother was laughing and Robbie had gone to bed. I had the quiet lady's musket ball in the palm of my hand and it felt lucky. I still had a window I could see the water from. We'd have school the day after tomorrow, and Joan would be there with me. That was the size of my world and I liked it that way.

Or none of that was true, and I was just hiding that morning. Just like my mother, laying perfect table settings over the scars and the cracks.

By the time the leaves fell down and clogged the gutters, my mother had stepped out of her movie-theater light and I couldn't tell where the edges of the world were anymore. Someone had switched the projector off and we were all disappearing into the smoky dark.

It was that night I found Beatrice. It had been two weeks since I'd finished my blue box, and I'd been taking the bus and the train around so I could use a random scattering of phone booths.

That night after dinner I put a couple of issues of the TAP newsletter in my backpack with a list of country codes. My mother was on the couch, reading *Shogun* and drinking a white-wine spritzer.

"Going over Joan's, Mom." I wasn't; I still didn't know where Joan was. But my mother never checked.

"Daisy! Wait."

I stopped in the hallway with the screen door in my hand.

"Come here a minute." She leaned over and patted the cushion by where her feet were curled up.

I put my backpack down by the door and went over to sit on the edge of the couch. I could see the roots of her hair and the distance in her eyes. Down where she was, in that well full of Valium and chardonnay, there was love. I could see the echo of it in the way she looked at me.

"What are you doing, Daisy?"

"I just told you. I'm going to Joan's. How's the book?"

"Sad. There was an earthquake. Do you need anything? Did you eat?"

"I ate with you, Mom."

She looked away for a minute, and then giggled. "I know that, silly Daisy. I meant are you full? Do you need anything? Want some cookies?"

"I'm good, Mom."

She put her hand in my hair. "You are, aren't you? Such a good kid."

"Yep. And I'll be home early. Okay?"

"Sure, but where are your other friends, honey?"

She slid the hand down to my cheek and I heard Robbie bouncing down the stairs.

"What other friends?"

"What other friends?" Robbie leaned his head into the living room. "Joan is his friend. He's gonna marry her."

"Don't joke like that, Robbie. It's not funny."

"I'm not going to marry Joan. That would be like incest."

Actually, I'd never really thought about it before. I turned the idea around in the air over the couch and tried to look at it from every angle.

"It isn't funny, Daisy," Mom said. "It's sad. People never accept the children from mixed marriages. They don't fit anywhere. Just an awful fact of life."

"You mean white people don't accept children from mixed marriages? Those kids grow up somewhere, Mom."

My words circled the room and disappeared out the window. She turned her head back and forth between me and Robbie like it was hard to follow the conversation.

Anyway, after I thought about it, I was pretty sure I didn't want to marry Joan. I just wanted to live in her house and make her breakfast every day and buy her an aquarium for her birthday and sit with her up in the trees, waiting for winter. And I didn't want her to marry anyone else.

"Got some work to do, Mom," Robbie said.

She smiled up at him. "Thank you, honey."

The screen door slammed behind Robbie, and I leaned my head down on my mother's knee. She breathed out a sigh of happiness that made me feel guilty, because I was only waiting until I heard Robbie pull away. Wherever he was going, I didn't want to know about it.

I stood up when I heard the Charger speed away around the curve of Jensen Road.

"Daisy?"

"Yeah?"

"I love you every minute," she said. "Every minute of my life."

"I know that. I can always tell, Mom. Honest."

It was like I'd let go of some string that was holding her upright. She fell back against the couch and closed her eyes.

I went out onto the porch and held the screen door until it clicked shut, then headed up through the woods to Beltaire Road. It was a warm night. Once I crossed 25A, I was beyond the breeze from the water. Particles of grit from the road stuck to my skin and my hair stuck to my neck. I had one of Robbie's old T-shirts on with some cutoffs. Standing in front of Casa Lucciola out on Meadowlark Road, I watched my scrawny limbs turn pink and blue in the blinking neon. Inside, there were families sitting in red leather booths eating shrimp fra diavolo and chicken Parmesan. A dad was laughing over his Sambuca while Mr. Pinissiaro patted him on the back and smiled. Everyone seemed connected, like they all had a place. Like it was me trapped behind the window glass and not them.

I looked at the phone booth on the corner. It was too close to home, but I went over and picked up the receiver anyway, just to listen while it sang its one-note song. Once I lifted that handset out of its cradle, I was inside the line. The circuit went through me. It was me between the earpiece and the keypad, making notes spark down the wires. I was part of a giant electric spiderweb the size of America. The size of the world. And I could make it do things.

I got out my blue box and dialed directory assistance in Boise, Idaho. Then I used it to open up a line to Atlanta, listening to the clicks and beeps chirping like birds inside the wires. I'd been working my way around Europe anyway, looking for people who spoke English. I guess it was because of the people in Casa Lucciola that I dialed a 39 number that night. Italy.

"Pronto." My grandmother used to say that. The voice was somewhere between a woman and a girl.

"Do you speak English? I'm sorry, I know it's late." I was pretty sure it was after midnight in Italy.

"Yes, and who are you?" It was English, but more beautiful. She had an accent and she was, not whispering exactly, but speaking low. Like there was no need to shout and all the time in the world.

"My name is Daisy."

"You are a girl? You don't sound like a girl."

"Um, no. It's my nickname. I have blond hair and I'm really pale, I guess."

"You should be the Lion."

"I don't think I look like a lion. Pretty much a Daisy."

"The lion. It's a flower."

"Dandelion?"

"Yes. It's more like a man."

Just like that. She never even asked why I called. She didn't want to know where I lived, but I told her anyway. When I asked her where she was, she wouldn't say.

"It's warm," she said. "There is no air. I'm sitting in the window." Later, she said, "I am married, but too young. Not happy."

It was months before I wondered what would make a person pick up a phone and say those things to a stranger. Right then I just said them right back.

"My mother is . . . kind of lost. My brother is doing bad things. I can't tell anyone. I don't know how to help them."

We stayed on for an hour, that first time. The whole time, I pictured our words traveling a trunk cable under the Atlantic, back and forth between us while sea creatures swam overhead. Beatrice was sitting in a window somewhere in the humid air, smelling the Mediterranean Sea and talking to me like I was the very person she wanted to be in a conversation with. Like it was easy.

Now I'm at Aunt Regina's house, without a blue box or a pay phone. Beatrice was part of it all, but not the way Joan thought. Working the phones made me free. Inside the phone system I was like Joan holding her breath underwater. I was pushing through to another world, made only of electricity and sound. I could say whatever I needed to. I didn't need to hide because I was already invisible.

THE WATERY BREATH THAT SHAPED THEM

joan

I TOLD YOU about Mr. Johnson's microscope so you'd know I'd been looking at protozoa for a month already by the time school started. I was excited about biology, but once I got there I realized I already knew everything we were covering. I decided it was going to be boring. I wish I could say I was never so wrong in my life, but I have been. I've been wrong so much, I'm having a hard time putting my mistakes in order and weighing them up.

The day the teacher first brought out the microscopes, the leaves outside had started turning and the sun was so bright he had to close the blinds so we could see our slides.

The first strange thing about Mr. Tomaszewski was that he assigned me a cheerleader for a lab partner. Usually teachers put me with the rest of the freaks. I thought Charlie Ferguson would be my lab partner, or Una, the German girl who played the French horn.

The next weird thing about Mr. Tomaszewski was that when he noticed me labeling all the parts on the diagram of the protozoan without paying attention to him or looking at my book, it didn't piss him off. He didn't say anything sarcastic or accuse me of cheating. He just tapped my paper and nodded at the cheerleader like she should learn from me. Also, I should mention that he wore jeans to school and had hair down below his ears.

When the bell rang, I took my time putting stuff in my backpack while Mr. Tomaszewski opened the blinds and put the tray of slides in his sink.

"Joan Harris?" he said when I was heading out the door. I turned around and he said, "That's you, isn't it?"

"Yes." Maybe he *was* pissed off that I knew the names of all the parts on the protozoan.

"You like biology?"

I shrugged. "I like water. I like to know how stuff works."

"Oh, right." He laughed like he knew what I meant better than I did.

He didn't know what I meant. Nobody did.

"Maybe you should do some extra credit," Mr. Tomaszewski said. "You might get bored with this stuff. Seems like you know it already."

Well, I wasn't expecting that. My whole life, teachers had only ever talked to me like I was either a criminal or a charity case. Do you know how weird it is, having a teacher talk to you like you're a person for the first time? Maybe he did get it? I took a big breath and dove straight into Nick Tomaszewski without checking first to see how shallow he was.

He went over to the windows and started cranking open the blinds. The sunlight came streaking into the quiet and lit up the two of us, alone in the room now, and the dust in the air. I turned around and wove my way through the metal stools to the door. When I opened it, the sound of two thousand kids leaving class came rushing in like a storm wave full of rocks.

"Thanks, Mr. Tomaszewski. Bye," I said, but the words got lost in the crowd of voices, and I stepped out into the hallway without looking back.

Maybe he was the first thing I didn't tell Daisy, and maybe it was because Daisy never asked. He was spending all his time talking to some woman in Italy on the phone. Or maybe because he lied to me first. It makes me sound like a baby when I say it, but it might be true. I could see the things he knew hiding in his eyes. He was pretending they weren't there, so why should I be the honest one?

I kept quiet, and a space started to open up between us. Once it was there, things started pouring into it. By October, it was all changing so fast that sometimes I got dizzy just standing still. My parents. Robbie. Andre riding around in Robbie's car. Daisy refusing to talk to me. Teresa. *Beatrice*. Mr. Tomaszewski. I spent the whole fall semester feeling like the ground was moving beneath me.

* * *

My mom was in the city working on a production. She called that night to talk to me and Andre about school. I looked out the kitchen window at the sunset, so her voice on the phone was just background.

Is there a reason why the inside of clamshells look like sunsets? I mean, that way that things in nature always echo each other—it's weird, right? Whirlpools and galaxies, roots and veins, music and math.

"Joan?"

"What?"

"Well, hello to you, too. How's school?"

"Fine."

It's because there are only three rules to the universe. That's why everything repeats, I mean. Gravity, inertia, action and reaction. You put some really simple stuff in the middle of a void with three basic rules and you get all this. Daisy and jellyfish, whiskey and trains, electricity and angel dust, cops and spider crabs and the telephone network. It's all full of repeating patterns, if you can figure out where to look.

"Have you made any new friends?"

"No. Well, maybe, but not at school."

"You planning to join this conversation at all?"

"What for?"

"So, it's gonna be you, huh?"

"Me what?"

"I've been waiting for the boys to get angry. You, I expected to understand."

"Understand what?!" Then I was mad at myself for yelling. Like she'd scored off me.

"Okay, well, I'll see you soon, honey."

I put the receiver down on the counter and left it there for Andre. Maybe she said she loved me, but something jumped in the harbor right then so I wasn't listening. A sea bass, maybe. It was getting dark so I couldn't tell.

I went into my room and got out the *Encyclopedia of Animal Life*, but something was distracting me. I kept looking from the diagram of the cuttlefish to the empty ceiling, and there was this feeling in my stomach. My chest, maybe. Pressure. It worked its way up into my throat, trying to choke me or turn into tears.

Out the window, bats were diving over the water and the stars were stabbing their way into the sky. X-Ray Spex was thumping through the wall of Andre's room. He wasn't even in there; he was on the phone. How was anybody supposed to think in our house? If it wasn't the silence it was the noise.

I threw the encyclopedia on the floor and went out through the kitchen and down the steps. The tide was halfway in, so I sat on the bottom step to take my shoes off and roll up my jeans. The moon was hidden and the air was still, but I could feel the chill sinking down onto the water just outside the porch light. Maybe the darkness was telling me things, but I wasn't interested. I only wanted to know one thing. How do I make everything simple again? How do I put the world back together?

I took my bicycle from under the porch and went through the water to the Abbates' landing. The water spun up off my tires and onto my legs, and a cloud blew away from in front of the moon. All I could see was the spray glittering and the path of the moon on the water, until I rounded the curve and the orange lights of town blotted out everything under the trees. By the time I'd dragged the bike through the woods barefoot, I was covered in scratches and one foot was bleeding, but I needed the bike and I didn't want anyone to see me.

Robbie was dangerous and complicated and in the way. He was the lie between us, or at least at the time I thought he was the only one.

If Robbie went to the park, I could get on my bicycle and follow him. I could leave it up on Baywater Avenue where he couldn't see me and maybe get close enough to hear what he was saying. If I could find out what he was up to, I could make a call. I wanted someone to come and take him away in handcuffs so the space between me and Daisy would be clear again. Because seriously, Robbie McNamara? I'm sorry, but he just didn't matter to me. Waste of space. Space in the middle of my best friend's life. Prime real estate.

You don't have to call me heartless. Trust me, I know already. You'll see. But all I wanted was to tell on him, I swear. All I wanted was to make him stop so Daisy and Andre and even Teresa would all be safe again.

I put my shoes back on and waited. The dark under the trees was still whispering to me, and I still wasn't listening.

Robbie went by at about eight thirty. He was by himself, smoking, with the window down and Bruce Springsteen on the tape deck. I got on my bike and followed him through the intersection at the bottom of Main Street. There were some kids on the grass in the park, but nobody noticed me. I puffed up the hill underneath all the lights in all the living room windows on Baywater Avenue, shining like some kind of Victorian Christmas card in September. All warm glow and no televisions. People on Baywater Avenue do not have televisions in their front rooms.

By the time I leaned my bike against the bushes above the back of the park, I was boiling hot. I peeled off Arthur's army jacket and threw it over the crossbar. It was a boy's bike, obviously. I have two older brothers, remember? Pretty much everything I have used to belong to a boy, except the underwear my mother's always buying me.

The voice came from about six inches behind my head.

"Everything okay here, young lady?"

I jumped and then turned around. He had his radio in one hand and his cop hat in the other.

"Didn't mean to startle you. Why so nervous?"

I wanted to point to Robbie and say he was carrying shit and he was violent, but everything that was clogging up my throat came back again. I just stood there in my tank top while he looked me up and down. I shivered and wanted to put Arthur's jacket back on, but I couldn't move.

"What's your name?"

"Joan Harris."

"Where are you riding that bike to at this hour on a school night?"

"The dog ran away." I still hadn't caught my breath. "I was just looking one last time before bed."

He asked what the dog looked like, and said he'd keep an eye out. Then he took two steps closer to me, and I backed into the bushes. He walked right inside the invisible wall around me and then said I lived down Jensen Road, didn't I? Just so I'd know he knew.

We were both quiet for a minute, but he didn't back up.

"Thank you," I said, because that seemed like a conversation-ending thing to say.

He waited long enough to let me know he didn't have to take my cues, and then said, "My name's Officer Kemp. I'll see you around, Miss Harris," and walked away.

Then I was sitting on the curb with Arthur's jacket on my lap. I put it on and felt around for cigarettes. I wished I had my scalpel. I wished I had a sledgehammer. Okay, I wished I had Daisy.

I guess I kind of woke up a few minutes later, on the other side of one of those experiences you can't tell people about. I couldn't tell Daisy because he wouldn't get it, Arthur or Dad because they'd lose their shit, and my mom because why would I? I just pushed that memory under the surface and carried it with me, down through the bushes into the park.

And yes, Robbie was behind the bandstand, but he wasn't threatening anybody. He was hanging out with some people, and Teresa wasn't there. Whatever they were doing, it was mellow. Nobody was saying anything. They all looked like they were listening to the same music, but there wasn't any music. There was no conversation either. Maybe that's what people get out of smack, never having to think of something to say. I could see how that's restful.

I hung around for a while, then wondered why. Robbie McNamara was a lost-it who was capable of pretty much anything, but I knew that already. I'd known that since I was about eight years old. And whatever he was doing, I sure wasn't going to tell it to Officer Kemp and his friends.

For a couple months I convinced myself that I was making a big deal out of nothing. People said that to me so much that I just gave in and believed it.

You can't open people up and see how they work, anyway. Everything they do is just the surface effect of some infinite, screwed-up mess of synapses firing and misfiring, complicated by whatever drugs they do to slow that down or speed it up or make it stop. You could open up a brain and look at it for years; it wouldn't tell you anything about what that person did. Or what they'd do next.

I went up and got back on my bike. On Baywater Avenue, I took my feet off the pedals and just let go. Like a strong enough breeze could blow everything back into place, put my mother back, and blow away all the silent cobwebs in my house. Wipe away Robbie's heroin and Daisy's lies.

I went back to thinking about the cuttlefish while Arthur's jacket filled up with cold air and lifted off my body.

Then I heard one whoop of a siren and red light splashed over me. I leaned back on the brakes and fell onto one foot. I was at the bottom of Main Street looking at the hood of Officer Kemp's car. He leaned out the window and pointed at me.

"You should watch out, Miss Harris," he said. "Another time, the driver might not stop."

And that was Highbone. Kids got lost and people freaked out. Every few years somebody crashed into the wall on Jensen Road. Guys sold pretty much anything that would get you high right in our park. Sometimes they overdosed or beat each other up over it. Housewives were drowning in their own living rooms and the cops were hassling us for nothing while the dads went to jail for what the papers called "white-collar crime." You'd think that would be enough. You'd think everyone in town would already be wandering around with hollow, shocked looks in their eyes.

But no, there was more coming. Before New Year's, all that had faded into the background and no one talked about it anymore. Highbone had become a completely different place by then. Someone had peeled back the surface of our town, and the whole country saw what was underneath. By Easter 1980, we were creepier than Amityville.

That Saturday, I left a note for Daisy and took the train to Hicksville. I knew Teresa lived right behind the station, so it was easy to find her. She was on the balcony, combing a little boy's hair. She was talking to him, but I couldn't understand. I figured that was because I sucked at Spanish. I passed the tests, but they were hard, and I forgot it all right away.

Teresa was wearing a jean jacket and a floppy hat. She looked like she just got back from Woodstock.

"Joan from Highbone. Hey, it rhymes!"

"Hi. I hope you don't mind?"

"Mind? Only if you're here to preach at me. You're not gonna try to make me pray or anything, are you? 'Cause the Jehovahs just left."

"I'm not really religious."

The little boy was squirming. She tightened her legs around him and said, "This is Clygee."

"Hi, Clygee." I waved and felt stupid. I'm not that great with little kids.

"Clyde, you'd say. C-L-Y-D-E."

"I guess you must ace Spanish in school. I barely pass."

"I don't speak Spanish." She smirked at me. "It's Portuguese. My parents are from Brazil."

"Wow."

"Not really." She waved a hand at everything around us and rolled her eyes. "I was born here."

"Sorry. I've never been anywhere. Well, North Carolina a couple times, but it was just a housing development and one trip to the beach."

"You better come in. My mother will want to look at you to see if you pass the test."

"What's the test?"

"Nobody knows, but it's definitely a pass/fail. My mother doesn't really do anything in between."

Teresa's mother had the blender going in the kitchen. Teresa leaned her head in to introduce me.

"Mom, my friend Joan. Joan, Mrs. Maia."

Mrs. Maia took her hand off the blender and smiled in the sudden quiet. That was it.

"I think you passed." Teresa went down the hallway in a zig-zag, using her hands to push back and forth from wall to wall. She threw her head back and shouted, "Come on down!" at the ceiling.

She shared her room with Clyde, but you could tell which side was hers. There was a poster of Princess Leia, half-covered with pastel drawings of butterflies and flowers and sunsets. She had one of those collapsing hat racks nailed up, full of necklaces and scarves.

"You're a real girl," I said. "My mother would be so happy if my room looked like this."

She hung her floppy hat over her necklaces and sat down on the bed.

"You think I'm a slut."

I sat down too, even though she hadn't asked me. She'd knocked the breath right out of me. I'd come all the way on the train, thinking we could be friends.

Her mother came in right then with two tall glasses of juice, grapefruit and lime.

"Drink it. It's good for you." She said and smiled at me before she left.

"You definitely passed if she's worrying about your vitamin C intake."

The juice was full of pulp, but it was good and it gave me something to do for a minute.

"I don't think you're a slut." It sounded like a lie, but it wasn't, and I felt helpless. Language is so messy. The meaning of everything changes depending on what voice you use to say it. "I just figured you might not know about Robbie. He's not as nice as he seems."

"Look around, Joan. This is where I am all the time, unless I'm in school. During the summer, it's work. Sometimes I just want to get out a little."

"I get it. Trust me."

"Don't go all social worker on me, either. My parents are good people. We all work hard. I get good grades. A lot of shit goes on around here, but we stay out of it."

"A lot of shit goes on in Highbone, too. It's just that in Highbone everybody refuses to talk about it."

She gave her bitter laugh. The cynical one.

"I like you," she said. "I'm not a slut. It's just sometimes I want to do the thing that isn't safe. I just want to go the wrong way on the escalator and see how it feels, you know?"

"I guess. When I see someone going the wrong way I just want to know why. I want to yell at them to turn around."

"You're fucked up too, you know."

Teresa doesn't exactly pull punches. Maybe she takes after her mother. No gray area. No in between.

So that was when I started riding trains around Long Island. When everyone who mattered started to spread out along the big network of steel and sleepers that connects the seamy underside of all the towns. I used to have a tide table; now I have a timetable. The world is so much bigger than it was a year ago.

The guy on the loudspeaker is calling the Montauk train. I laugh when he gets to Speonk, even though Daisy isn't here. People look at me like I'm crazy, and I head down the ramp into the platform for the Huntington train, breathing in the smell of crowds that have been dead for decades, looking at a hundred years of dirt lying on the sleepers. If Daisy were here, he'd tell me when they electrified. He'd put his face up to the window and shade it with his hands so he could see the sparks fly up off the rails.

daisy

ONE WEEKEND AT the beginning of October, I took the boat across to Carter's Bay in the dark, so I could call Beatrice before anyone was up. At five in the morning it would be the middle of the day where she was. I went into the phone booth by the Wheelhouse Inn and filled it up with cigarette smoke while I worked up my courage.

A raccoon flashed its green eyes at me from the edge of the parking lot before it wandered off into the woods. There was a rat, too, by the Dumpster. It was just me and the rodents and the moths hanging in a cloud around the streetlight. Then the hiss and clicking of the long-distance line, and then Beatrice's voice.

She didn't say *"pronto"*; she just picked up and said my name.

I said hers.

"It must be very early," she said. "Are you well?"

"Yeah."

"Good. You should not call me in the day. Nighttime is better."

"Oh, I'm sorry. We have school now. It might be my last chance for a while."

"Are you going to ask me if I'm well?"

"I think I'm not well really, Beatrice. Something's wrong with my mother."

"Marriage is like prison," she said, and I had to laugh. "It is not a joke."

"No, it's just that my father is in real prison. You know, he got arrested. He's in jail."

"Is he a bad person?"

"I don't know. Maybe. He fixed some books. Sorry, I mean he helped some people hide money."

"Oh. That is bad. Not the money, but what they do with it. It could be very bad."

"Anyway, my mother needs him. She kind of floats off, you know? She can't pay attention to anything when he's not around."

"Once, my husband hit me."

"God. I'm sorry, Beatrice."

"With his hand open, but still it hurt me. He hit me because I wasn't happy. It did not make me happier."

I looked up at the sky getting lighter over Highbone. We listened to the hissing on the line and to each other breathing.

"She needs to know he will come back," she said.

"If your husband went away, would you want him to come back?"

"Yes."

"Why?"

"Your mother, she needs hope. She needs something to get ready for. A family house is like a prison for the wife. We love the jailer. Like . . . hostages."

"Beatrice?"

"Yes?"

"No one should hit you."

"Go and play, Daisy. Go and be happy today."

I rowed back across and tied up to our post. The bottom of the boat scraped into the sand as the water lapped its way down and away. I closed my eyes and listened for the sound of the Harrises' kitchen door opening. For Andre's music, for Arthur running up the front stairs. I waited to smell the coffee Mr. Jensen, Joan's grandfather, likes to drink on the back porch. Beatrice's voice melted into the air over the road, chased away by the sounds of Andre's radio and Mr. Jensen closing the screen door. Maybe I fell asleep. The sound of them moving around each other, every one of them awake and connected, made me feel safe.

I didn't hear Andre's window open. The clicking of the shutter melted into my dream and then woke me up. I opened my eyes and Andre was leaning over me with a Pentax.

"Don't move," he said. "You look like you're dead."

"Thanks." I shut my eyes.

"I meant it in a good way. Like a dead Viking or something. Like you're in *The Lord of the Rings*."

"I'm so not, but okay."

"You can move now. Why are you sleeping in the boat?"

"I went to Carter's Bay. I had to make a phone call."

"You're weird, McNamara, but I guess Joan gets you."

Andre made me a print of that picture, but I gave it away. I wish I had it now, so I could use it to help me remember that morning. The feeling of the warm wood with the sun on it. The sound of the boat, scraping the sandy mud.

An hour later Joan still hadn't come out. Waiting for her in the mornings was making me jumpy and sick. I never knew when she would be there and when she wouldn't. If she went off somewhere without telling me, I'd have to sit at home under the weight of my mother's dreamy silence and her disconnected smiles.

I thought I could hide at Hatchet Mary's, lie by the ponds, and think about Beatrice. I could make another plan for getting my mother to the beach. Maybe to Planting Fields, where she always loved the greenhouses. If I worked her up to it, maybe I could get her to the water-lily room at MOMA. We could sit on the benches and imagine what it would be like to love nothing but color and then lose your sight. She would smile a sad smile, but it would be relevant.

At the bottom of the hill on Seaview Road, where you turn off to the beach, there's a wooden fence and a load of brambles. If you crouch down and crawl under them, you come out into an abandoned estate. No one ever seems to care that kids hang out there. Even now, after everything, I don't know what that place connects to, where you would be if you walked all the way through.

Later, in the papers, they called the place the name of the people who owned it, but all the kids in Highbone call it Hatchet Mary's. I don't know why, maybe it has something to do with the graves.

By the pond at Hatchet Mary's, everyone whispers. There are willows, and the water has a layer of duckweed on the surface. The green in there presses down on you from above, turning the sunshine into underwater light. The gravestones are covered in yellow lichen that looks like lace, and the light filtering through the leaves makes everything seem sleepy. You feel like if you're too loud, you might wake up the dead world in there. The ground will heave up and the pond water will clear and the leaves will fall away, leaving you exposed in the middle of some rich Victorian guy's lawn. You'll be thrown backward into some other Long Island, without Levittown or malls or police.

It was hot and still under there when I found Ray Velker and Patrick Jervis sitting by the little waterfall.

I've known Patrick my whole life because he uses our bus stop. If he didn't wear a denim jacket with the sleeves cut off, he'd be a nerd. He's round and freckled and his hair is the straightest, shiniest hair in Highbone. He pulls it off somehow, though, mainly by slouching a lot and not saying much.

"Hey, little McNamara." Patrick's voice was quiet, like I said.

"Hey."

"Wanna smoke?"

Ray had a baggie full of some strangely clean gold weed and a brass pipe with a chamber. He nodded and said nothing at all.

That was cool; I'd gone to Hatchet Mary's for the silence anyway.

Looking back, I guess the weed didn't look normal. Also, it was really harsh, and we all kept coughing.

"Where's Joan?" Patrick said. "Don't think I ever saw you without Joan before."

"Don't know. I think she might be avoiding me."

"Remember when nuns weren't allowed to walk around alone?" Patrick said. "When my brother was little he saw a nun alone and he pointed and shouted at my mom, 'Look, Mom, half a nun!' Without Joan Harris, it's like you're like half a kid right now."

That is probably the only perceptive thing Patrick Jervis has said in his whole pointless life. It definitely seemed profound after a couple bowls of Ray's weird gold weed. I looked into the pond and thought about where I ended and Joan began. I thought about my beating heart and the blood in my veins, like a dead open circuit that didn't complete. No pathway for current. No spark and no wave.

I looked at the carp turning and slipping under the cloudy water. One day all Joan's practice would pay off and she would finally be able to stop breathing. She'd slide into the water and never have to come out again. She'd turn into who she was meant to be all along, and I wouldn't be able to follow her without drowning.

"Sometimes Joan goes places without me," I said. "It's not like we're attached at the hip or something."

While I was with Ray and Patrick I felt pretty normal. Stoned, but normal. Then it all got a little weird, but still, normal weird. I said goodbye and thanks for the smoke and wondered whether I was acting like a freak. I didn't want to go home, but there wasn't anyplace else. I must not have been paying attention when I crawled out onto the corner of Seaview Road, because when I got to the fence my arms were full of scratches. Little beads of blood were bubbling up out of the rips in my skin. I stared at them for a while and then walked down the broken edge of asphalt between the double yellow line and the woods.

That was when I started sinking into the road. The surface of the pavement came up to my knees and then it was crushing my chest. I couldn't breathe and the whole world turned the blue color of reflected televisions. My mind split in half. There were two of me, and one of them knew it wasn't really happening, but that one wasn't helping. The road was rising up my ribcage. There was air all around me but I couldn't suck any of it down my throat because the pavement was crushing my lungs.

Something in the weed.

I heard a squirrel running through the leaves, and the sound was so loud it scraped the inside of my skull. I told my legs they weren't really trapped and they should move, but they wouldn't. After a while the other half of my brain started chanting, "It's only a drug. It's only a drug." That wasn't helping either. A car made the curve behind me and rushed by so close I would have jumped sideways if my reflexes had been working. My heart choked up into my throat and I started to sweat. I went back to chanting, out loud this time.

Then I took one step. The blue air laughed at me, and the sound made little sparks like electric rain. The road pushed tighter against my chest. I could see every pebble embedded in the asphalt and every separate, specific glint in the coal tar between them. If I closed my eyes I wouldn't see that, but I'd probably see something much worse, or nothing at all. I might fall out of myself and into the nothing. I pushed as hard as I could and took another step, then started running. I ran all the way back to Jensen Road and up into the attic, knowing if I stopped or even slowed down, the ground would swell up and swallow me.

Our attic has a big gap in the floorboards, a line that runs right across under the eaves. I imagined it holding everything down, and the attic floor tilted back and forth on that axis, trying to rise up. I crawled into the dormer window and pulled my knees up, afraid to take my eyes off that crack. I guess I spent all afternoon and half the night staring at it and saying, "It's only a drug, it's only a drug," using the power of my mind to hold down the floor.

Around two in the morning, I looked down at the lights and the jagged silhouettes of the treetops around the harbor. I wondered where Joan had gone, and what kind of trouble Robbie would get into next.

Was he going to knife somebody or just step out into traffic? Maybe he'd slow down so much he'd stop moving, get into Mom's prescriptions and start staying at home, staring at the walls. To be honest, that would make my life a lot easier. At least Joan would stop asking questions.

I thought about my dad, too. My mom said he didn't do what the cops said, but she never gave us any details. He's an accountant; how bad could it be? Did I want to visit him, or still be there when he got back, or ever see him again at all? I needed to think about what the alternative was, about my room and my attic and whether I could live without them.

I didn't think about Ray, because why would I? Him and Patrick were off somewhere, laughing at me. If I told Robbie what they did, he'd probably beat them up. I wasn't going to do that, and the rest of it didn't matter. So I didn't make any special place in my imagination for the picture of Ray Velker at Hatchet Mary's, sitting up with his fingers moving and light in his eyes. I didn't know how much that picture would matter, later when the world froze and we all changed.

I did think about Beatrice, with the gray finger marks from an open hand on her cheek. I wondered whether she wore her hair up or down. Whether she was twenty-five or forty-three. Why she wasn't happy.

The answers to all my questions came eventually, and I didn't want any of them. Sometimes I wonder why I stayed conscious. Why I stayed sane. I could have let go that night, let go of the half of me that knew what was real. If I'd let myself sink into the pavement, would I have stopped breathing? Would it have been like when you die in a dream and your heart stops? When your body just lets your mind throw you over a cliff and jump out of you while you're falling? Your dream self hits the ground and shatters and your sleeping body rots at the crooked edge of the road under the leaves.

Or maybe I didn't wonder any of that then. Not yet. Maybe I thought, *Patrick Jervis dosed me and he's a shithead, but everything's fine now.*

In a few hours I'll find Joan, and everything will be fine.

When morning came, I went downstairs and turned the oven on, so the kitchen would be warm when I got out of the shower. I looked in the refrigerator, then shut it again and drank a glass of water.

When I went to the bus, Joan was leaning against the wall on the blind curve of Jensen Road. It was one of those sharp, golden days when you suddenly have more energy and you can feel the future right in front of you. I ran when I saw her, but I had to stop and catch my breath before I got there. I hadn't eaten breakfast, and the whole world felt jagged and loud. I was still hollow and shaky and thinking about myself. Maybe her, too. I should warn her about Patrick and Ray and anybody else with suspiciously clean weed.

"You look pretty, Joan."

"Shut up."

"You can deny it; it's still true."

I wasn't hitting on her. It wasn't like that. Or anyway if it was, I was too stupid to realize it until way later. The reason I ran when I saw her was because I thought the air around her would be softer. The truth is, I used Joan to block out all the noise. We'd been part of each other so long, I never thought about the space between us. I get that now, but it's too late.

Patrick didn't show up for the bus, which was good because what was I going to say to him? He came the next day and saved me the hassle by completely ignoring me.

The sun sliced a shadow across the retaining wall, and the air smelled like hot tar.

When the bus came, we sat in the back with the burnouts and let ourselves sink down into the babble. If we needed to say anything we had to lean over and cup a hand around the other person's ear.

"Where were you yesterday, in Hicksville again?"

"Maybe."

It took me a minute to do something with the look on my face. I looked out the window and over into a delivery truck. The guy had a page of *Playboy* taped to his dashboard and an AA chip hanging from his rearview.

"What's in Hicksville?"

"A friend. What are you, my mother?"

"All right. I was just wondering. Jeez."

"No. You were just shocked that anybody else would hang out with me."

"Why are you mad at me? What did I do?"

"I went to see Teresa, if you have to know. You know, the girl whose life your brother is trying to ruin?"

"I told you, Joan. Robbie's a screwup, but he's not mean. Even if he was, he's not organized enough to be good at it. You know that."

"Forget it. Where's your lunch, Daisy?"

"My mom was asleep."

"She didn't get up and make a big production out of bananas and tuna salad? No lecture about not letting people pick on you from the person who nicknamed you Daisy?"

"She sleeps a lot lately. Everything with my dad makes her tired."

When the bus pulled up at school, there were kids all over the football field and the halls were still empty. I wanted to go straight to Mrs. Farrow's room, but Joan dragged me to the cafeteria for hash browns and orange juice. We sat by an open window and leaned our faces out to breathe in the smell that came up off the cut grass when the sun hit it. After a minute, she turned away from the window and caught me looking.

"What, Daisy? What is it now?"

"My mother thought I wanted to marry you."

"Wow, I wonder how that conversation went."

"Beatrice said her husband hit her."

"You talked to Beatrice again?"

"Yeah, a few times."

"You don't even know who she really is, Daisy. She might not even be married."

"Can me and you just share a houseboat without being married, though? Or maybe a sailboat even?"

"Yeah, me and you and the people from the yacht club. That'll work right out."

"We could put in a glass bottom. It'd be your version of heaven."

"Heaven is a ridiculous concept. Surely your guru Arthur explained that to you already."

"I'm just saying, we should start making plans. We'll be out of here in two years. We could do anything."

The idea that we might go in separate directions honestly didn't occur to me. I wasn't scared of it, because I didn't think it was possible. I just thought about whether heaven was a glass-bottomed boat or whether Joan wanted something else. I found out later that we'd been in heaven all along. That heaven had no bottom. Turned out we could let go and fall forever.

I took metal shop, mainly because there wasn't a class for people who wanted to figure out the phone system. I could take mechanics if I was willing to go on the BOCES bus, but I got enough shit from people already. I tried to get Joan to take metal shop with me. She said, "I am not gonna be the first girl to take metal shop. Live without me for fifty-five minutes." Turned out I could do that. Just about.

Metal shop was full of greasy hair and cutoff jean jackets. The big ambition in that room was fixing carburetors for the Hells Angels on East Fourth Street. The first thing we made was a pair of bookends out of sheet metal. Later, I painted flames on them. That day it was just the T square and the tin snips, though. The shop was noisy, good for thinking in. I was wondering about when my house would be empty so I could turn the circuit breakers off and wire an answering machine into my bedroom light switch. I wasn't really paying attention to the conversation until they got around to the angel dust.

"Hey, Daisy, I heard you had a bad trip."

A bunch of guys laughed, and I tried to look like I still wasn't paying attention. Ray didn't say anything either. At least I don't think he did. I was concentrating so hard on being invisible, I might have missed it.

"I heard you freaked out and ran away." Aaron Woolf laughed and pushed up against me.

"It was cool," I said. "I just had to go home."

I finished with the tin snips and made my body relax before I walked across to hang them up. I was just trying to breathe my way through it, stay calm until they moved on to something else. I'm not proud of it, but it's the truth, and it's one more thing I didn't tell Joan. How could I?

They started talking about going to a concert at Stonybrook, who was driving and who had some hash and could somebody get backstage passes.

"Backstage, that's where you find some desperate ass."

"Wanna come, Ray? Maybe you could finally get laid."

See? If you just stay calm, they get bored and start on someone else.

"I got business to take care of." Ray looked at me when he said that. I knew he meant business with Robbie.

"Yeah, you better stay home with your record player and your porn stash and a couple of old socks," Aaron said. "Safer bet."

So, that was the level of conversation at Highbone High School. You really wonder why me and Joan stayed home building blue boxes and taking apart fish? I put my metal shop stuff in a cubbyhole with my name on it and Ray came up to put his next to mine.

"Listen, you won't say anything will you?" I could barely hear him. He wasn't even looking at me.

"To who? What am I gonna say, Ray? That you're a dick? Everyone knows that already."

"It was Patrick's idea about the angel dust. If Robbie thinks it was me, he'll go nuts."

"Relax, Ray. I don't even care."

It was true. I wasn't mad at him. I was busy worrying I'd have to spend the rest of my life in that kind of conversation. If not for Joan and the telephone network, I was lost in a world of jean jackets and jerk-off jokes. I walked away from him and went into the commons to find her.

That was the last time I ever saw Ray Velker. I don't have to wonder if he's in any of my memories after that. If I'm imagining things. Sometime in those next few days, Ray disappeared.

I've spent months trying to unpick that memory, but even if they'd put me on the stand, I wouldn't have been able to say for sure that was how the conversation went. How much those guys were hassling Ray. Whether he looked scared. I was too focused on myself at the time. Anyway, they never even questioned me. Not about that, anyway.

* * *

Last year they put televisions in the commons. The lockers are in these wells with benches in the middle. When we got back to school in September, every well had a TV on a rolling stand. Before Christmas, they started playing *Video Concert Hall* at lunchtime to prove how hip they were. I found Joan behind one of the televisions with her biology textbook and her five-subject notebook. I had to shout over "Video Killed the Radio Star" to get her attention, but I just thought it was the noise.

"Metal shop was okay. Thanks for asking."

She looked up and brought her eyes into focus.

"We're making bookends. Why are you behind the TV?"

"Anthony McNamara, bookend maker. It has a cool ring to it. This could be your vocation. Come on, there's loads of wires back here. You'll like it."

I slid my back along the wall and sat down next to her behind the television cart.

"How was biology?"

"Boring. How's Robbie?"

"He's fine, Joan. Stop it."

"I'm only asking."

"When are we going to see your mother in the city? I went to all that trouble to get you the address."

"You loved it. Riding around Long Island playing with pay phones is your nirvana."

"I have to randomize so they can't put my house at the center of a pattern."

"Just put a colander on your head and get it over with. The FBI doesn't care what you do. You're paranoid."

"Not true, Joan. So not true. The FBI are AT&T's personal collection agency."

"So, there's a load of weirdos like you all over the country, using fake names and playing with the phone system?"

"Yes! If not for them, I never would have talked to Beatrice."

"You've never even seen Beatrice, Daisy! What if she's a dog?"

"Why are you being mean? We don't want look at each other, we want to talk to each other."

"Can't you just stash some pornography under your bed and fail math like a normal guy?"

"I suck at normal. Which, by the way, so do you, Ms. Fish Guts. Now when are we going to see your mother?"

"What if I don't want to? Did you even think of that, or am I just part of your phone game?"

"I was trying to help. We need to start doing things for ourselves. Nothing's going to happen to us if we just sit here waiting for it."

"Daisy, shit is happening to us. You're just pretending it isn't."

"What shit?"

"Really? God, you're just like my family!" I think she meant that as a criticism.

"Well, you're nothing like mine."

And then we were quiet for a while. There was a silence into which I could have said something. I could have told her about the angel dust, about being hassled in metal shop. That she wasn't wrong about Robbie. Instead we sat underneath "Watching the Detectives" and said nothing. We avoided each other's eyes and looked up at all the cheerleaders gossiping by their lockers, at the art room kids moving through the commons in a scruffy bunch. In my memory I see Ray Velker walking with them, even though I know he wasn't.

When I tell people here in Rockaway that I went to Highbone High School, they don't know where I'm talking about. Then I say, "You know, Ray Velker?" and they go, "Oh!" or "Shit, man," or something. Ray Velker is the thing that defines us now, but right then he was just part of the background noise.

Thinking back, I can almost feel the air in the commons that day, the things eddying around us. We were breathing in violence and desperation and other people's hallucinations, but it was all invisible to us then. Like the fluoride in the water or the radiation from Brookhaven, the DDT and the Valium and the strontium 90. All the heavy atoms and alkaloid molecules that shape us and then break us apart.

joan

IT WAS THE cheerleader who told me Ray Velker was missing, during lab. I remember the moment exactly.

"Nah," I said. "Ray can only take so much school or his head explodes. I saw it once in eighth grade. It was messy."

The cheerleader looked at me like she didn't know black girls could do sarcasm. Or maybe there just wasn't any room for sarcasm in between those Farrah Fawcett wings. I wished Charlie Ferguson was my lab partner, then I'd get to do all my labs alone.

"No really," she said. "His parents called the police. My dad's a social worker. He got called in. Ray's missing, for real."

Her name was Eileen, but it should have been Cindy. Or maybe Betty.

"He'll show up. He probably drove to someplace like Robert Moses to get high and forgot to come back. You ready to dissect a cow's eye? It's next week." I said it on purpose, to see her cringe.

I don't know. She just pissed me off, with her tits and her blow-dry and her fake squeaky voice. Maybe she's a perfectly nice person underneath all that, but she doesn't occupy a perfectly nice place in the world. So what's the difference? Last year, all the questions were like that. The ones science can't answer.

I hung around after class to talk to Mr. Tomaszewski so I wouldn't have to walk home with everyone else. I guess you could say I was avoiding Daisy.

Mr. Tomaszewski was trying to convince me to do an independent study.

"Okay, here's what you do." He was stuffing a pile of pop quizzes about cellular energy into his bag. "Go to the library and write me a report about Aristotle."

"What's Aristotle have to do with biology?"

"Go find out." Subtle guy, Nick Tomaszewski.

When I came out of the side doors of school, Officer Kemp was parked across the road. He turned off his engine and raised one hand at me without waving it. I looked at the reflection of the science wing in his rear window and buttoned my jacket.

But Officer Kemp wasn't the only reason I said yes when Mr. Tomaszewski invited me into his car. I let him drive me home because I knew he wasn't going to give me the lecture about the value of education or the one about how I'd see things differently in ten years' time. Not even the one about the value of truth and beauty. Science teachers don't usually do that one. Anyway, at that point he seemed like the only person who would look me in the eye.

"I told you, you should call me Nick," he said, "at least while we're in the car." He laughed. "It saves a lot of time; my last name takes a while."

"It'd be weird, calling you Nick." I shuddered a little, even. Not because it was creepy, because being in his car did something to my nervous system. The hairs were standing up on the back of my neck and I felt hollow inside.

"Why is it weird, though?" He turned the engine over and looked at me. "Think about it. Isn't that just a way to enforce hierarchy? I visited a school in the city where all the teachers went by their first names."

"Wow, can I go there?"

"It costs five grand a year. Seems like only the rich can afford to be egalitarian."

"Yeah, because they're already not."

He laughed. "Were you born like this?"

"Like what?"

"You see right through everything. That's a valuable quality—you get that, right?"

"Yeah, it means people don't want to talk to you or tell you anything. It's really great."

"Well, you've earned the right to call me Nick. Once you say it a few times, it'll stop being weird."

He wasn't that much older than me. Twenty-four, maybe, but I'm just guessing. He never told me. Nowhere near thirty, anyway. Not even ten years older than me, which is why it was so ridiculous for Daisy to freak out about the whole thing.

"Mr. Tomaszewski's a communist," Daisy said later, like that was the same as serial killer.

"Daisy, you don't even think there's anything wrong with being a communist. Say what you really mean."

"I mean it's creepy, Joan. He's old enough to be your . . . He's a teacher. He has authority and shit. Also, socialist is what I said there wasn't anything wrong with. Get it right."

"You only said that because Arthur said it. All your ideas are really Arthur's ideas."

"What's wrong with Arthur all of a sudden? What did he ever do to you?"

"Nothing's wrong with Arthur. Except he's not the one who's supposed to be your best friend."

Inside Nick's car there was no Daisy. No family. No bullshit. That's what I thought, anyway. When I was around him it was like none of that had to exist at all.

His car was French. He called it a *deux chevaux*. Two horses. When you sat in the front seat your legs were so close to the road you could practically feel it scraping by underneath you. The seats were made of thick foam. You could see it through the rips in the leather, because Mr. Tomaszewski's car had clearly been lived in. Possibly fought in and slept in, and definitely partied in. Sometimes you could smell the weed.

He had peace signs and anti-nuke stickers all over the dashboard, and there was always a load of flyers on the floor in back, shouting in big letters about railroad strikes and No Nukes demonstrations and strontium 90 in mother's milk. He had a forked piece of deer antler hanging from the rearview.

I had him drop me by the Narragansett, so no one would see us. I didn't want to hear about it from my brothers, and Daisy was already mad at me for trying to be friends with Teresa. I stayed out on the mud until dinnertime, then went through the back and knocked on Andre's door.

Maybe Andre is the thing that changed the most last year. By New Year's he had a fade and pipe-leg jeans and wouldn't listen to anything that wasn't an import. He had a job on Saturdays, stocking the bins at Nervous Records. He thought working at Nervous Records made him cool, and Nervous Records thought hiring Andre made *them* cool.

"Enter." Who says that when you knock on their door? Andre.

He was stretched out on his bed with a sketchbook, wearing his Japanese house socks with the separate space for his big toe. He has long skinny legs anyway. The socks don't help.

"You look like a tree frog."

"Thanks. You look like a homeless person." He shut his sketchbook and raised an eyebrow. "Anything else?"

I glanced around and realized I hadn't been in there in a while. There was a big poster of David Bowie on the back of the door, and his records took up practically a whole wall. Above his bed were all the black-and-white prints he'd made in the dark-room at school. Pictures of Gramps and Arthur and me and the quiet lady. There was even one of Robbie, getting out of his car.

"Okay, so this is creepy."

"Creepy, how? You're my family."

"Robbie McNamara is not your family, Andre."

"Yeah, but I love the way that jacket shines in the street light. If you use a long exposure it makes him look like he's about to dematerialize, like on *Star Trek*."

Down in the corner, I noticed my mom. She was out on the floating dock at low tide, with her legs drawn up and the sun shining on the stretch of mud between her and the camera. It was recent; I could tell by her hair.

I pointed. "She let you take that?"

"Yeah, I asked her where she wanted to pose, and she said the floating dock."

"She actually posed for you?"

"She said when she was my age she used to lie out there all day, reading."

If you didn't know her and you looked at that picture, you'd never guess she had a husband and kids. She looked all the way inside her own self, like no one had ever been ripped painfully out of her.

"She never tells me stuff like that."

"Maybe you don't ask," he said.

"What is going on with Mom and Dad, Andre?"

"What do you mean?"

"Seriously? You too? She stays away for weeks at a time."

"She works in the city. What's weird?"

"They never even touch each other!"

"How do you know that? Personally, I'm good without them making out in front of me. They're fine. Have you heard the way other people's parents talk to each other?"

I opened Andre's window and took one of his cigarettes off the night table, then lit it with a wooden match from his brass box. Andre is the kind of guy who keeps his matches in an antique box.

"They're not in love, Andre." I dropped the match and watched the ember disappear into the dark.

"How is that any of your business? Show some respect."

"Respect? They're my parents."

He laughed, but not like it was funny. Someone made a splash out on the water but I couldn't see who, or what they were doing.

"They're supposed to be here for us, Andre. If it's all so perfectly fine, why won't anybody admit it's even happening?"

"There's a difference between being private and denying something. You have a house and clothes and food, and you can go to college. You can't really accuse them of slacking. They both work their asses off. For us."

I stared straight into the lamp on Andre's bedside table and then out into the dark at the image it left burned into my eyes.

"Do girls at school like you, Andre?"

He was quiet for so long I turned back around and blinked at him. He was smirking at me.

"I didn't ask if you liked them. I asked if they liked you."

"Sometimes, I guess. Ruth Carter likes me, but as a friend, I think. I hope."

"How do you know?"

"It isn't hard to figure out, Joan. Mostly, nobody in school looks at me like I exist. Except Mrs. Farrow."

"That's bleak."

"Yep. At least you have Daisy."

"Not really. Not anymore. He's in love with some Italian lady he talks to on the phone."

"Seriously? Don't you think that's a little far-fetched?"

"No. He can do all kinds of stuff with phones for free."

"I'm telling you, he probably invented her to make you jealous."

"What were you really doing in Robbie's car, Andre? Taking his picture?"

"I already told you, Joan. Get a life and stop spying on people."

I like Andre, but me and Arthur have always been closer. I'm looking back and thinking maybe even that is because of Daisy. Daisy barnacled himself onto Arthur when we were about nine, and I was always with Daisy.

I don't know. Andre is just one of those kids who seems like he got pasted into the wrong family. At least I always thought so, until that night when I realized he'd been hanging out doing arty shit with my mom the whole time. I guess he belongs in the city, too, with his 501 button-flies and his 2 Tone Records.

He loves me, though. They all love me, like Daisy keeps saying. Well, good for them. Turns out, once I step outside my own front door, all that love is worth exactly nothing.

joan

WHENEVER MY MOTHER was there, all the questions just drained out of me. Then as soon as she was gone, they rushed back up into my chest and started suffocating me. Meanwhile, she hung out with Andre posing for pictures and communing about truth and beauty or whatever people like them think is important. Me? I needed some solid evidence.

I spent a whole day going through stuff in the attic. That's where our family keeps all the pieces that don't fit. Our attic is just like everything else in our family. It's full of more gaps than facts. You read letters you just know your grandparents would never write, but that's their signature at the bottom. You look at pictures that can't possibly be your parents. They look so happy, so relaxed. Something a little bit badass glinting in their eyes, even. Then the dust makes you cough and it's too hot up there and you go back downstairs into the silence. At least down there I know what to expect from people. Pretty much nothing.

One Thursday after school I went into my dad's room. He leaves for work at two thirty, and Gramps doesn't get back from playing chess with Mr. Johnson until it's time to cook dinner. I grabbed a dust rag and a broom so I'd look industrious if anyone caught me.

My father's room faces the woods. The maples and beeches were turning red and gold outside his window that day, but it was still open. He always leaves it open a crack, even in the winter. Like my mother is a feral cat and maybe she'll jump back in and curl up on the bed if he pretends he isn't looking.

There is a picture of my mother on the dresser in there. She has some kind of fifties hairdo and gold earrings on. The photographer had her turn three-quarters then look around at the camera so it's like you just said something interesting and she's caught by it. Listening and looking at the camera like whoever is behind it matters. She has beautiful eyebrows.

Every time I look at that picture, I feel like a failure. I'll never be that interesting or that beautiful. I don't even want to be.

The frame is older than the picture. Everything in our house is old. I don't mean shabby. I mean passed-down objects and secret histories. Everything whispers at you, telling you all the time that you only know half the story. I wish my ancestors had left a catalog with detailed descriptions, so you'd understand exactly what kind of happiness or pain you were lifting when you moved something to dust the coffee table.

First, I went for the shoeboxes in the back of the closet. My father thinks shoes should always stay perfect and last your whole life. He keeps his wrapped in tissue paper. He was fashionable once, in about 1955, and he's sticking to it. Turned out there was nothing in the shoeboxes but shoes.

What was I looking for? I don't know. Maybe I thought she was really from another family. I'd find a document with her picture and some other person's name and I could wave it at her and call her bluff. Maybe I thought they were divorced already and I'd find the decree. Then Andre and Arthur would finally have to believe something was wrong. Maybe I was going a little crazy. It's possible.

I gave up on the closet and went to Dad's desk. There it was: her geometry notebook. I could have missed it, except I looked twice because it was such a weird thing to save, in among the birth certificates and Gramps's discharge papers. So I flipped through and saw the pages in the back, filled with words. The date, just the year, was added later with a different pen. The clock in the living room struck five, and I took the notebook out of the room with me. I stuffed it in my backpack, thinking I'd bring it in and stash it in my locker at school.

Then the hurricane happened, and school got cancelled.

Daisy called while we were sitting in front of the six-o'clock news, waiting for the weather report. The preview said the hurricane was a category three, out to sea off Hatteras Island.

"You have to come over for it."

"I can't, Daisy. They're not gonna let me stay at your house overnight, not even during a hurricane."

I'd pulled the phone around onto the back stairs and shut the door on the cord.

"Think of something."

"Why?"

"What if a tree falls on your house, Joan?"

"What if a tree falls on *your* house?"

"You're farther down."

"So, you're saying I should leave and let the tree fall on Dad and Gramps and my brothers?"

"No, I'm saying the tide is gonna come way up and they should all leave. You should come here. We can watch from the attic."

"You're the one that loves storms. I just want to take a sleeping pill and wake up when it's over."

"I love *thunderstorms*. There's not gonna be any lightning in a hurricane."

"Bummer for you. Also, incidentally, people might get killed."

"What happens to everything in the water, anyway? Where do the fish go?"

"They go way out and then dive. They probably felt it coming last week. Humans are complete morons compared to octopuses. Even clams have more common sense."

"I gotta go tape up the windows. Think up an excuse, Joan. Come over."

When I went back in the living room, Andre said, "It's gonna hit Jones Beach tomorrow at lunchtime. We staying here or what, Gramps?"

In the morning, a fireman came while Dad was sleeping and told Gramps we should leave. Later, they were arguing about whether to go to the church because there wasn't enough room at Howard Earle's apartment. It turned out to be easy for me to say I'd just go up the hill and stay with Daisy and his mom.

Andre spent a while freaking out about his records and moving them all up into the attic in case it flooded. Then he decided the roof might leak and put them down in Arthur's room. In the end he took the British imports with him. Gramps gave him a twelve-record limit and he practically hyperventilated.

Arthur just brought *The Prison Notebooks* and a box of Marlboros. Panic was beneath him. He was more worried about getting bored. Gramps packed all the food into the picnic basket. *Hamper* is maybe a better word; our picnic basket is the size of Rockefeller Center. He made Andre walk me up to Daisy's before they left. Mom's notebook was in my backpack with volume five of the *Encyclopedia of Animal Life.*

Andre was supposed to check with Mrs. McNamara when he dropped me off, but Daisy said she was still sleeping. He was in the kitchen making macaroni salad with the radio on, some newscaster circulating panic and pretending it was helpful. I turned it off.

"People lived through hurricanes before they had radios."

"Cool. Let's pretend there's no electricity and no news. We have to look at the sky and smell the air to figure out what's going to happen."

"What would you do without electricity, Daisy?"

I kept my backpack on and looked out at the dark sky. There wasn't any wind yet. The drops pattering onto the window were like any old rain. The ocean was taking a big breath and getting ready to slam into us, but you wouldn't have known it.

We brought the macaroni salad and two sleeping bags up into the dormer window. Daisy's attic was the opposite of mine. It's just as old, but completely empty. There was no history up there, nothing to weigh us down.

"The little stuff will die," I said.

"Huh?"

"You asked what happens to everything that lives in the water. The big stuff goes way out and dives. That's how the fishermen used to know a big storm was coming. But a lot of the little stuff dies."

"Don't cry, Joanie."

"Fuck off. There's gonna be a lot of cool stuff out on the mud tomorrow."

"Yeah, like pieces of your house."

"My house has been through at least twenty hurricanes, Daisy. Think about it. Gramps said there was one in 1938 that was so bad a bunch of people died. Tomorrow, there'll be dead stuff that doesn't normally come this far in. I'm hoping for an eel. I really want to look inside an eel. Maybe another spider crab, or even a horseshoe crab this time."

"Horseshoe crabs are gross, Joan."

"Shut up. They're amazing. They have the best defense mechanism ever. Hide everything but the weapon, then stab first and ask questions later."

"How is that cool? It's insane thinking of something that looks like that being vicious. Does it even have a brain? There's a reason why Hollywood aliens look like the underneath of horseshoe crabs. I still have nightmares about the freaking spider crab."

"Pussy."

By the time we got comfortable, the wind was picking up. The tops of the trees were waving and tossing their branches against the sky. Daisy's eyes were wide and far away, watching his world get churned up.

"Teresa's nice," I said.

"She works at the Lagoon."

"Cleaning. So? What if she was a dancer? Who the hell are you, Jerry Falwell?"

"I'm just saying, your mom and dad don't even like *me*. What are they gonna think of her?"

"You'd like her if you met her. Absolutely no bullshit about her. It's almost scary."

"Beatrice says people's eyes are like diamonds. If you look at their eyes in the light, you can see the flaws. She said honest people's eyes are as rare as perfect diamonds."

"Beatrice isn't real, Daisy."

"Yes, she is!"

"You made a bunch of calls around the world and accidentally found some married lady in Italy who talks the exact same crap you do? In English?"

"Yes," he said. "I guess that's what a miracle feels like." Then he looked out at the storm and smiled.

Before Beatrice, everything Daisy knew was inside the circle of that window. Sometimes he stayed up all night, looking out of it. He likes my microscope for the same reason he likes that window. Not because he can see what's invisible, but because he can't see himself while he's looking through it. When you think about it, it makes sense that he'd make friends through the telephone, with people who couldn't see him.

Later when I couldn't picture where he was, I worried about what he'd do without the attic window. Without a frame for the world and a piece of glass to keep him separate from it. Right then, he put his hand up against the pane, millimeters from the hurricane, and looked like he was trying to breathe in the storm. I heard the front door slam.

"Is that your mom?"

"Maybe. Or it could be Robbie."

I should have realized there was something wrong with his voice then, but my mother's notebook was burning a hole in my backpack, distracting me. I hadn't even looked at it yet. The whole world was pounding onto the window six inches from our heads. Gusts of wind slapping it and raindrops falling on the roof so hard they sounded like a thousand rocks a minute.

"Daisy, what kind of thing could happen and you would

keep it a secret, even from me? Something bad or embarrassing or dangerous or what?"

"I don't know, Joan. That's a weird question. I'm gonna go down and make hot chocolate. Stay here and make sure the roof doesn't blow off."

As soon as his head disappeared down the stairs I took the notebook out, but it was too dark to read it. All I could make out were a few parallelograms. I ran my hands over the pages trying to imagine what kind of secrets were spilled out on them. Just before you get ahold of something, answers seem so possible. Like you'll actually be able to fill in all the blanks and understand. You don't realize how stupid that is until later, do you? While the words in that notebook were still unread, they held every answer I needed.

I looked up and thought about the light switch. Then I fished in my pockets for matches.

Just as I struck one I heard the crack and then the crash. I thought someone's house had fallen down. I looked out and the glare nearly blinded me. An oak had split and dropped a branch onto the power line over Jensen Road. Daisy came running back empty-handed and pressed his face up to the dormer window. I sat back, but he grabbed my hand and pulled me up next to him. The power line was writhing around on the asphalt, sending out sprays of blue sparks. Daisy was mesmerized. It was even better than lightning.

When we were little, I used to think he was some sea creature that got lost or robbed of his gills and wound up trapped in the world of air. That night, when I watched his face bathed in the electric light from our power lines, I realized it wasn't water he was made for. It was electricity. In Daisy's perfect world, electricity wouldn't be trapped in circuits; it would be free and everyone would breathe it. The air would crackle, and Daisy's weird transparent arms would wave around, full of charge, looking for contact.

We must have stared at that power line for an hour. It kept snaking around, and the cold fire kept spitting out of it. Sometimes it caught the water and the raindrops lit up all around it.

I look back on myself in that dormer window and all I can think is how blind I was. It wasn't that what I knew about Daisy wasn't true, just that each thing was hiding something else, something worse and deeper that had nothing to do with me. If I couldn't see anything that was happening to him, how was I supposed to rescue him like the helpful sidekick from the movies?

I didn't save anybody. I'll tell you that up front.

The electricity went off about three in the morning. The cable in the road flopped and went still, then disappeared into the dark. Then the world was nothing but sound, nothing but wind and pounding water and Daisy's hand on the window.

We had to light a fire in the fireplace to warm up the hot chocolate. Daisy got out a flashlight he'd made out of a Palmolive liquid bottle and the bulb from a brake light, but it kept dying if you squeezed it the wrong way. We lit candles and went down the stairs with our shoulders against the wall so we wouldn't fall. We burned the sides of the saucepan and the hot chocolate came out lumpy, but we put it in a thermos and took it back up to the attic anyway.

When Daisy went down to the bathroom I pulled out the notebook again and tried to make the flashlight work so I could look at my mother's handwriting under the flickering bulb. I didn't even read the words. I just kept studying the loops and curls to see how she made her *J*s and whether her *R*s were always the same. I thought about changing my name to Joan Jensen. Then I thought about changing it to something that had nothing to do with my family at all, just scrubbing them and their weird silences out of my life completely. If I moved to a city somewhere, I could make up a life and change it every time I met someone new. Hiding the notebook from Daisy was my first lie, but I could feel the attraction right away.

When I heard Daisy coming back up the stairs, I panicked and shoved the notebook behind the insulation. I tried to act normal while I thought about how I was going to get it back out again without him knowing.

Why should I tell him? I was Daisy's friend, which is why his brother came to my house looking for him and ended up dripping blood on my life. But when he needed someone to talk to, he picked Beatrice instead of me. She was too far away to get caught up in his mess. I was right in the middle of it, and he left me blind.

Daisy lit a lighter and then a candle. He held his hand in front the flame so I could see the red glow of the blood inside him. Then we took turns holding our hands over the candle while the other one counted. That was the first time Daisy ever won that game. I guess I was tired of being tough. Anyway, neither of us was tough enough for what came next.

Let me tell you what happened that night. A chaos of wind and water and power came in off the ocean and ripped the surface off our world. Stripped us bare. That's not even a metaphor. After that night everything was raw, wide-open, and exposed to the pitiless sky.

School was closed for two days while LILCO fixed the power lines and they cleared the trees off the roads. The morning after the hurricane, we went out to look at all the things that had been picked up and tossed all over Highbone. Roof tiles and clapboards and pieces of birch bark. Sail covers and hubcaps and tar paper. The tide was in, so we walked around the harbor over to the Narragansett, but it was closed. There was kelp up on the road, which is weird because it's deep-water stuff and doesn't even grow in the harbor.

We were examining our beech tree for damage when I heard my mother honking a horn up on the road. Well, I guess it wasn't her honking because there was some other guy driving with his girlfriend in the passenger seat. When I got to the top of the steps she had the back window rolled down and her head laid down on her arms.

"Joan! Gimme some sugar," she said.

"Hi, Mom."

"Hi? That's it? Did the house blow away? Please say the house blew away. Morgan and Marian and I risked life and limb getting out here to check on you. Give me more than 'hi,' girl."

"Hello? Are you okay? Did you see any dead people on the highway?"

"Where is everybody?"

"Hi, Mrs. Harris." Daisy was still three steps down, looking over the edge of the road and wondering if he should keep coming up. My mother always stopped Daisy at the threshold. If she'd been around more, we might never have been friends.

"Joan! I said, where is everybody?" She ignored Daisy like he hadn't even spoken.

"They went to Howard Earle's."

She rolled her eyes. She thinks Howard is a philistine. "And left you here alone?"

"I was at Daisy's."

She gasped. Very theatrically. "You were—we'll talk about that later."

Then she pulled her head in and opened the door, jumped out, and stuck her head back in the car. "Come on, you two. My industrious young daughter will make us some coffee inside."

She had on a skirt and about six necklaces. Her hair was in two braids and she had red boots. At first I thought the boots were cool, but when I looked closer, they weren't.

In the kitchen, I sat with the lady who turned out to be Marian while Mom showed Morgan up to the attic.

"So, Joan, is it? You're in high school? What's your favorite subject?"

"Facts."

That stopped the rest of whatever bullshit Marian was going to hand over, and I looked out the window while the water boiled. Daisy was trying to be useful, looking for a milk pitcher. I didn't point to the right cabinet because I figured the longer it took him to find one the less time he'd have to spend figuring out what else to do.

After I put a cup in front of her, Marian came up with, "Facts are good, but what about feelings? People your age should read poetry. You're the perfect age for poetry."

"Just poke around up there, Morgan," I could hear my mother yelling up from the bottom of the stairs. "You'll find something good, I promise!"

"Poetry is a scam," I said to Marian.

She gave up then.

Mom came back in and took over the coffee like I wasn't all the way qualified. She put cinnamon in it.

"Morgan is writing a piece for us," she said. "I've been telling him he needs to come out here and riffle our attic for material."

"So you thought a hurricane would be a good time?"

"The phones are down. I was worried about you all." Even Marian didn't seem convinced by that.

By the time Mom put Morgan and Marian back in the car, they were carrying a whole box of irreplaceable things that belonged to my family. The tide was on its way back out.

My mother folded her arms on the car door and laid her head on them again.

"You two be careful. I'll be back Wednesday for rehearsal."

She stood watching their taillights.

"You're staying?"

"Well, try not to sound so thrilled about it. Tell me who the hell thought it would be a good idea for you to be sleeping over a boy's house? You're fourteen, for Jesus' sake."

"Fifteen. And it's not *a boy*; it's Daisy."

"Well, I'm sure even Daisy McNamara has working parts."

In case you're wondering whether my mother ever had "the talk" with me, that was it right there. Hope you didn't blink and miss it.

"I'll be speaking to Dad later. Let's make some hot food for when the boys get back." Now she was Susie Homemaker?

When she said "Dad" she meant Gramps. When she said "the boys" that included my dad. Like he was just one of the cumbersome children she had to cluck over half-heartedly every once in a while.

"I gotta go out, Mom."

She yelled after me, but I ignored her. I found Daisy on Arthur's bed turning the pages of *The Stranger* like he was reading it.

"Arthur said I could. He said I could read his books whenever I wanted."

"I don't care. Help me find an eel, come on."

"I'm reading, Joan."

"No, you're not."

"How's your mom?"

"I don't fucking know. Come on, I went over your house for the hurricane; now you have to help me find an eel."

There wasn't an eel, but there was a bicycle wheel, two different shoes, a young dogfish, and about nine tons of plastic garbage. We took the dogfish to the floating dock, and I went back in the house for my encyclopedia and my new scalpel. I'd oiled it, like the guy said.

"Look at the gills," I said to Daisy.

You have to make the cut down the side, not in the stomach like you do when you're cleaning a fish to eat.

"Why, Joan? Why would I want to look at the gills?"

He was rolling the bicycle wheel around the floating dock. It was so bent it wobbled and made wavy lines in the mud.

"See how many gills there are? That's because dogfish are old."

"Some of them must be babies."

"Stop being stupid on purpose. This one is a baby. I mean old in evolutionary terms. Sharks are like roaches, man. They've been here forever."

"They're squidgy." But he leaned over to look while I pulled one of the gills back with my new scalpel.

"Why are you cutting it open? Just hang it up and all the guts will fall out the mouth. Remember?"

We saw that once, me and Daisy. After *Jaws* came out, they used to get people to hang around the fishing tournaments by bringing in big sharks and hanging them up. No one was going to eat them or study them. They just killed them for crowd pleasers and hung them up until the guts fell out of their mouths. Go figure. The insides fall out because sharks have no bones to hold them together. Sharks have been around longer than bones.

When I draw my own anatomy book, the pictures will look like big a pink-and-gray mess you have to pick through. Because that's what it's actually like. Not all neat and color-coded. Death is wet and messy and confusing. It took me fifteen minutes to find the long, skinny lungs and lift them out. Daisy wouldn't even look at the pipe that carries the water through between the sets of gills.

The dogfish's skin was like sandpaper, and the pink inside of it was fading into no color at all. Even the sky over us seemed like it had been dredged up and then drained. The mud at the bottom of the harbor smelled terrible. I remember Daisy's breath, sounding slow and damp and then getting faster when I opened up the shark and showed him the truth inside.

daisy

AUNT REGINA MAKES braciola and manicotti. Every time I go out and come back, there's some dead thing roasting in the oven. Beef joints and chickens and one time a whole octopus in a pot, I swear to God. I can never get away with taking my dinner up to my room; I have to sit at her table that is permanently set. I get up in the morning and everything is already there, the place mats and the ceramic salt and pepper shakers and the bowl of fake dahlias. She crochets covers for the spare toilet paper.

I eat it all and look in the mirror every day to see if my arms are filling out. She tickles me, counting my ribs like I'm five years old. "I'm breaking the bank, trying to put some meat on you," she says.

I wonder if my mother grew up in a house like this, with plastic over the furniture and everyone endlessly cooking. Sometimes

I shut my eyes on my square window with its view of all the other square windows and try to picture it. Frank Sinatra on the radio in a house somewhere in Astoria. My mother in bobby socks, trying to breathe.

I couldn't stop thinking about what Beatrice had said, about housewives and hopelessness. She said the reason my mother was drifting away was lack of hope. My dad shipwrecked our family and left her stranded on the rocks. That's why I called home and pretended to be someone else, so I could make her feel like a rescue was coming. I was trying to help. I swear.

I went all the way to Greenport, on a day when the sky was one big cloud and the wind was relentless. It was one of those middle-of-the-day trains with hardly any people on it. I stood between the cars and did some math in my head: the population of Long Island divided by the number of calls I made a month. How many people could they rule out? How many calls did the average person make, daily? How many pay phones were there on the whole island? I should start going into Nassau, maybe Queens. I should have been going to other states, but even *my* family might notice that.

It was a few days before the hurricane, but the waves in Greenport were already huge. All the summer places were closed, and the sand from the dunes had blown onto the edges of the road.

I made the call from a boarded-up clam shack across from the beach. Sea gulls came screaming around me, thinking maybe

French fries were coming back early. I had to wait half an hour for them to give up and go away.

Then there was the wind. I could hear it whistling through the receiver and up into my ears, so I took my jacket off and made a little tent over the phone. Then I could hardly see. I had to work the blue box by feel.

My mother's voice went to Illinois and came back to me sounding higher and thinner than it really was. It made me wonder how different Beatrice would sound in person. How I sounded if you were sitting in a window in Italy.

"Hello? Hello!" my mother said. "I can hardly hear you."

I had a handkerchief over the mouthpiece and I was doing an English accent. I don't know why. I couldn't think of anything else but truck driver, and that seemed too obvious. Too much like a movie about gangsters.

"He'll be out soon, Mrs. McNamara."

"What? Who is this?"

"Don't you worry about your husband, ma'am. We're taking care of it. He'll be coming home soon."

There was a long silence and then she took in a big, slow breath. When I heard her crying, I hung up.

I came out from under my jacket and the seagulls started screaming again. I used up nearly all my matches, trying to light a cigarette. The wind was forcing every breath of ocean air back down my throat. Finally, I went into the dunes and lay in a hollow. I was out of the wind there, but if I reached up I could put my hand in it. I looked up at the silhouettes of the birds against the sky, thinking I'd done something good. I'd made the world better. Thinking, *Wait till I tell Joan.*

On the way home, the train rode slantways into the sunset, throwing a parallelogram shadow onto gravel and the weeds. I sat in the facing seats at the end of the car and put my backpack behind my head. Down the aisle there were some old people coming back from a week at the beach, and a bunch of off-duty conductors riding back to Jamaica.

I leaned back to look out at the strip malls and the wrecking yards and the lights glowing into the pink air. I put my feet up and thought about hope, how easy it was.

"You using all these seats or what?"

I looked over at a pair of stockings full of holes and then up at a blue Mohawk. I hadn't even realized she was standing over me.

I said, "Sorry," and moved my feet, even though there were only about five other people in the whole car.

There was a guy standing next to her, but he didn't say anything. They sat down across from me and she put her feet up between me and my window.

"Cool jacket," she said.

"I got it from my brother."

"Well, it's cool on you. Where you going?"

"South Highbone. You?"

"South Highbone, on this train?"

"It's complicated. Where are you going?"

"Ronkonkoma. This is my cousin Kevin. He doesn't say much."

He raised a hand and said, "Hey." He had black hair and black eyes and a Swiss army coat.

"You don't look like a Kevin."

He laughed. "Yeah, my parents are Greek. My mom thought Kevin was a hardcore American name. She thought it would make me blend in."

"You guys live in Ronkonkoma?"

"Kevin lives in Bay Ridge. They send him out here for the fresh air." She looked out at a container yard and smirked.

"I thought you were from the city, too."

She laughed. "Why, 'cause I don't look like a cheerleader?"

"Don't people hassle you?"

"I live in Commack. What do you think?" But she smiled. "Where you been?"

"Greenport. I had to make a phone call and I couldn't do it from home."

Then I had to explain a little about the phones. Kevin wasn't saying anything, but he was looking at me like I was about to do something he didn't want to miss. It made me feel a little uncomfortable, but also a little more like I mattered.

"You gonna tell me your name?" I said to the Mohawk girl. I sounded like Robbie. Like talking to people didn't faze me at all.

"Anne."

"Seriously?" I looked at her net vest, held together with safety pins, and the *PiL* button on her jacket. "Anne doesn't seem good enough."

"Okay, what's yours? Alexander Graham Bell?"

"Daisy. Well, it's been Daisy ever since I was three." I nodded at Kevin. "My mom wasn't thinking about the whole blending-in thing. Technically my name's Anthony."

"Nah, Daisy is definitely better," Anne said. "It's tough on you."

That was the first time I realized that when you're talking to strangers, everything about you is new. There's no expectation. No context. In Anne's ears, my name sounded completely different than it did to the people who knew me. I could feel the world get a little bit bigger.

"You go to school in Brooklyn?" I asked Kevin.

"College. Hunter."

He was nineteen and he was taking fine art. They don't make people like Kevin in Highbone. But then, I didn't think they made people like Anne on Long Island either.

Before she got off the train, Anne asked me for a piece of paper. All I had was my empty matchbook. She borrowed a pencil from Kevin.

While she was writing she said, "Kevin's going to meet me in Westbury in January. We're going to see the Slits at My Father's Place. You should come."

She stood over me while she undid one of her safety pins. Then she used it to pin the matchbook to my jacket. On it was her number.

"'Cause I know you're good with the phone," she said. Then

she kicked my feet off the seat and ran off the train laughing.

"Cool to meet you," Kevin said, and swung down the steps after her.

I leaned back and looked out the window, listening to the buzzing in my veins. Since the middle of summer, I'd been trapped in a parallel circuit. Joan. Robbie. My mother. All of them were pathways through resistance. Until that day, when I stepped outside the trap. I went the other way, didn't ask first, didn't tell anyone, and did what I figured was right.

It felt good at the time. At the time, I thought Anne and Kevin were proof that I had shifted something. I actually believed I'd just manufactured hope out of thin air.

Two days before the hurricane hit we turned on the news while my mother sorted through the mail. A whole week's worth was piled up on the bricks of the hearth, bills and circulars on top of a pile of old *Pennysavers*. The hurricane was still a tropical storm in the Caribbean, but the weatherman kept showing us pictures of it swirling toward us.

"This is his once-in-a-lifetime chance," my mother said. "He's hoping it'll be bad."

"The leaves'll be great this year, Mom. Can we drive upstate?"

She wasn't listening. "If people get evacuated and maybe a couple of them die, he'll go coast-to-coast."

"I'm sure that's not what he's thinking, Mom. Anyway, how bad can a hurricane be in October?"

In the end the leaves never got a chance last year. The hurricane came and ripped them away while they were still halfway green.

"You seem happy today, Mom. Something cheered you up?"

She picked up her coffee cup and said, "I can't take this anymore. I wasn't cut out for this."

I was so used to those two phrases coming out of her mouth; I hardly heard them by that point. She sighed and went upstairs with her coffee and a water bill trailing from her other hand. I watched the big swirling storm on the weather map and the sun coming in the windows and thought, *How bad can it be?*

My mother came back downstairs all dressed up. I looked at her blond hair, shining in the sunlight coming from the front hallway. I'd gotten used to the dark line down the middle of her head. She'd been slipping for at least a year at that point, smudges on her nails, her color growing out. The truth kept creeping up out of her body no matter what she did to hold it back. Now her nails had gone back to the right color red.

"You look nice, Mom. What's the big occasion?"

She looked at me and tilted her head. I looked into her eyes, but they didn't seem to lead anywhere.

"Nothing, Daisy. Hold my hands." She held her new fingernails out to me and I reached past them to touch her palms. Her eyes went misty and she smiled like someone had just said they loved her but she didn't love them back. Not the way they wanted.

I should have known it was a sign of something when the

blond went all the way to her scalp again. I did know, but I read it wrong. I was looking, but I wasn't listening. She was wearing dressy sandals and she seemed bright, full of energy. I thought she was coming back to us. When I close my eyes and look at that last image of her on the couch in the morning light, I can still feel my own happiness. I thought my phone call had fixed her. Everything was about to get better.

"Best boy," she said. "Tell me about your week."

"I told you before, Mom. I had metal shop. We did quadratic equations in math. Arthur lent me a book named *The Street*. It's really sad."

The other thing I'd done was wire a tape recorder to my light switch. When you hit the light it said, "Hello, Daisy. Come on in. Relax." But that stuff made her nervous, so I didn't mention it.

"Where's Robbie?"

"No idea."

"I'll have to go up and see your dad. Will you two take care of each other?" She meant that as a serious question. I know she did. In her mind, Robbie could take care of me.

"Yeah, Mom. We'll do the leaves, too. If Robbie helps me, I can clean out the gutters for real this time."

"You're so good, Daisy. Someone lucky is gonna marry you."

She left the next day. It had rained overnight, regular rain, not hurricane rain yet. There were piles of wet leaves on the driveway. She made Robbie get out of bed and started talking to him about emergencies and the mortgage and the savings account.

She put her arm around me and looked over at him. "You know he's special, right?" She meant me.

"Yeah, Mom," Robbie said. "I'm gonna make sure he's okay. He's going to be a college genius, if I have to carry him there on my back." He meant that, too. He would have done anything to take care of me. He did.

The wind came up and blew some beech leaves around in circles, while the telephone wires swayed back and forth over Jensen Road. I stood next to Robbie in the driveway, watching while she took the Chevy down the hill. When the sun hit the copper paint, you could see it had glitter in it. There were maple leaves stuck to the back windshield and the white vinyl hardtop. Her brake lights went on at the bottom of the driveway and again before she hit the curve by the Narragansett.

I grew up on a road to nowhere, that's for sure. It carried people around that curve and right out of existence. All those people who crashed into the wall when we were little, and my dad, then my mother, and all the others, too. When I think about it, they all went around that curve before they disappeared. Even me.

daisy

THE HURRICANE STALKED us for a couple days, winding its way up the coast and feinting a few blows at the coast of Virginia and Maryland. People unplugged things, and the sound of televisions was replaced with the sound of battery-powered radios.

I taped up the windows and called Joan.

We spent a lot of that night in the dormer window watching the crazy wind. We talked about Ray Velker. Nobody had seen him in a couple of weeks by that point. We wondered for a minute if he'd gone back home because of the hurricane. Showed up to help his parents unplug the appliances and tape the windows.

"Where's your mom tonight?" I asked her.

"In the city, where else?"

But of course I was really wondering about mine. Where was

my mother that night? Was she up the Hudson somewhere, safe inside four walls? Dry? Sitting in a rest stop watching the wipers and the rain glistening red in the tail lights?

"Do you wonder what their lives were like before we got here?" Joan was saying.

"Huh?" I pulled our pan of hot chocolate out of the fireplace and poured it.

"You're not listening." Joan poked my arm and made me spill some onto the bricks.

"Sorry. I was thinking about Robbie."

"Yeah, but before Robbie, before Arthur, what were they like?"

"What was who like?"

"Our parents, Daisy! You ever think whatever they are now is because of us? We're in the way of them being who they're supposed to be."

That was so obviously not true about either of my parents, or Joan's mother. Except for Joan's dad, none of our parents even let us slow them down. I couldn't say that, though.

"No, Joan. I don't. I don't think being who you're supposed to be means you get everything you want. It's how you deal with what you get."

"Put that shit on a Hallmark card, McNamara. That's good enough to keep a hundred housewives quiet for a whole month."

I took the hot chocolate upstairs so we could sit in our sleeping bags and drink it in the attic window. Now I'm trying to figure out which things had happened by the time the hurricane came. What was on her mind at that point?

Me? I was hiding in the middle of a hundred-mile-an-hour wind. Everyone around me was moving, but I was standing still.

The best thing that happened that night was when the old oak fell down across Jensen Road. It took down a power line and it was at least three hours before LILCO cut the juice. It was like somebody opened a vein and let the lifeblood out of the suburbs, blue and white and spitting. I looked out at that writhing wire and then over at Joan. She was burning, too. I could see it. Things were growing and changing inside her, and she was reaching out to touch the world.

The raindrops lit up and the televisions died and everything that kept our lives circulating came free of its casing and seeped out into the storm.

For days, the world was full of garbage. Pieces of trees and pieces of boats and junk out of people's backyards blown around everywhere. The abandoned house had fallen another foot, and for months we were afraid to go in it. I woke up in the middle of one night and looked down at the dead power lines at the side of the road. There were striped sawhorses with flashing yellow lights around them.

I came downstairs and found Robbie at the dining room table with the checkbook. He had some ground-up pills sitting in the mortar and pestle with a rolled up twenty, but he was doing the math. I checked it.

"Hey, Robbie. Want some coffee?"

"Daisy."

"Yeah, I'm the only other person here now, remember? So, coffee?"

"This one's red." He held up an envelope. "We need to do this one."

"Okay, Robbie." I started making the coffee anyway.

"Daisy, some kids are dealing some weird shit in the school. Stay away from it, okay?"

"I already know. The other day—"

I was about to tell him about Patrick and Ray dosing me. I was about to say how I sat there trying to keep the floor down all night. I thought we'd both laugh. Then it hit me. He probably already knew. He might even know where Ray was. Robbie was dealing, Ray was meeting him in the driveway, and I was so busy trying to stop Joan from asking questions, I hadn't really asked myself.

I never finished my sentence, but Robbie didn't notice anyway.

"You hear me? None of that dust and shit, right?"

"Right, Robbie. How much sugar?"

Turned out we didn't have any sugar. Robbie said he was making a list and pulled out the telephone pad from under a stack of bills. He wrote "SUGAR" on it in capitals.

"It's a weird high, anyway. You wouldn't like it." He wasn't wrong about that.

How did Robbie know about what kind of shit was going around school? Well, that's the sixty-four-thousand-dollar question, isn't it? I guess I knew right then that the angel dust Patrick and Ray gave me at Hatchet Mary's came from Robbie. I'd spent a whole day and a night crouched in the attic window, trying to keep the walls of reality from falling in and crushing me, and it was probably Robbie's fault. I turned my head and looked outside so I didn't have to look at the facts.

It was so dark out, all I could see in the kitchen window was the kitchen. And me looking back at myself in a T-shirt with *Oxum Oaxaca* written on it backward. It was four a.m., no point going back to sleep.

"This one's red," Robbie said again. "We have to do this one."

"Okay, Robbie. Let me check your math."

"Go for it. You're the college genius."

Like I said, it was right. He couldn't even remember five minutes back, but he could add and subtract and balance two columns, as long as one of them wasn't made out of something that could get you high. Spawn of an accountant, Robbie McNamara.

I took a shower before the sun came up. When I got out, Robbie was asleep in the living room chair. I made pancakes, but when I tried to wake Robbie up he just ran into the bathroom and threw up then went back to sleep on the couch.

I never call Joan in the mornings because her dad works late and sleeps late. So I finished off the maple syrup and put it on the list, then ate the pancakes myself. While I was eating, the sun came up washed my reflection out of the kitchen window. When it lit the tops of the trees in Carter's Bay, I went up into the attic so I could get a look at the world before I went out into it. I saw

Joan heading to the bus stop, but I didn't shout. I didn't want her to come in and see Robbie.

When I got out onto the road, Joan was leaning against the cement wall with a cop standing over her. Arthur's car was parked at the top of the Harrises' stairs and the people from the Narragansett were cleaning all the hurricane junk out of their parking lot. Then all that disappeared into the image of Joan with her head leaning back against the wall, looking past that uniform at the sky. The cop was tall and so skinny his uniform was baggy at the waist. The weather was getting cold, and the breath was condensing between them, turning gold in the sideways sun.

When you walk along that wall the sound of your steps bounces off it and out over the harbor. You can't sneak up on anybody right there, not even with bare feet. When I hit the road along the wall, the cop turned his sunglasses on me, then he said something I couldn't hear and nodded at Joan.

"Hey, Joan!" I ran the rest of the way.

Not because I was really worried, but because you just do, don't you? When we were little we ran everywhere, down under the trees, splashing through the shallow water, crunching the snow in January, up and down the attic stairs. If you took your shoes off in the halls at school you could get up a run and then slide. We liked doing that in the art hallway next to the graffiti wall. Maybe last year was the year we stopped running. The year we slowed down and everything caught up to us.

The cop was parked on the inside of the curve with his flashers on. You wouldn't see the flashers until you were on top of him, but what did he care? If someone hit his car, he'd get a new one and the other person's life would be fucked. He opened his door and got in, didn't even look at me when he pulled away.

"You rob a bank or what, Joan?"

"Or what."

"Seriously, what did the cop want?"

"I don't know, Daisy. What do cops want? Ask Sigmund Freud."

We climbed onto the bus and I leaned into the back seat, looking up at the blue sky and down at the reflection of bare branches moving on the water. There should have been a whole circle of red and gold around the harbor, but the hurricane had ripped it away. I looked over at Joan and she looked fine. Well, maybe a little grumpy and fed up with me, but that was normal.

I just didn't think about it.

I'm looking out my window now, at the place where Joan just disappeared. There's no curve here; Rockaway is nothing but right angles. It must be an hour since she made the corner outside, but I can still see the shape of her fading from the edge of the street light. And I can still see her there against the wall on Jensen Road, too. I'll never stop seeing it, now that I know what I was looking at. Officer Kemp turned out to be the cop's name, but I didn't find that out until he'd forgotten it himself.

SKIPPED, BEAT

joan

THE DAY OFFICER Kemp pulled up at the bus stop, I had the notebook in my backpack. It was the end of October, almost a week after the hurricane, but there was still a load of broken branches and trash all around the edge of the harbor. I got to the bus stop before Daisy, before anyone, and stood against the wall feeling my mother's life against my back.

She had a brother. He died, in the army, I think. At first I thought it was a boyfriend, but then I did the math on her age during the war. Also I realized the whole family wouldn't be crumpled up with grief over just some boy my mom had a crush on. So. I had an uncle and no one had bothered to tell me. That was my family all over. Pick any corner in my house and shine a light in it, I'd find some fact that made one of my relatives into someone I'd never met before. Truth was their enemy.

I didn't even know his name or where he died. Did they send his body home to get buried? Was there a grave? Did Gramps go to visit it when we all thought he was playing chess with Mr. Johnson?

"Joan Harris?"

I hadn't even heard him pull up. His car was sitting on the curve of Jensen Road with the light going around but no siren. All I could think was, if you're a cop you don't need to use flashers.

I just nodded.

"Your brothers are Arthur and Andre Harris?" Crap.

"Yes."

"Tell me how long your brothers have known Ray Velker."

"What? My brothers don't know Ray. He's in my grade."

"Someone's distributing some dangerous drugs in the high school, Miss Harris. I'm sure you've heard something about it."

"No, sir. I don't do drugs."

He switched gears so fast it took me a minute to catch up.

"You're all grown-up, aren't you?" He ran his eyes over my T-shirt, and I felt like someone was smearing dirt on me. I kept quiet. What was I going to say? He put one hand against the wall next to my head.

"Well, I hope your brothers aren't involved. Don't you?"

He leaned his head so close to my neck I could smell the rancid cop coffee on his breath. I was so distracted by it that it took me a few seconds to feel his fingers on my belt loop.

"I like girls like you," he said. "You're just born knowing things, aren't you?"

He tugged my belt loop and then pushed up his sunglasses so I had to look at him. There was nothing else in front of me but those empty blue eyes. They reminded me of icebergs and the titanic sinking, of an ocean so cold it couldn't even carry sound.

"You can't do this." Count that as the stupidest thing I ever said. He just laughed.

"I guess I'll just have to ask your brothers myself."

His face blotted out the harbor and the trees and the sun that I hadn't even bothered to notice when I was standing there alone. The air in front of me that I hadn't even bothered to breathe.

"Joan!" Daisy's voice came bouncing of the cement wall, and his ridiculous feet started flapping faster down the asphalt.

The cop didn't move. He kept his face right where it was and then laughed again, under his breath. It seemed like forever before Daisy yelled my name again and the cop took his hand off my jeans. I felt like my body didn't belong to me anymore. I just wanted to get on the school bus without it, leave it there on the side of Jensen Road.

The cop got in his car and drove off.

"You rob a bank or what?" Daisy said.

I stayed after school to talk to Mr. Tomaszewski about the dogfish. Daylight savings was over and it was almost dark by the time I'd been to my locker, gone to the library for a book about Aristotle, and headed home. The oak leaves had been down so long they were drying out, and the wet maple leaves had left ghosts of themselves on the sidewalk. The rest of the trees had been stripped bare by the hurricane. If Daisy had been there, we would have gotten off the sidewalk and walked along the edge of the road, just to kick up the dry leaves and hear the rustling sound.

Even after that morning, I hadn't learned to be scared. Not yet. I was so glad to be alone, I even took the long way home. Which was why I ran into Robbie behind the library. I was circling my conversation with Mr. Tomaszewski around in my head, trying to understand how it felt. And I was thinking about my mother's brother, about the emptiness behind Gramps's eyes and what my dad knew about it. Did Arthur know too? The world around me disappeared while I tried to imagine a life for that picture of my mother, the one on my father's dresser. I tried to see her speaking and moving around the house, sad and angry or dreaming and excited by the world beyond the curve of Jensen Road.

I didn't realize anyone was behind the library with me until Robbie said my name. I woke up from my daydream and felt everything at once, the air going into my lungs, the size of the space around me, the distance between me and home. Robbie was by the bushes next to his car. I looked away at the library but it was empty and dark.

"Hi, Robbie. You waiting for somebody?"

He looked confused for a minute. Then he stood up and took a step toward me. "Where the fuck did you take Teresa?"

A gust of wind blew through my insides like the hurricane had suddenly woken up again, but I kept walking. I just wanted to be in the road, in the traffic, in my own kitchen, with or without my mother. I wanted to be in the bottom of our boat with nothing but water on three sides and the sky on the other.

"In the park? We just went for a smoke," I said. "That was weeks ago, Robbie." I took a few steps toward the corner of the building.

"I brought her," he said. "I would have taken her home. You should mind your own business, Joan."

He stood between his car and the side of the library, legs spread out and hands hanging loose, blocking the way out of the parking lot. I still don't know if he was threatening me or if he didn't even realize what he was doing with his own limbs. Either one was possible.

"I wasn't being nosy, Robbie. I was just being friendly. I like Teresa."

"Don't bring her around the house. I don't want Daisy hanging around with girls like that."

"Girls like what?"

"Never mind, Joan. Just leave Teresa alone, right?"

"Sure," I lied. "Robbie, can I say something to you?"

"You want a ride home?"

"No, I'm good. Daisy needs you. He needs you to be okay. You're his big brother."

"Hey, make sure you and Daisy don't do any of that shit that's going around school. I told him; now I'm telling you."

"Yeah, we won't. What about you? The thing with your

parents is already killing him, Robbie."

All of a sudden his back got very straight and his eyes cleared up.

"Something you want to say about my parents, Joan?"

"Never mind."

I didn't want to walk past him, so I cut through behind the gas station, in the opposite direction from home. From the scrubby trees behind Dunkin' Donuts you can see the traffic on 25A, but it can't see you. I stood there and smoked a cigarette, trying to guess where the people inside the cars were going.

Did Robbie just want to get Teresa high and sleep with her, or was it worse than that? I couldn't put him on a scale and weigh his intentions. I couldn't measure the shape of whatever was wrong about him lately. According to Mr. Tomaszewski I just needed more information and a logical system. According to people like my mother and Daisy, I needed extra metaphors. I needed to appreciate the poetry of everything, even this shitty little patch of trees under the flat black sky. I was supposed to see the universal truth and beauty through the exhaust fumes and the selfish intentions and the greed.

What I could see was this: Everything was more confusing than it needed to be. Everything would be simpler if Robbie would just go away.

daisy

WE STILL HAD normal days. I was still pretending my mother would be home soon. I was still lying to Joan about her being gone at all. Robbie was still there the day I got home from school and smelled autumn. Things were rotting under the trees. The tree branches were just dark shadows poking into the sky. You wouldn't know it was fall from the leaves turning because the hurricane had whipped all the color out of the world.

I loaded some dishes and made some macaroni and cheese. Then I called Joan to tell her my mom was out and the *National Geographic* special was in Morocco.

"Camels," she said.

"It isn't camels; it's mountains. Just come over."

"I don't want to watch a show about sand. I want jellyfish."

"Morocco has beaches, Joan. Look at a map."

"Yeah, but no one ever films them. They just want to talk about spice markets and camels."

"You know you're coming. We can't know where we want to live until we see everywhere."

"I like it here."

"No, you don't. This place pisses you off. I'll make you hot milk with honey and ginger. I'll let you tell me about jellyfish brains."

"Jellyfish don't have brains, Daisy! That is my point, which just proves you don't listen."

We ate the macaroni and cheese and Joan made coffee with cinnamon in it. Robbie came in and stuck his nose in stuff, like he couldn't tell what it all was from the kitchen doorway. He leaned against the counter and smiled.

"You two should get married before Mom comes back."

"Shut up, Robbie." I walked into the pantry and stood there until the blush left my face.

"You remember what I said, right?" I heard him say to Joan.

Silence.

"We made one good thing in this family." He lowered his voice, but I could still hear him. "That's Daisy. It's my job to take care of him while my dad's away. You think I don't know that?"

"Yeah, I know. You're the man now." You'd only know that was sarcasm if you'd been listening to Joan your whole life.

"I know you're more grown-up. Keep him away from that shit at school, you hear me?"

I stayed in the pantry until he went back upstairs, then we ate at the table, in between the bills and the newspapers. When it was time, I got my grandmother's blanket, and we brought some hot chocolate into the living room. While we were watching the Atlas Mountains, Joan took a *No Nukes* button off her jacket and stuck me with it.

"Ouch! Joan, what the fuck?"

"That's it. You see that part where you flinched and felt pain and yanked your arm away? That's all they have."

"All who has? What are you talking about, and why did you stab me, you complete nutcase?"

"Jellyfish, Daisy. All they have is the flinching and maybe the pain, the twitching and pulling away. The part where you felt surprised and pissed off and betrayed, like why would my friend do that to me? They don't have that. No brains. Just nerves."

"You could have just told me that. Psycho."

"Yeah, but you won't forget now, will you?"

"Okay, let's make sure they never let you be a teacher. Where'd you get the button anyway?"

"Nick gave it to me."

"Who the hell is Nick?"

"Mr. Tomaszewski. He was telling me about this big demonstration in Battery Park. The cops tried to ride horses right over them while they were sitting on the pavement."

"When did Mr. Tomaszewski get to be Nick? That's creepy."

"It's not creepy. He talks to me like I'm a person. What's wrong with that?"

"Oh my God, he's perving on you!"

That was the moment. I should have said something right then, but all I was thinking about was me. She was looking right at me and saying only Mr. Tomaszewski talked to her like she was a person. It hurt. I didn't think about Joan, or what she was missing or why she thought it would be so cool to have nerves but no brain.

"Did Robbie go out?" she said.

"I don't know, Joan. Why are you so obsessed with older guys lately?"

"Eww! I just want to know what he's up to. So would you if you paid attention."

"Sorry. I was a little distracted by you being brainwashed by a teacher."

"See, if you have brains people can wash 'em, which is a drawback. Can't brainwash a jellyfish. Anyway, you oughta know by now my brain is unwashable. I'm special that way."

"I bet if the administrators knew he was talking to you about peace demonstrations and giving you rides home, he'd get in trouble."

"The principal is your moral compass now?"

"Okay, you want to talk about shit? Why are you so mad all the time lately? Are you still pissed at your mom or what?"

"I don't know, Daisy. Nothing adds up these days. I feel like I'm playing that game where you have to guess who's giving the signals. Like everybody knows but me."

"Joan, you should forget about the Robbie thing. For real.

Let's go see where your mom stays." Maybe I was trying to distract her. I don't know.

"I don't know if I want to. I told you that. Why are you always hassling me about it?"

I looked around the living room at the emptiness where my mother used to be. It was so wide and cold, our house felt like the windows were open all the time. Like the wind was blowing through the hallways and the walls didn't matter anymore. There was no difference between inside and outside. I didn't want any of that to spill over into Joan's life. I didn't want it to touch the two of us. I was up to my neck, drowning. But I still thought I could cling on to her and keep her dry at the same time.

Worse, even after what happened when I tried to fix my mother, I tried to fix Joan, too.

We did go to the city. We cut school, took an early train, and ended up squished between some old commuters playing cards. On the concourse at Penn Station, we were hemmed in on all sides by people in suits.

We heard the rattle of the CC train and saw the rats scattering and the light in the tunnel. A guy was living at the end of the platform and another guy was playing the saxophone behind us.

We got on the train and tried to stand up without holding on. Then we hung on to the pole and swung around each other.

"Is your mother gonna be pissed at us?"

"I don't care."

I fell onto the seat, dizzy, and looked up at a tag made with a fat marker. It said, *They still haven't caught The Zephyr.*

"She already doesn't like me, Joan."

We sped through a ghost station. A light like cathedrals was falling through the grating from the street and down the walls. Every inch of the place was covered with tags. I pictured the kids jumping down in there and climbing out again. Inhaling spray paint fumes and standing on each other's shoulders while hot wind blew down the tunnels and over them. That light making them saintly while rats scurried around them and colors came out of their hands. That could be our lives, but it wasn't.

"Believe me," Joan said. "My mother doesn't think about you enough to dislike you. She doesn't even think about me that much."

The train screeched into Ninety-Sixth Street and the doors opened on the smell of piss and engine grease.

Mrs. Harris's building had a doorman and a guy working the old-fashioned elevator. We asked for her, and the doorman said no one with that name lived in the building.

Joan looked out the doors at the wall and the park and then said her mother's maiden name. "Jensen. We're looking for Eva Jensen. She's in 5B."

"Oh, of course," the doorman said, and Joan laughed at him.

He called up and said Joan's name into the phone behind the desk. A little mouse shriek came through so loud we could hear it from where we were standing, then something lower. He pointed to the elevator.

We told the elevator guy where we were going and he said nothing at all, just pulled his big lever and looked at the wall.

There were two doors in the hallway, and Mrs. Harris was standing in one of them with one hand on her hip and the other on the door frame.

"Joan, what the hell are you doing here?" she said.

"Nice to see you too, Mom."

"See? That is the kind of thing people do. Force you into saying something and then blame it on you. You are worrying me, child." She nodded at me. "Daisy. What's going on with you two?"

Joan moved in front of me. "I just wanted to see where you live."

"So why didn't you call first and ask, like people? You know better than this. I'm a guest here."

Joan looked at her feet. "Can we come in or what?"

"Yes, of course you can come in. Stop being ridiculous." We'd been there a minute and a half and it was already a fight.

"Do you want me to wait downstairs?"

"Don't be silly," Mrs. Harris said. "Come in and I'll get you kids something hot to drink."

But it was Joan I was asking, really.

When we came through the door of 5B, it turned out to be connected to 5A on the inside. The two front doors were both on one long hallway. There was light down to the left, and the sound of something classical on a stereo.

"This way." Mrs. Harris stood back and pointed down into the dark on the right. "All the way back."

The hallway smelled like dust and cigarettes and naphthalene. We passed a series of shadowy rooms full of boxes, with old tennis rackets and school uniforms piled on the beds. There were bookshelves and dead plants and mirrors reflecting the light that leaked from Central Park West around the drapes.

"This is where you live?" Joan said.

"I don't live here; I live with you. The Novaks like my work, honey. They invited me to stay so I could be closer to the theater. But I only live when I'm with you all."

"That's bullshit."

"Watch your mouth. And sit down."

We passed a little kitchen and stopped at a room with the blinds up and the surfaces mostly cleared. There was a table and a desk looking out over the park.

"This place is creepy." Joan sat down so hard the chair jerked back and scraped the floor.

"It reminds me of home," Mrs. Harris said. "Did you see those rooms down the hall? Full of empty husks, full of ghosts. Doesn't it remind you of Jensen Road?"

"So, you don't want to have the same name as us?"

"I use Jensen for the theater. It's the name I grew up with. It feels right."

I just kept quiet and worked on being invisible.

"The same name as your brother, you mean?"

I didn't know what she was talking about at the time. Joan didn't tell me about the notebook or the dead uncle until everything was over.

"What are you . . . ? Who talked to you about that?" Mrs. Harris looked like someone had taken the life right out of her, like there were big sad oceans in her eyes.

"So, what, you thought I would never find out? You think that's okay?"

Joan wasn't trying to be mean. She was just feeling around trying to find out where everything was. She was just trying to pull the blinders off.

Mrs. Harris said, "Daisy, do you like sugar in your coffee?"

I just nodded. I didn't want to add a single breath to that situation. I wanted to go out the window, scale down the wall of the building, and run away into the park.

She put coffees in front of us and got out a box of cookies.

"Okay, honey, what do you want to know?" She turned the desk chair around and sat facing us.

"Seriously?! Where do I start? Why the hell is everyone lying all the time?"

"No one's lying, Joan. What did anyone lie about?"

"Fucking everything!"

"I said, watch your language. Not talking about something that happened before you were born isn't the same as lying. Your gramps has suffered a lot of grief. I guess we started by not wanting to upset him, and then it just became a no-go subject."

"That's a cop-out. What about you? You don't talk about anything. Why don't you live at home?"

"I do live at home. I just stay here for work. And I did talk, to your father." She went quiet for a minute. "I used to talk to your father about it all the time, when Arthur was a baby."

"You talk to Andre, too. Why not me?"

"You're not understanding. The minute I saw Arthur I was terrified. I could just see him falling and crashing and breaking apart. I was afraid to hold him, even."

"Jesus!" Joan stood up. "Get over it. People need you."

"I know that. And I'm doing what I can about it. Being myself is part of it, honey. One day you'll see."

"No, I will not. I have no interest in seeing." Joan got up and turned toward the doorway. "You can fuck off."

I started to follow her, then turned around in the hall. Mrs. Harris didn't even get up. She just put down her coffee and looked out the window. The way she stared made me think of Joan. The two of them are bigger inside than other people.

By the time I caught up with Joan, the elevator man was already sliding back the folding door of his cage. He pulled the lever and looked at the wall. The weights rose and we dropped to the lobby. Downstairs, we crossed the street and stood on a bench to climb over the wall into the park. There were bag people everywhere. It seemed like somebody was living in every hollow under the trees. We found an empty spot though, on a slope under some sycamores. The ground was freezing. We could see the tops of people's heads and the taxis going by.

I'd never been to the city without my mom before. The people made me dizzy. Not because there were so many of them, exactly. It was because every single one had a story. They all had voices and histories and pain, sparking over the surface of Manhattan in a pattern so complex no one could read it. I was thinking how every time they crossed over or into each other, a whole new set of futures was born.

It was like the phone lines. It occurred to me they must be more complicated in Manhattan than anywhere on earth. I thought about the old movies where the exchanges still had names. "Murray Hill three-two-nine," a lady with marcelled hair would say, and another lady with a cheaper dress and a Brooklyn accent would unplug a wire and plug it in somewhere else. My mother told me my grandmother had that job. She worked in a big exchange wearing roller skates.

"Let's go to the museum," Joan said.

She jumped over the wall and down off the bench and headed downtown before I'd even stood up.

I just sat there for a minute, caught in a sea of voices and multifrequency signals, crackling through wires underneath and above me. Every one of them was carrying a conversation as inaccurate and painful as the one I'd just seen. The world was made of strangled voices and tears and blue sparks.

We walked in and stood under the murals, looking up at the T. rex. The main thing I remember now is the musty darkness. The light was just like in those bedrooms at the Novaks' apartment. The Museum of Natural History goes on forever, chock-full of the suspended dead. Leopards stuffed with straw and skins flattened all over the walls. The whole place is cold and shadowy and full of marble eyes.

Joan wanted to see some jellyfish that were made by glassblowers in Massachusetts. They were pinned up on boards, sparkling against black velvet. It was the only place in the whole museum that seemed to have enough light. The only place where I was pretty sure I wasn't breathing in the skin cells of dead animals.

Joan walked all the way around the room once fast, and then started again slower.

"I hate them," she said.

I was bent over a Portuguese man-of-war. "No, look! They got all the details."

They'd even tried to make movement in wavy glass.

"I am looking. You can see they weigh a hundred times more than real jellyfish. If you dropped one of them in the ocean it'd sink straight to the bottom."

"I think they're graceful."

"They made it all, except the most important thing."

Joan was looking for the motion, the resistance, the watery breath that shaped them.

"They look all correct, but it's a trick."

She was right, of course. They had the wrong weight, the wrong gravity, no motion, no cell division, no change.

"Everything is dead, Daisy."

"Okay, you had a weird day. It'll be better tomorrow."

"No, I mean, everything is frozen. Stopped. Like all those jars of pickled things upstairs. Time isn't right in here."

"I thought you'd love it here. You're always cutting up dead stuff."

"I never want to do this. I was wrong. I've been wrong the

whole time. I want to look at stuff that's alive."

"Cool. It'll be so much less gross for your friends."

"I don't give a shit what my mother does anymore."

"Okay. Maybe you're just pissed off at her right now?"

"Actually, no. I just don't care."

It was dark by the time we got back to Penn Station. We came down the stairs in the middle of that sea of commuters in suits, all taller than us. "Baaa-aah," we said to their backs. Nobody even turned to look.

We couldn't find a seat, so we stood at the end of the smoking car, flashing through Woodlawn and Forest Hills and into the tangle of tracks outside Jamaica.

"They have dead people, you know."

"What?"

"In that museum, they have dead people. They don't put them on display anymore. They keep them in the basement. Arthur told me."

"Jesus! Isn't that illegal?"

"They're not white people, Daisy."

I looked over at Joan, straining like a hot air balloon with one of the strings cut free. Someone had thrown some weight off, tilted her sideways and lightened her. She was breaking loose, from Jensen Road and childhood and the laws of gravity. I couldn't see the whole thing yet, but it was beginning. I felt it.

daisy

IT WAS JUST before Christmas the night Robbie came home with his hand bandaged up and his neck covered in purple fingerprints. I was in my mother's bathroom when I heard the front door slam.

She wasn't there on the bed behind me, sleeping. She wasn't downstairs making artichoke quiche. Her bedroom was starting to smell like dust, but the lights around the mirror were still warm and yellow. They still made whoever stood in them glow like a movie goddess. The thing was, we weren't in a movie. Not even my mother. Nothing was going to tie up neatly and make perfect sense after an hour and a half.

"Daisy!" Robbie's voice sounded hoarse but it didn't really register. Why would it?

I was thinking about doing something with that circuit that

lit up the mirror. It had to be pretty complicated, because if you unscrewed one bulb the others stayed lit. What kind of things could you put in there? Fans and pinwheels and different colored lights and maybe the speakers from phone receivers.

"Daisy! Need to talk to you."

I looked down into the front hallway and saw the blood on his shirt before I saw the bandages. I could see his nerves singing and twitching too, but it turned out he wasn't high. Or anyway that wasn't the reason he was humming like a LILCO wire.

You couldn't live with Robbie unless you learned not to panic too quick. Whatever it was might get better or it might get worse, but that wouldn't have anything to do with how you reacted to him. Mainly I was thinking, *God damn it, Joan's coming over. Not now, Robbie.*

"Come in here," he said, and went through the living room doorway.

By the time I got down there he was pouring double shots of Jameson into our grandfather's Waterford glasses. Whatever it was, he thought it was big. I noticed he wasn't breathing all the way.

"Sit down." He was hurt bad. When he saw me staring he said, "For real, you shoulda seen the other guy."

"Robbie, we need to go to the emergency room."

"Don't worry about it. I got seen to already."

"By a doctor?"

"Sort of. Listen, Daisy. I'm gonna have to do something a little dangerous. If I don't come back, you need to be careful. I'm pretty sure no one'll bother you, but if you don't see me just watch out."

"Robbie, I think you probably need to calm down. Who'd you get in a fight with?"

"You're gonna have to take some of this on, Daisy." He waved his hand around at the house.

"What? I'm doing more stuff than you, Robbie. Who do you think raked the leaves? Who do you think keeps putting stuff in the dishwasher?"

"You know what? Before you came I was the golden boy. When I was little Dad used to look at me like now that I was in the world, he could stand up straight and feel no pain. Later, he started staying away, and Mom kind of went to sleep and stopped taking care of her hair."

"I'm sorry, Robbie. But none of that is our fault."

"When you came, it cheered us all up for a while, even her. By the time you could walk everybody could see you were smarter than me. Weedy, but smart as fuck. Mom said it wasn't just your yellow head that made her call you Daisy. It was your weedy sweetness, she said."

He put a hand out toward me. "I just always wanted them to look at me again the way they did before you were born. But I love you though, man. I want you to be okay."

I looked at the rug and then out the window, because I couldn't stop myself thinking, *You're just making excuses for why you're a fuckup. It isn't their fault, and it definitely isn't mine. Get a grip.* If I opened my mouth, that was what would come out, and I didn't want it to.

I picked up the glass. "What happened today, Robbie?"

"Mike Johnson was disrespecting Dad."

"Who's Mike Johnson?"

"I guess I was so mad my body was moving faster than my brain. By the time I even noticed what I was doing, there was blood everywhere. I had one hand around his throat and I was hammering him with the other one until his eye socket cracked."

He held up his bandaged hand and said, "That's how this happened. I might have used a piece of the chair, too. I don't remember. I stood up and went out to my car, and no one even tried to stop me."

"Jesus, Robbie!"

"Dad's in jail because he's a soldier. Mike Johnson shouldn't have been disrespecting him."

"This isn't an Al Pacino movie, Robbie. Dad's not a soldier. He's an accountant."

"Okay, see?" He was pulling on a clean T-shirt. Moving his arm made him wince. "Everybody always protects you, Daisy. That's gotta stop now. I'm sorry man; I love you as much as they do, but it's time to step up."

"I stepped up, trust me. I've done plenty. You just need to calm down."

"We need more cash. I'm gonna have to do some drastic shit, and it might not work."

"No, Robbie, you don't have to do anything. You could just get a job."

"That wouldn't be fast enough. It wouldn't be enough money.

You're gonna have to grow up a little, man."

He said it like he was equipped for survival and I wasn't. Like he had the skills to even walk down the road without falling down and breaking something. And he believed himself too.

"Mom could come back anytime; you just gotta hold down the fort. I'm leaving you the checkbook."

"Robbie, you can't leave."

It wasn't me I was worried about. Robbie could barely tie his own shoes without hitting himself in the face or swallowing poison. How was he gonna survive whatever crazy crap he was planning?

"Don't spend too much. If this doesn't work, there might not be more for a while."

Robbie went into the garage and came back with the big crescent wrench. I looked down at my glass and realized it was empty, except for the syrupy liquid that clung to the sides. I'd never drunk whiskey before. It tasted like vinegar and dead leaves at the back of my throat.

He actually hugged me before he went out the door and got in his car. In the driveway he said, "I should be back in the morning, but if I'm not you can totally do this, man. You're smarter than all three of us put together."

He had to reach over and shut the car door with his right hand. The window was rolled down even though it was cold. I opened my mouth and nothing but condensed breath came out.

I tried to yell but I was trapped in a vacuum. No medium for sound, no air in my throat, and my ribs collapsing under the pressure differential. I wanted to grab at him and scream for him to stay, but I couldn't move.

Finally, I shouted something useless like, "Please don't, Robbie." He was already hyped up and crazy and bleeding, and he was going for more. He was half-dead already, and he thought he was on a roll.

Did I love Robbie? I don't know. I just wanted my world to stop tearing apart. I love him now. He was my brother.

Robbie's instinct for self-preservation was just missing. Even before he started trying to fry his own brain and get himself mangled and crushed, he got his kicks from doing crazy shit other kids wouldn't do. My first memory of Robbie is him standing out on a branch over the harbor while another bunch of kids stood around shouting. I was maybe three. He jumped into the water and it was only three feet deep. One of his ankles twisted on the bottom and swelled up. Dad was home, and Robbie sat around the living room smiling with his foot up for a week.

Later he climbed the water tower, rode his bike down the steps and right out onto the curve of Jensen Road, raced his car without a seat belt, and started dealing speed in the Lagoon. The shape of Jensen Road was how Robbie saw the universe. He was always riding a curve.

I watched him pull into the Narragansett and sit there for a while, then pull out again. As soon as his taillights disappeared, I started counting the minutes until Joan got to me. I watched until all the lights in the Harrises' house went out. I wanted her to come in my front door and shove my arm and explain why I didn't need to be scared after all. I wanted us to stay up all night telling each other everything, behind the attic window where nothing could touch us.

None of that happened because she never showed up that night. The next time I saw her she was sixteen, walking up the road wrapped inside a whole new world.

joan

WHEN TERESA CALLED, I was standing at my bedroom window with my mother's notebook, looking at the water rising and the light stretching out sideways through the cold atmosphere. The tiled roof of the abandoned house was showing through the branches, and there were a few scraps of cloud sitting on the harbor.

My mother had written in the notebook about the day she met my dad, and then some other things after. About her college friends and how she was only studying to be a nurse because her parents wanted her to. How she had to do whatever they wanted now, because of the dead brother.

I jumped when Andre opened my door and said, "Phone."

There was coffee in the kitchen, so I poured some and pulled the telephone through the storm door. The heat rose out of my cup into the air. The weatherman had said we'd get the first snow before morning. I had to dangle the receiver over the back railing to let the cord untwist. A little tinny version of Teresa's voice came out of the mouthpiece, circling over the harbor.

"Just a minute," I shouted at her. "I'm untwisting."

By the time I got the phone to my ear it burned me with cold.

"Robbie got in a fight at work," she said.

"At the Lagoon? See? Told you he wasn't as nice as he seems."

"No, listen. It was like watching a building blow up. All of a sudden, furniture was flying around and all the air heated up. There was blood all over the floor."

"Crap. Are you okay?"

"I'm fine. I called to say you were right."

"It happens sometimes. Glad you figured it out, though. You seem cool."

"I mean, it wasn't what you thought, but he tried to get me to do hard stuff. So I'd keep buying it off him. So I'd owe him money."

"Please tell me somebody put him in the hospital."

"He drove away."

"He lives in a house with my best friend and his mom, Teresa. What should I do?"

"Talk to him. Your friend, I mean."

"I tried. It doesn't work anymore."

"Want to meet me at the mall?" she said. "We can ride the escalator the wrong way."

"I probably won't be able to go anywhere now until after Christmas."

"Say what you mean, Joan Harris."

"I kind of like one of my teachers. I think my mom and dad might break up. My best friend is lying to me. All the time. And seriously, it's gonna be family stuff from now until after Christmas."

"Wow. Nothing that interesting happens to me. Just the whole dealers-trying-to-kill-each-other-in-the-strip-joint-where-I-work thing."

"Fuck off. How about the day school starts? Meet me at twelve."

"I can't cut school," Teresa said. "They'll call here. Meet me the Saturday before."

"Fine."

"I'll wear my hat, so you can spot me."

"Right. I'll be the one with the security guard following me around."

She hung up and I sat down with my back against the railing and my cold coffee in my hands, holding the phone against my shoulder. I needed to talk to someone. Should I try my dad?

When I read my mother's notebook, I hardly recognized the person who I knew must be my father. The guy who wore those shoes he keeps in the closet. The guy who called her a queen and was studying political science. What the hell happened to them?

The phone sounded one long beep in my ear, then changed

pitch and screeched. I had to go inside to get a dial tone back so I could call Daisy's number.

"I'm coming over, Daisy."

"Cool. No one's home but me. Hurry up."

"You're going to tell me the truth. Tonight."

Silence. Not even any sound on the line.

"No one even likes me hanging out with you," I said. "Your brother's a menace, and you commit felonies in phone booths on a daily basis, but you are my best friend. That only works if you tell me everything."

"Okay, Joan. Okay."

But those were just words. From where Daisy was, I was just a voice. My words traveled across the road and up the hill to his kitchen through the wires. But all the things I wasn't saying stayed right there with me. I hung up.

After the house went quiet, I climbed out the window and up the hill, thinking me and Daisy would watch TV with the sound turned down until the color bars came on. Daisy would tell me everything and then we'd go up and sit in the attic window. I'd show him the notebook and explain about my parents, and this time he'd get it. Daisy would help me fit Nick Tomaszewski and my dead uncle and my father's sad eyes into the world. We'd breathe out and let ourselves go. Daisy would talk on and on about the phone system and the English exam.

None of that happened. That fantasy didn't even make it all the way across the road.

At the bottom of the driveway I saw Robbie's yellow Charger, and suddenly I knew the answer was in there. I just climbed in. It wasn't until I was lying on the floor in the back with Andre's duffle coat over me that I even thought about what I was doing. I was going to get the truth and bring it back so Daisy couldn't deny it anymore. We could tell people what Robbie was up to. He'd stop or go away, and everything would be fine again.

I hadn't thought about the interior light. It seemed to take five minutes to go off and I lay there imagining what I would say when Robbie stuck his head in and went, "Uh, Joan, why are you on the floor of my car, man?"

Then I heard Daisy.

"Robbie, listen to me. This isn't a good idea." His voice was high-pitched and choking.

"You're all good, man. It'll be fine. I'll probably be home before you wake up."

"I'm asking you, please, Robbie. What do I tell Mom if something happens to you?"

So there I was on the floor of Robbie's car when I realized there was a reason Daisy needed me. When I realized that mattered. According to Teresa, Robbie had already practically killed somebody that night. Whatever he was up to was killing Daisy, too. I'd heard it in his voice. Inside Daisy was a life as big as the ocean, and I'd been looking at it with a microscope. It was like trying to open the sky with a scalpel. There was a whole world of hidden pain in his voice, and all I'd been thinking about was the facts.

Then Robbie opened the car door, and it was too late for me

to get up and say anything. I stared up at the roof of the car and out at the tops of the McNamaras' pine trees. If he'd looked in the back he would have seen me, but he was Robbie, so he didn't.

Daisy yelled "please" one more time while Robbie made a hairpin turn and headed out onto Jensen Road. I had to hang on to the back of the passenger seat to keep from rolling all over the place. We didn't go far at first. Robbie pulled into the Narragansett parking lot and opened the glove compartment. I looked up at the sign that said "Crabs. Stuffed clams. Beer on tap," listening to the sound of his razor blade clicking on mirror glass. When we pulled out again, he went through his gears so fast I rolled up against the back seat and came uncovered. He put Pink Floyd on the tape deck and I breathed out, pulling the coat back over me.

He went across 25A and parked in front of a house on Meadowlark Road. He was in there so long I sat up and rolled down the back window to smoke a cigarette. It wasn't until later that I thought what would have happened if anyone over there caught me. By the time I had the sense to be scared the whole thing was almost over.

I sat on the floor of the car with my knees folded up, trying not to think of the sound of Daisy's voice. I thought about Teresa and her floppy hat. My father's shoes and my mother's photograph. I tried to think of smart things to say to Mr. Tomaszewski about Aristotle and his cuttlefish. Did I mention it was freezing? I shook my legs every once in a while to keep the blood flowing. I thought about my mother's brother. What did he look like? When did they hide all the pictures of him? Maybe I'd seen his face in a box in the attic and I didn't even know it.

Did Andre know about him? Was I the only one they didn't trust?

I don't know, maybe if I was someone else I would have cried. Okay, maybe I held my eyes open so the tears would circle back down and I could swallow them. But then they burned my throat and made me want to scream at people.

Anyway, I'd grabbed ahold of one thing out of all the weird confusing things. I was going to follow it until I found out where it led to. Then I was going to fix it.

Guess how that worked out?

By the time I heard Robbie saying goodbye on the front porch, it was the middle of the night and my legs were numb. The next place he went was the Stella Maris Chapel. He parked around back where there weren't any lights. There was no moon and no surf, either. The gulls were asleep, and the partiers at Fiddler's Cove had gone home. Robbie got out of the car and slammed the door behind him without looking back.

I counted to fifty before I lifted my head and looked out the driver's-side window. Into absolutely nothing. I couldn't see Robbie or anything else either, except the outline of the chapel that made the darkness darker in between me and the road. I had to hope Robbie was on the other side of that square of blindness when I opened the door. I got out and nearly fell over. My legs were so numb it was like they weren't even there underneath me. I leaned back against the door and tried to click it shut as quietly as I could so the light would go off.

I made for the chapel and felt my way around it. My legs came back full of stinging pain, but I ignored that. When I looked around the corner of the building I saw Robbie in the street light, crossing the road into the Fiddler's Cove parking lot. He wasn't going to the beach, though. He went back into the marsh and disappeared. I went along the road behind the trees so I wouldn't show up in the street light. There were two lights by the showers that stayed on all night, but they only fell halfway across the parking lot before the shadows took over.

Robbie was suddenly nowhere. I wanted to curse out loud and break one of the streetlights, but instead I slid down against a tree and stared at nothing while all the implications of what I'd been doing hit me. I stretched my legs out and moved my toes. The blood rushed back down and burned my skin. After a while the pins and needles stopped, but by that time my ass was frozen. I strained my eyes trying to see my cold breath in the dark, but it didn't seem to be there.

He'd gotten away from me again. I couldn't wander through the marsh looking for him without a flashlight, and if I had a flashlight he'd see me.

I was going to have to walk home. It was three miles away and three o'clock in the morning and I didn't even have to wonder which cops were on the night shift. Not with my luck. If I tried to go the whole way off the road, I'd be filthy and late for breakfast by the time I got anywhere near Jensen Road. One more time, I wished I had my scalpel.

Just as I gave up and pushed myself up against the tree at my back a car pulled in, a green Mustang with two guys in it. They drove over to the dark side of the parking lot and right to the edge of the asphalt, then turned on their lights and shined them out onto the water. Everything outside that pathway of light went dark and I heard Robbie stumble and curse under his breath. He hadn't gone into the marsh at all. He was about twenty feet from me and I thought any minute he was going to say, "Joan Harris, what the fuck!" Pull me out and send me home or back to his car.

He didn't say anything, though, and I'll never know if that was because he didn't notice me or because he didn't want those other guys to know we were there. We stood right near each other on the edge of the marsh, watching those beams of light and the little ripples the wind was making on the water. And I guess those were the last fifteen minutes Robbie McNamara spent near anybody who knew him or cared. I don't know.

I got distracted looking for Daisy's boat in the stars and didn't notice when a real boat pulled up and idled just at the edge of those headlights. The two guys got out of the Mustang, and one of them walked right past us, heading to the parking lot entrance. He stood looking down the road, and Robbie strode past me swinging something heavy in one hand. That was when I noticed he wasn't moving too good. He held his other hand against him like it was useless. I realized he must have driven all that way one-handed. Also, he was barefoot. There was frost on the grass and that crazy junkie wasn't even wearing socks. He snuck up from behind and swung once at the lookout's head. Robbie was tall and it was lucky hit. The air whooshed out of the guy and he crumpled down without making a sound.

Well, I was right. And wrong. Robbie was a lot scarier than anybody thought, or a lot more desperate. Daisy knew already, and he was hiding it from me. He thought I needed to be protected. Daisy. Me. Everything was upside down in ways I hadn't even dreamed of.

Robbie left the lookout lying on the pavement and circled through the shadows at the edge of the parking lot. He passed within five feet of me. Three steps would have put me in his path. I could have reached out a hand and stopped him, but I just leaned against that tree and held my breath.

The trunk of the Mustang was open, and the other guy was helping unload stuff from the boat. He waded back with his arms full of something wrapped in blue tarp and the boat started its engine and turned back out into the Sound. It was gone before he even got back to the car. I was still watching the water when the boat's light went on and started shrinking toward Connecticut. I guess Robbie swung at the other guy and missed because I heard the shout and looked back in time to see the guy grab on to Robbie's bandaged arm. The lookout came cursing and stumbling across the parking lot.

They threw Robbie against the car and started talking to him in loud whispers I couldn't make out. He yelled once when they twisted his bad arm again and they told him to shut up. Those were the only words I heard.

The lookout punched Robbie so hard I heard the roof of the car buckle when his head hit it. Then he threw him across the back seat while the other guy took his waders off. They slammed the door on him and drove away so fast I was looking at their taillights before I was done wondering how much damage that punch would do. One minute after Robbie's head bounced off the roof of that Mustang I was standing in the dark by myself. I needed to get to Daisy, but I was pretty sure the keys to Robbie's car were still in his pocket.

It did take me almost three hours to cut through all the woods and backyards between Fiddler's Cove and Jensen Road. I had plenty of time to think, and it wasn't about my mother or Nick Tomaszewski. That scene at the beach washed through me like turpentine, burning all the confusion away. The scale of what mattered and what didn't and how much there was to hide had brand-new proportions.

The way I figured it, there were three possibilities. Either Robbie was already dead, or he'd have to wise up, or he'd run away. Any one of those would make life better for Daisy and his mom. But I wasn't wishing for any of it. I swear.

I felt like I'd tried to shove a bully out of the way and they'd stumbled in front of a moving truck. How could I tell Daisy?

I'd found out everything I needed to know, but none of it mattered. Robbie McNamara's life was just blood and blunt instruments and need. When you open a dogfish you see a mess of guts; when you open up a person like Robbie you see selfish blindness and meaningless violence. People call guys like him animals but they're not. Animals only kill each other when they're hungry.

When I got home, I went back in my window and straight to

Andre's room. He opened his eyes when I bounced onto the edge of the bed.

"Wake up. Now."

He looked at the wall and then pulled his blanket over his head.

"Joan, what the fuck?"

"Get up, Andre. I want the truth and I'm not leaving you alone until I get it."

"Puberty is turning you crazy. You get that, right?"

"Why were you in Robbie McNamara's car?"

"What the hell are you talking about? I've haven't even seen the guy since October."

"You were in his car, back before school started. Twice. You told me he just happened to see you and give you a ride home. That's bullshit, Andre. Tell me the real reason or I'll tell Dad you like boys."

"You need permanent Valium, you know that?" Andre sat up and hugged his knees. "Will you at least get me some water?"

"No."

"Jesus! He wanted me to sell shit for him. And by the way, I did just happen to run into him and he did offer me a ride home. Not everyone is lying all the time, Joan."

"Yes, they are, and you know it. Did you know Mom had a brother?"

"What? Will you stop tripping?" He looked at his alarm clock. "It's six thirty!"

"Why would Robbie ask you to sell his shit, Andre? You won't even take aspirin."

"Aspirin is bad for you. And I'm the only black kid in the entire senior class. Do you have any idea how many times a day kids ask me for weed?"

"Robbie wanted you to sell his weed?"

"Not weed. Forget about it, Joan. You should stay away from the McNamaras. I know Daisy is your soul mate or whatever, but Robbie is not cool. Seriously."

"Daisy is not my soul mate. He's my best friend and I need to know what kind of shit is going on in his house. What was it?"

"Angel dust. He must have found somebody to move it because it's everywhere at school. Kids are smoking that shit before class. Can you imagine?"

"Not really. And Mom did have a brother. He died. Ask her, since you're best friends."

I ran out of breath and ground to a halt. There was nothing more to find out.

"Please get out now," Andre said. "I have twenty minutes before I have to get up for work." He slid down and pulled the blankets back over his head.

When it got dark again I went and looked over at the McNamaras' driveway, hoping to see Robbie's car and hoping not to. I stood staring at their front door, feeling numb. There was either too much going on or not enough, but I couldn't make myself feel it either way. The next day was my birthday, and turning sixteen didn't matter at all.

joan

MY MOTHER WAS home, and she wasn't even mad at me for going to the city. Gramps made me a cake and sang "Sixteen Candles" and everyone laughed. Arthur stood by the light switch while Mom lit the candles, and then the room went dark, candlelight in everyone's sparkling eyes. I can almost see it in the train window now. If I unfocus my eyes I can feel my way back to that kitchen full of people trying so hard. Full of secrets and lies and a whole other kind of light.

All the time, I felt like Robbie was on the edge of the circle of candlelight, just outside, bleeding and struggling for breath.

It was carrot cake, because that's my favorite. We played Scrabble at the table. Except Andre because obviously his new pipe-leg jeans had made him too cool for board games. He stood by the wall saying, "That's not a word," and "Normal people don't do this on their sixteenth birthday." I knew what I was doing, though. Mr. Tomaszewski said he'd meet me at the Narragansett at eleven. I just wanted to climb into his Deux Chevaux, where nobody knew anything about angel dust or missing kids or the McNamaras. I wanted to talk to him about cnidarians and echinoderms and anything else that didn't have a brain.

When everyone started to drift off, Dad called me from his room. Mom was with Gramps in the kitchen, murmuring together and drying the dishes. It was ten fifteen and I was getting nervous. I sat on the bed next to Dad and tried to look interested while I jerked one foot up and down.

"There's something I want you to have, Joan."

When he went to the closet and started moving things out of the way, I was sure he'd go in the desk next and find out the notebook was missing. He was after something else, though, a little wooden crate with six square holes, made for bottles.

"They used to keep soda-water siphons in here," he said, "back in the day. My father got it from the old bar car."

He lifted out something wrapped in tissue and uncovered it. It was a glass the color of blood. No, rubies. People say rubies are the color of blood but they're not. People are unobservant and then they're innacurate. Rubies are purpler, blood is more orange. He held the glass up and looked at the lamp through it, then handed it to me.

"They were my grandmother's," he said. They must have been made around 1900. There used to be twelve, but things get broken over the years."

I held the glass up and looked through it at the ruby world. It was so thin, it could have been a soap bubble.

"What do you drink out of them?" I didn't know what else to say.

"Punch, I guess, originally. Or whatever you want. They're yours now."

"Dad! I can't keep these. I can't even keep my sneakers clean. I'll break 'em."

"Everything in this house is your mother's. I only have a few family things, and you're the only girl. Woman, now." He actually put his arm around me. I got distracted trying to remember the last time that had happened. "They should be yours."

"Tell me about Nana." My dad grew up in a house with a regular mother in it. I was trying to imagine that.

"She was happy enough. And just good. Listen, Joan. You know, sometimes it seems like you're . . . supposed to be with someone."

Oh, crap. Now he wanted to have the talk? Really?

"It's so good when it seems like someone understands you. Being around someone, you get comfortable."

"Don't worry, Dad. Nobody makes me feel comfortable. I don't really like people. Except Daisy, and he doesn't count."

"Well, what I'm saying is, we take things—people—for granted. We don't always see the whole situation. People tend to assume everyone sees things the way they do."

"You lost me, Dad."

It was ten thirty. I needed to be out my window in twenty

minutes. All I could think was, why couldn't this meaning-of-life shit come tomorrow or the next day? I already had more truth inside than I could keep down. It was making me sick.

"I'm saying the way you feel about someone isn't always the way they're gonna feel about you."

Then it hit me. He was talking about Daisy. He thought I was dreaming some kind of white-picket-fence dreams about Daisy McNamara.

"Dad, seriously. I don't feel any kind of way about anybody. I promise."

"It can sneak up on you, Joan. You could always talk to me. Or your mother."

My mother? Was he serious?

Then I looked over at him. His eyes were wandering around the room while he rustled some of the packing paper from the box with one hand. Right then I realized he was broken. Someone had ripped the guts out of him a long time ago. Just the weight of the everyday air was so much he could hardly hold himself up. I watched him sitting there, and even his breath looked painful.

I held up a ruby glass and looked at him through it. The glass was lighter than those jellyfish at the Natural History. You could imagine it as liquid too hot to touch, blossoming out of the glass-blowing rod. You could see the frozen movement in it. Those jellyfish makers should have studied my great-grandmother's glasses. Dad leaned forward through the red world, put his elbows on his knees, and sighed.

Both of us had spent the past few minutes thinking he was

talking about me. I think we realized together that he was talking about himself. That night I figured out my dad was invisible. He was the one nobody noticed. I should have thrown myself onto him right then, crawled inside his arms and knocked all those glasses onto the floor. I should have acted like I was his daughter.

I just stood up and said, "Thanks, Dad. They're really beautiful."

He shook his head and smiled at me.

"Try to keep them safe. It'll be good for you to take care of something that's been around longer than you."

I put the crate of glasses on top of my dresser, closed my bedroom door, and forgot about my father's pain. I'm not proud of it, but at the time all I could think about was where I was going next.

Arthur had gone out, and I could hear The Selecter coming from behind Andre's door. From my window you could hang down over the back stairs, and the drop was only a few inches. Maybe my uncle used to do it too, in some 1940s world of big band and roll-your-own cigarettes. I still don't know which room was his. One of us must sleep in his bed.

The tide was out, and I went across the mud to the Narragansett parking lot. All I'd worn was a sweater because I couldn't jump out the window in Andre's duffle coat. There were only four cars in the lot, and none of them was Nick's. I sat on the steps behind the deck and lit a cigarette. There were patches of ice on the planks and icicles hanging from the railings, but somehow the cold didn't touch me. I sat in a shadow, hoping Daisy wouldn't see me if he looked out the attic window. I'd told him I had to spend the whole night with my family. I didn't want to face him after what I'd seen. I thought I could keep it to myself and he'd never have to know.

Nick pulled up twenty minutes late and shined his headlights on me. I looked straight into them and blinded myself, then squinted my way around to the passenger door.

"Guess where I was today?" Nick said.

I shut the door and took my mittens off. "Model airplane club? Weight Watchers?"

"No."

"Home watching *Jeopardy!*? Moral Majority fundraiser?"

"Yes, you are very witty, Ms. Harris. I was at a science teacher's conference."

"Be still my heart. Were there a ton of pocket protectors?"

"Ha, ha. I got something for you."

Nick drove until we got halfway down Herman Road, to a sign that said, "Liberty Diner, twenty-four hours." Someplace no one from Highbone High School was going to be at midnight. He reached in the back seat and grabbed some catalogs, then slammed his door. I locked mine; he didn't.

"If anyone really needs it more than me, they're welcome to it," he said. "I have insurance."

The walls of the diner were aluminum with red-and-green neon chevrons down them and pointy milk-glass sconces. The waitress looked at us like we were criminals. Nick ordered souvlaki and made me get something big, too. I went for a Spanish omelet and a strawberry shake, then thought about my grandmother's glasses and asked for red Jell-O, too. When it came, it was the wrong color. Everything was wrong under those lights.

The catalogs were from UC San Diego and the summer program at Woods Hole. Nick thought I should go to Woods Hole before I started eleventh grade.

"People don't talk about science like it's a talent, but it is, and you have it, Joan."

"Yeah, yeah, 'a mind is a terrible thing to waste.' I heard it already."

"Joke about it all you want. It's still true. Don't you want to get off Long Island?"

"Not really. Why? My family's been here so long I'm pretty sure I'd get sick and die if I drank the water anywhere else. And there's no lack of sea life. Why can't I just stay here?"

"Because the programs you need are in other places. If you don't do it, you'll regret it later."

"There would be people. I really don't like people."

"People like you, though. You're very personable, Joan. That's a talent, too."

Personable. Think about that for a minute. What the hell does that mean? Available to be made into a person?

"People are crazy and violent and selfish. I don't care what psychologists say; there's no science that can tell you why."

"Some people aren't any of those things. I promise."

"Mr. Tomaszewski, you have no idea."

He really didn't. From where he was sitting, people like Robbie McNamara were invisible. The topless bars and the angel dust and the pointless junkie violence didn't touch him. At least not until the next thing happened. The next thing touched us all.

"I don't have to go to San Diego. I could just go to the South Shore. It's a whole other world down there. Open ocean stuff. I haven't seen enough of Long Island yet."

"The whole world is trying to get you to think small, Joan. Don't buy into that."

"Please don't be one of those people who wants to dump your experience on me. I have plenty of that, trust me. I'm all good for the when-I-was-your-age crap."

"How about the 'you're special' crap? Because you are."

I guess things got a little uncomfortable right then. He didn't stare into my eyes or anything. There was just a weird silence and some kind of extra weight in the air. When I say uncomfortable, I don't mean it in a bad way. Just that something shifted and suddenly I was in a situation I didn't recognize. No, that's not true. I'd never seen it before, but I knew what it was.

Then I thought I had imagined it. It was so far-fetched.

"Anyway, I'm not gonna stop bugging you about it," he said. "Get used to it."

He dropped me off back at the Narragansett. I didn't tell him it was my birthday until I got out of the car.

"Sixteen?" he said. "Wow, I didn't even get you anything."

"I don't want anything. I got enough weird things from

people in the past twenty-four hours to keep me weighed down for a while. I'm not good at opening presents. I never know what to say."

"That's okay. You're good at pretty much everything else."

The tide was coming in, so I walked around by the road and down the steps. Andre's window was shut but his light was on. I climbed around the house and stood on the railing so I could reach my window and pull myself back in.

That night, I dreamed about red jellyfish and Nick's hands. The jellyfish looked like my grandmother's ruby glasses, and the underwater current was made out of my father's voice. I was with Nick inside blue sunlight, breathing water.

But when I opened my eyes in the morning, I was thinking of Robbie. It was seven thirty, not even light yet. I took the bike out, but I had to walk it through town because there was so much ice on the roads. The middle of Seaview Road was clear, so I went down the yellow line and around the corner into the wind whipping around the Stella Maris Chapel. The smokestacks were blinking at the big empty pit of the Sound. No light and nothing moving. No one in the chapel. There never was in the winter.

Nothing in the parking lot. No cars.

I stood there feeling grains of cold sand in the wind and watching the sky turn orange behind the LILCO plant. I watched the sun rise on empty asphalt and resurrected Robbie in my mind.

It was a little more than forty-eight hours since I'd seen him right here, trying to turn his life into a gangster movie with an existentialist ending. There hadn't been enough time for the car to get reported and picked up by the county. The obvious explanation was Robbie himself, slouching his shoulders and sliding sideways out of consequences. That was his specialty, wasn't it? Robbie limping back the next day, beat-up but breathing, popping Steve Miller in the tape deck and driving off to the Lagoon, leaving Daisy alone to deal with his mother's disconnected smiles.

I dropped the bike and sat down on the cold asphalt. My shoulders let go and I exhaled the breath I'd been holding for two days, but the wind shoved it back down my throat.

Last winter was cold. The kind of cold that burns your lungs and makes your bones feel like they're going to crack. There was ice everywhere, people slipping and falling in parking lots and skidding around the curve on our road. In that kind of weather, all you can do is pull into yourself and try to keep your blood moving. I felt like even my nerves were frozen. I couldn't tell how I felt about Robbie surviving, but I believed it. I swear.

joan

THREE WEEKS AFTER my birthday, I was staring at the ceiling in Nick Tomaszewski's apartment thinking, *This is it*? No one knew where I was, not even Daisy. I want to say I felt different, but I didn't really feel anything. Maybe that was different. The parts of me were suddenly cut off from each other, failing to communicate.

I tried to focus on the inside of myself. How much was just glands and nerves and how much was my brain, complicating everything? We were smoking and I was still wearing my T-shirt, because now my life was a gritty movie.

Whatever teachers got paid, Nick wasn't spending it on his apartment. Maybe he had a sick grandma. Thinking back, he told me pretty much nothing about his family or his life. The mattress was on the floor, and everything in the apartment was really neat.

Mostly because there was hardly any of it. I listened to my breath slowing down and my heart falling back into my chest while my brain made two kinds of calculations at once.

You could count all the examples of each class of object on your fingers.

Five dishes: various types.

So that was it. People write poetry and kill each other over that?

Eight books: five biology, two Hermann Hesse, one Emma Goldman.

Is it better for other people?

Three shirts on three hangers, hanging from a coat hook.

Is it better the second time?

One ashtray, actually an abalone shell: thirty-seven Marlboro butts.

Will there be a second time?

Two windows, one street lamp, no moon.

"How will you get home?"

"I didn't think about it." I'd just assumed he'd take me back to the Narragansett, like before.

"I don't think it's a good idea if I drive you. I mean, we could get in trouble now, you know? I don't think people should see us together. You get that, right?"

"Yeah, sorry. I wasn't thinking."

Ray Velker had been missing for months. His absence was seeping into the air of Highbone and people were getting jumpy. Nick stood in his downstairs doorway and said, "Be careful. Be safe."

The road was covered with a sheet of ice and the leaves crunched in the ditch at the side. Every sound I made rang back at me like I was trapped in a metal room. I walked down to 25A and then cut through behind the library. Every time a car passed, my heartbeat bubbled up into my throat and choked me. A couple of times I heard one coming and ducked off the road into the bushes.

Snow melted into my shoes and my face started to hurt. I came down onto Jensen Road and wondered where the fish were, which ones could do that carp thing where they go into stasis in the ice. It made me think of the Arctic, what lived under the ice floes, what the temperature and the light were like down there.

There was one dead car left in the Narragansett parking lot. I felt bare and hollowed out. The cold peels everything back and turns it brittle. Winter takes the skin off the world.

I've only told two people about that night, and they both judged me for it. Not for sleeping with Nick, for walking home after. Like that was the fatal mistake. Like I'm stupid and worthless for not making him drive me home. The first person was Daisy.

I heard him call me from his driveway and felt relieved and pissed off at the same time. Now there were two things I couldn't tell him. I knew I couldn't tell him that his brother was trying to be a gangster and royally fucking it up. Daisy was always trying to save his family. Robbie was beyond saving and beyond caring who he pulled down with him. I thought I could protect Daisy from that.

The other thing I couldn't explain was how my body felt, or that I was starting to understand why people used metaphors involving hearts, or that I couldn't tell whether mine was full or broken. I couldn't even tell him the bare facts.

His voice gave me a lump in my throat. I pretended not to hear it. The next thing, there he was, sliding all over the ice in his socks and shouting at me.

"Shhhh! You want someone to come out here and ground me for the rest of my life?"

"What the hell are you doing walking home in the middle of the night?" He grabbed on to my arm to steady himself.

"Never mind. Are you gonna make me some oatmeal or what?"

When we got inside Daisy made me run my hands under the cold water in the kitchen sink and change my socks. He asked me three times where I'd been, but I didn't tell him.

We went back out and climbed our beech tree before it got light. The cold branches cracked into the silence and the air prickled into our lungs like broken glass.

"Joan, why won't you look at me?"

"Shut up. What are you talking about?"

I looked into his eyes and tried to remember the color of Robbie's. Things flashed in my mind, those headlights on the water and the street light coming through the Indian bedspread that covered Nick's window. I had to look away, and then he knew he was right and it was pointless pretending. I still tried, though.

"I'm talking about why you're being weird, Joan. You can't

hide from me, you know. Something's the matter."

"No, it isn't. Where's Robbie?"

"I don't know. Around. He stays away a lot."

"When was the last time you saw him?"

"I don't know, Joan. Stop changing the subject."

But there was no subject. There was no shared language anymore, no reference point. We couldn't even hide our lies from each other, but we were still telling them.

The tracks at Jamaica are always freezing, even in the summer. And my head is still wet from the ocean. My skin is covered in salt and the feeling of Daisy's long, translucent fingers in my hand. If I close my eyes, I can see the rushing water full of little bubbles and grains of sand. I can feel the ocean pulling us under. I have to shake my head and remember to breathe so I can think what happened next.

daisy

I DIDN'T FINISH Joan's birthday present until about a week after she turned sixteen. I put it in a box on the dining room table, and it sat there for another two weeks. By January she was out all the time and telling her grandfather she was with me. If I called, she'd get in trouble.

I talked to Anne from the train a few times, but I didn't go to meet her and Kevin at My Father's Place. I didn't go out at all unless I had to. What if Mom or Robbie came home and I wasn't there? When everyone else was turning sixteen and going to concerts, me and Joan were busy hiding from each other, each wrapped in our own cocoon of lies. I did see Kevin, but that was much later. When it was all over, it was Kevin who taught me to breathe again.

One night it snowed two feet before it got too cold to snow

anymore. The harbor had been frozen for a week already. Most years that didn't happen at all, but last winter it froze from Christmas until after my birthday. That morning I'd had to pour boiling water along the bottom of the screen door to unfreeze it before I could get it open.

The night I saw Joan in the road at three in the morning, the Big Dipper was sitting up over Carter's Bay. I tried to use it to find the North Star, but when I moved my eyes over that way, all the stars disappeared into the lights over Jensen Road. That glare took me back to childhood and summer and days when the only deaths between us were creatures out of the water and mosquitoes on the wall.

My childhood memories are made of light so bright they wash together and flash back into me every time my eyes get caught in headlights or flashbulbs. In all my early memories, me and Joan are wearing shorts. It's always warm and it never rains. Just before Joan came down the road that night, I was remembering the first time she ever gutted a fish in front of me.

The day was bright and burning and we rowed out to the very edge of our permission. We were maybe twelve, and we weren't allowed to take the boat out of sight of Joan's house. We went as far as we could and looked around the bend. From there, we could see the moorings at the end of Main Street, the sailboats coming and going from the Sound, and the chartered fishing trips carrying tourists out in search of imaginary marlin. I sat in the boat and pictured me and Joan, grown-up and living a life full of oysters and champagne and ship radios. We could live right there, maybe fix up the abandoned house. We'd have a magic laboratory and people would come to consult with us about all our special knowledge. When Joan threw the sea bass in the boat and it started thumping around, I jumped and we almost capsized.

"Hit it!" she shouted at me.

"What? Why?"

"It's suffocating, Daisy. You're supposed to club it."

"You club it. God damn!" I was only twelve; I still cursed like my father.

She hit it with her shoe, but it kept thrashing. I just stared at its weird pouty mouth and all the extra fins. Its jaw kept opening on big gulps of nothing.

"Calm down, Daisy. It's not even a big one."

"Put it back, Joan. Please?"

"No. This is fishing. People do it all the time."

The sea bass went still, and Joan looked at the net in her hand. She put it down under the seat and picked up her oar.

"Let's go back. I need a knife."

She left me and the sea bass on the floating dock and went back to her kitchen for the knife. The fish was still glistening. I reached out to feel its skin, then pulled back with slime on my fingertip.

"You slice along the belly, right here." She drew a line with her finger, then put the knife in below the gills. There was a small ripping sound, like someone tearing wet canvas. The guts came out all in one package, organs joined together by transparent sinews. Joan spread them out on the dock and started naming them. I jerked my head away and looked up into the sky, just trying not to see for a minute. My gaze fell right on the sun and everything else disappeared like stars in street light.

The sound of footsteps brought me back to the middle of the January night. Someone was walking fast along the wall on Jensen Road, steps echoing out over the water and up into the trees. I swung the round window on its hinges and looked out. There was Joan in Andre's duffle coat with her knees sticking out through the ripped-up jeans that made her grandfather mad.

I thought about calling her but everyone would hear, so I ran out to catch her before she hit the Harrises' stairs. I didn't realize I wasn't wearing shoes until I felt the ice sticking to my socks.

"Joan!" I used a shouty whisper, but it still seemed like the loudest thing I ever heard. I thought Arthur would come out and grab us by our collars any minute.

She looked up at me and didn't even seem surprised.

"Joan, where were you? It's three o'clock in the morning."

She put a finger to her lips and looked over toward her house.

"Come in." I whispered.

When we got to my porch she said, "Jesus, Daisy, you left the front door open."

I put the teakettle on the stove and got out some cups, then leaned against the counter to take my wet socks off. I was waiting for Joan to say, *What the hell is wrong with you? Your feet are frozen. Christ, Daisy, make a fire and get warm,* but she didn't say any of that. When I looked back at her, she was staring at the stove light with four hundred miles in her eyes.

"Joan. It's dark and the roads are icy. You shouldn't be walking on the road. Where the hell were you?"

"Leave it. Seriously. Is there oatmeal?"

I made Quaker Oats and we sat across the table from each other in just the light from the stove, not saying anything. I don't know about her, but I was trying to think of something besides, *Who were you with?* I wasn't sure I wanted the answer to that.

I guess we talked about cuttlefish and telephones and how life on Mars would evolve if there was any. I don't remember. By the time I remembered her birthday present, it was almost six o'clock.

Joan put out a cigarette and said, "Let's go out to the tree. It'll be light soon."

We put on two of Robbie's old hockey hats. I took Joan's present off the dining room table and gave her a pair of Robbie's socks so hers could dry.

While we were crossing the road, Joan looked at me and said, "What's in the box?"

"I'm getting to that."

I thought if I started with the present, we could work backward. She could tell me why she was avoiding me, where she kept going, and what she was going to do about her parents, and what the other the thing was. The invisible thing that was always shouting in her other ear while I was trying to talk to her, making her so scared and so mad all the time. I could explain about

Robbie and why my mother left and why I didn't tell her sooner. Right then, it all seemed possible.

I slipped on the frozen leaves when we went down off the road and slid all the way to the beech tree. When I shouted for Joan, the echoes banged into each other and came back jangling in the emptiness. It wasn't daylight yet, but the moon was still up, and there was snow everywhere. It was so bright we could sec our breath. Under the tree, you sank down into the snow up to your knees.

I reminded her about the sea bass. Then she told me where she'd been all night, and my visions disappeared like the light in my mother's eyes.

"I don't want to tell you what . . . I mean, I don't . . . Shit, Joan. I just don't think it's okay that you had to walk home alone in the middle of the night."

"I'm a big girl, Daisy. We're not six anymore."

I held my hands together so she could use them to get up to our branch.

"People are disappearing lately, Joan. It's not safe. You're the one that keeps telling me that."

"It isn't really strangers we have to worry about, though, is it?"

"When were you gonna tell me? You're having a torrid affair with your biology teacher. What the hell?"

"Why would you care, anyway? You're in love with some woman on the phone."

She held the trunk of the tree and stretched out a hand to help me up.

"It isn't love!" I swung up next to her. "She's like my mother."

"How do you know what she's like?"

"Okay, maybe not exactly like my mother, but—"

"You have no idea who she is, Daisy. But you'd still rather talk to her than me."

"Joan, you are pretty much the only person I ever want to talk to. You haven't been around, remember? At least now I know why."

But she was right. I was talking to invisible strangers so I didn't have to look Joan in the eyes and say the things I knew.

"Anyway," she said. "I don't think torrid is really an accurate description of what me and Nick are doing."

"Okay, maybe just good old nuts? Or we could always go with FUCKING ILLEGAL!"

"It is not illegal, Daisy. I'm sixteen. Of all the people on the planet, you should understand. You are supposed to get me."

I'm not saying I wish she hadn't told me. But it changed the shape of us. It was the kind of truth that shoves you out of one world and into another. I thought about the sea bass again and felt like all the blood and guts I'd ever seen had come back up out of me and stuck in my throat.

The things that came out of us that morning were sharp and cold and stayed visible on our breath. We could see our words becoming part of the frozen world. By the time we were half-way through that conversation, I was holding on to the branch while the weight of everything tried to push me backward into the snow. I kept Joan's birthday present inside my coat. Nothing I could ever give her would be enough, anyway.

I didn't tell her that my mother was gone. I didn't tell her how long it had been since I'd seen Robbie or that I was going to have to sell the stereo to pay the electricity bill and buy food.

When the sun came up, everything was naked and empty. There were no leaves to hide us; we were exposed to the sky. Unless you're a rabbit or an angel, it's impossible to hide when the world is covered in snow.

I looked over at Joan and she said it again. "I expected you to understand."

daisy

IT WAS MAYBE February when Patrick Jervis came up to hassle me in metal shop. I was pouring plastic into a mold.

"Where's your brother these days, McNamara?"

I was making a plastic handle for my screwdriver and thinking about Joan.

"Hey, Daisy! I said, where's your brother hiding?"

I guess he was being scary, but I didn't care. I wasn't hearing any of the usual noise, the music or the bullshit jokes or whatever Mr. Kronenberg was saying to people while he walked around the room.

"He's not hiding. He's around."

He wasn't. I hadn't seen him in at least a month.

"Well, he's got shit to do. People are getting kinda tense,

waiting for him. Tell him to stop snorting smack behind the bandstand and take care of business."

I turned the heat off and waited for the mold to cool. When class got out I could find Joan in the commons. We could make snow angels on the football field, or cut afternoon classes and go eat cannoli in Huntington. Patrick shoved his shoulder into my back, and I burned my arm on the casing of the mold.

"I don't feel like you're paying attention to me, McNamara. Kinda pisses me off."

I guess I was supposed to worry he might hit me, but I didn't really care if Patrick hit me. The whole idea of physical pain seemed so far away.

It was while we were putting things back on the shelves that I heard them talking about Ray. I didn't know it was about Ray at the time, though. I've gone over it a lot. There was no way I could have known.

"Seriously," Patrick said. "He'll take you up there and show you."

"Shut up. That's bullshit. If he was up there, the cops would know by now," Matt McBride said. He sounded scared, not skeptical. His voice was low and shaking.

"Find Scottie in the park and ask him. Fifty bucks I'm right."

I am sure he said Scottie's name. That's why it came back to me later.

I didn't notice at the time because I was thinking about the necklace I'd made Joan for her birthday. It took me three weeks to twist all those transistors together and then we got distracted that morning and I never gave it to her. She went in for breakfast and I went back to my house with the box still pressing into my ribs. In the end I wrapped it in a baggie and taped under the bench. I didn't want to see her open it. I didn't want her to have to pretend it mattered. Still, I kept hoping she'd say something.

I kept hoping she'd tell me she was only joking about Mr. Tomaszewski, about going away for the summer, about college and California. She would shove me and laugh and tell me how dumb I was, and I'd fall back onto the attic floorboards and let go of all the tension in my bones. The air in my lungs would stop fighting me, and I'd wait for her to tell me what was next.

My alarm went off that Saturday, because I'd set it out of habit. I was downstairs leaning against the kitchen counter drinking tea made out of yesterday's used bag by the time I realized it wasn't a school day.

I loaded the dishwasher and thought about what to sell. Whatever it was would have to be something small enough to carry on the bus and big enough to pay the LILCO bill. They were still delivering the *Newsday*, so I used the first few pages to wrap up the stereo speakers. Then I screwed the panel back on the amp and loaded it all onto a hand truck. The blank squares on the living room shelves made me realize how dusty everything was. Moving the stereo stirred up the flannel smell of settled time. Joan says dust is skin cells. The dust in people's houses mostly comes off their bodies. We're breathing each other in all the time. It felt kind of like company.

I'd already given up on the pawn shop up above Flannagan's in Highbone after the guy sniffed out my desperation and refused to give me more than twelve dollars for my grandmother's opal-and-emerald ring. I was ready to try the pawn shops in Huntington Station. I dragged the hand truck up the hill behind our house to make sure I didn't run into Joan.

From the top I could see the water and half the sky. The Harrises' roof had icicles hanging off it. I thought about them all underneath it, eating breakfast together and pretending to get on each other's nerves. I thought about Arthur and Joan, busy making philosophies of life that didn't have any room for all that love. About Andre and Mrs. Harris desperate to get away from it.

That swoop of air between the hill and the surface of the water was the size of the space that had opened out between our lives. It knocked the breath out of me. I was the only one who could see it and the only one who could cross it. If only I would just let go and speak the truth, throw myself onto the air and let her catch me. I turned my back on the harbor and dragged the hand truck over some tree roots onto Beltaire Road.

The bus cost me my last three quarters. If the pawn shop in Huntington Station was closed, I'd have to hitch home with the hand truck and the stereo.

But it was open. The guy asked where was my mother and told me please to go home and think about where my life was going. I felt bad and opened my mouth to try to explain, then realized it was impossible. Also, I'd already taken the tubes out of the amp so I needed to get out of there before he tested it. On the way home I spent $3.75 on tea bags and milk and eight boxes of macaroni and cheese.

The paper was still spread out on the table when I got back. By February they'd sent two red bills; I needed to call and tell them to stop delivering. I was looking for the crossword when I saw the thing I wasn't looking for.

"Unidentified Man Found Dead near Jamaica Bay" the headline said. It was on page five, but I'd used the first couple pages so it was staring up at me when I sat down. It could have been anybody, but I knew before I read the details. They didn't. They couldn't tell who he was or who the car belonged to because somebody had stripped the VIN, but it was a yellow Charger. They'd burned it, with Robbie inside. "Male in his early twenties," it said.

I bet people think that when someone you love has been missing that long, you wouldn't want to look at what was left of them. You wouldn't want to think about how people come apart—literally, how their bodies start to fall apart the minute whatever electric charge animates them is gone.

It's not like that. If something like that happens to you, you will want to know. Love means you know that body is it. All there is. You want to see where it's resting, half peeled away and turning from rot into mulch. To see that body turned back into moths and trees and birdsong. You want to be able to picture that, just so you can fill that blinding emptiness with something. Anything.

My first thought was, *She'll come home now.* I feel bad about that, but why lie? I pictured my mother's fingers turning the pages of the paper and smudging black with ink. I pictured her eyeliner running and her hands shaking. I thought, *She has to come back now.* My second thought was, *They must have taken pictures. Somewhere, there are pictures of what happened to Robbie.*

DAISY'S ELECTRIC MAP OF AMERICA

joan

MY MOTHER HAD a brother who died in a war. When she met my father she thought they were going to change the world. *My father.* Guess that didn't work out. And that was the big revelation of her notebook. Except inside the back cover, across the calendar of 1955, she had written: *Now everything is the future. Everything that happens will be after this* . . . And that was all the information I was going to get.

I woke up one Sunday in February and looked out my window, trying to see her there. There was a cloud of smoky moisture over the harbor and puddles of water where the sun was shining on the ice. In the notebook she said she would lie on the floating dock with her friend Deborah. Deborah would sing and my mother would daydream. I stepped out back, and the air was cold and wet.

When I got to the kitchen table, Andre had the Arts section of the *Times*, Gramps took the *Amsterdam News*, and all I had left was either the Travel section or the front page. There was so much snow in the city, they were putting it on flat train cars and sending it south until it melted.

"Lesser-known journalist who worked with Frederick Douglass?" Gramps said. "Seven letters." He was doing the crossword while he made hot milk with ginger and nutmeg in it.

A guy out fishing had called in a body in a burned car near JFK Airport—Gramps still called it Idlewild. It was an "unidentifiable male." In case you didn't grow up in the Tri-State area, "unidentifiable" means they took the fingertips off and smashed the teeth. The body had been dumped in a yellow Charger and burned out in the marsh.

"Fortune," Gramps said. "How about, island made by a sunken volcano? Four letters."

"Atol."

"Extra pancake for you, young lady!" He was in a good mood. I was about to ruin it.

After pancakes, we went out the back door and rested our cups on the railing. Me and Gramps liked to stand out there in the morning, even when it was cold.

"Gramps?"

"Yes, honey?"

"You don't believe in God, do you?"

He swept his arm out toward Carter's Bay. "Don't need to. Look."

I looked out at bare trees, at the pink sky and the disappearing mist on the water. I looked at the floating dock and the shadow it threw over toward the Narragansett parking lot.

"Yeah, I get what you're saying, but seriously, you don't think there's somebody sitting up there giving a shit what you do, right?"

"There's no need to say it like that, Joan."

I wasn't looking at him. I didn't see what that question did to his face at the time, but I can picture it now.

"Why take me to the church hall, then? Why make me listen to Mrs. Morris and them all day long? You don't even believe it. Don't you feel like a hypocrite?"

"Why, you think it's wrong what those ladies do for people?"

"No, that's not what I mean."

"So you just think it's beneath you?"

He was calm, but he was giving me the look. I thought maybe he'd found something out. Maybe he knew everything I'd been doing, everything I'd seen.

"No, Gramps. You're twisting it."

"Am I? Maybe I'm just saying it back so you can hear it."

There was so much space around I felt like there was nowhere I could hide from Gramps. All the things I'd seen and done lately had taken the shell off me. I felt there was nothing about me he couldn't see.

"If they're doing good, Joan, what difference does it make how they get there? Goodness comes out of people, and badness, too. I'm not too concerned with who put it there."

"No, I get that. I do. I just wish people would be honest sometimes. Just say what they actually think instead of everybody going through the motions and helping each other keep their delusions. I'm so sick of it lately."

"Careful what you wish for, child."

He turned around and opened the storm door, then turned back to take my cup out of my hand.

"Do you miss Grams?"

This time I was looking right in his eyes when my question hit him. Whatever was behind there had nothing to do with me at all. He didn't even answer me.

As the door was swinging shut, he said, "As for the other thing, no one up there cares what I do. I found that out all at once and thirty years ago."

It happened to him, too. It happens to everyone. The violent surprises, the split seconds that turn the world inside out. I just thought, *Why?* How did they all just keep going, keep pretending? I just wanted to shout at him: *How can you not feel it?!* There is so much silence and pain collected up in the corners of our house, people were choking on it and he was just handing out pancakes like Sunday-school prizes. I guess it was what my mother hated about home, but at least she could get away from it.

Sometimes I go to church with Gramps, even though Mom doesn't like it. Those ladies are so desperate to feel righteous and helpful, like there's a reason for God. I'm making them seem pathetic, but Gramps is right. They mean well. But believe me, if there was any kind of salvation there, I would have caught it by now. I looked hard, straight into their longing. All I saw was emptiness so big it made my throat close up and my eyes sting.

I hid my face back in the paper and read those words again: *unidentifiable male, yellow Charger,* but I was just distracting myself. I didn't do the math. How could I? The last time I saw Robbie he'd left his car behind. It was behind the chapel; those guys hadn't even seen it. Then it was gone, so it had to be Robbie who came back for it. How could him and his car both wind up in the middle of nowhere in Queens?

Anyway, I was thinking about how I needed to see my mother again. I wanted to put her back to the wall and make her tell me everything. Okay, maybe I thought if *I* told *her* everything she'd come home for a while.

I wasn't going to bring Daisy this time.

I could have cut school the very next day. Ridden the train through the tangled mess outside Jamaica Station and looked out the subway window at that underground graffiti palace on the CC line. I wouldn't have been there when the Suffolk County cops showed up at school. I wouldn't have had to know what they found.

The first thing I thought about when they searched our lockers was my mother's notebook. As if it was some kind of contraband. Ridiculous, but I was glad I'd left it under my bed that day.

The rumor started when I was in English listening to people talk about *Of Mice and Men*. It was the kind of conversation my mother would have loved. I was just thinking, *Who cares? None of this is real or true; somebody made it up.*

Notes and whispers started going around. You could feel the background noise get weighty and serious.

We weren't warned or asked before they searched our lockers, so of course some of the white parents flipped out and started shouting about the Bill of Rights. That kind of thing never happened to their kids, so it came as a shock. They kept us an extra twenty minutes in fourth period while the sound of metal doors moved closer, then farther away through the corridors. An extra twenty minutes of Steinbeck and "universal truth." I tuned out and tried to draw a diagram of everything I could remember about the inside of an eel.

By the time they let us out, there was no point going to gym class. I found Daisy behind our television in the commons.

"Shit. Thank God!" he said. "You didn't leave anything in your locker, did you?"

"Like what? Those nuclear launch codes we stole last week? My Russian dictionary? A pound of smack?"

Actually, I was just as relieved as he was.

"Fuck off, Joan. I was worried about you. What have you heard?"

"Mostly a bunch of bullshit about undermining the pastoral and the failure of the American dream. What have you heard?"

"They found something in Kieran Johnson's locker. They arrested him."

"Found what?"

"Nobody knows."

While we were talking, the cops were taking Kieran away in cuffs. We didn't get to the front doors until he was already in the back of the cop car. The whole world gathered into whispering circles of people with haunted eyes, standing in the bus circle watching the cops pull away.

Here's the thing: some of them knew. Right then, that day when they took Kieran away, some of them already knew where Ray Velker was and what had happened to him. What was still happening to him. It would be slowing down, out there in the cold under the leaves, but what was happening to Ray was unstoppable.

For the rest of us, the truth didn't sink in until much later. Truth is what they print in the papers, right? Right. So here's some.

They were bones. Human bones. It turned out Kieran Johnson and his friends were into getting wasted and digging up the graveyard. They'd take away parts of rotten people and sit around them smoking angel dust and building bonfires. I guess then they'd have creepy rituals or something. But they weren't Ray's bones, anyway. They were pieces of old forgotten people, so they charged Kieran with something pretty minor and let him go. Probably sent him to a shrink.

Yeah, that's what I'm telling you. Kids keep human femurs and finger bones in their lockers at my high school, and it isn't anywhere near the worst thing they do.

That's what you find when you lift up the surface of Highbone and look underneath. Follow anything in that town far enough, and you're going to find things you can't unlearn. Stuff you'll never be able to not see. It happened to Daisy, and it happened to me, and it happened to every kid who already knew where Ray was.

That Saturday I woke Daisy up and we took the bus to the mall. We got there at ten after twelve, and Teresa was standing by the south entrance in her floppy hat, wearing actual bell-bottoms like she just stepped out of the summer of love. Like Cambodia and punk had never happened and people still thought you could change the world by sticking flowers in the ends of rifles.

"This is Daisy," I said, waving a hand between them. "Teresa."

"Oh my GOD!" she walked all the way around Daisy in a circle, looking him up and down. She reached out and ran her fingers down his arm like he was a new coat and she wanted to see how he would feel on her skin. "I get it!" she said.

"Hi," Daisy said. He looked away at the parking lot while the blood flushed to the surface all over him.

"Joan says you're having an affair with a glamorous Italian on the phone."

Daisy glared at me. "Joan should talk."

"Do you get beat up? I mean, I think you look amazing, but I guess you don't exactly blend in at school."

"I don't get beat up. Joan exaggerates."

"I didn't say anything!" I wondered if it had been a good idea, putting them together.

Daisy swallowed, and I watched his Adam's apple go up and down. "Do you blend in?"

"Oh, yeah," Teresa said. "I'm a regular chameleon."

"Right," I said. "We going in or what? Daisy wants some copper wire."

The mall was full of milky light. There were two pigeons trapped in one of the hallways, cooing up under the glass ceiling. The escalator stretched up out of the big marble space with nothing on either side of it, so you could feel like you were being carried up to consumer heaven.

"Come on."

Teresa made for the down escalator, but when she put her foot out, Daisy grabbed her arm.

"That's the wrong one." He looked embarrassed and pulled his hand away.

"I know," Teresa said.

She jumped and started running up. Every few steps she let go and put her arms out while the escalator carried her back down for a minute. Then she ran again.

I looked at Daisy. "Well?"

Teresa got to the top and leaned over panting with her hands on her knees. Her floppy hat fell onto the shining floor.

Daisy looked up, shading his eyes from the scattered light. "She looks like an angel," he said. "I don't mean all sweet and floaty. I mean like an actual angel. The biblical kind."

"Well, she does kind of trumpet out the truth a lot. Do you like her?"

He stared some more and then turned to give me an unfocused look. "I don't know. I feel like she's from another planet. One where people don't keep bones in their lockers."

For a minute we understood each other again. We had a shorthand language that nobody but us would understand. It was all about body parts and crazy death, but it was ours. Maybe Daisy was right. He added poetry to the world, and sometimes we both needed it. We looked up together at that Long Island version of heaven, imagined angels, and tried to rise above the bones.

I waved at Teresa, leaning on the railing and singing some weird song about home down at us so loud everyone was looking at her.

"Can't you see why I don't want Robbie to mess with her?"

"Yeah. I didn't want Robbie to mess with you either, Joan."

I swear it didn't register. Now that I'm playing it over in my head, though, I'm sure he used the past tense right then.

daisy

I WAS IN Port Jefferson when I heard the cops telling each other the story of Robbie's death. I'd taken the train there for a phone booth, and gotten onto what AT&T calls a *verify trunk line.* From there I could listen in. I had three numbers I'd gotten from listening to a tip line and I'd been trying them all week. All I wanted was a name. A name that was either Robbie's or it wasn't.

I stood there, leaning on the folding door and feeling like a point on a map, like someone somewhere was sticking a pin into me at that very moment. The phone cops would catch me soon. I shook and smoked and realized I'd forgotten to eat again. It was sunny, and the surface of the ice was melting. Water was running past the phone booth along the curb and into a sewer.

Even though I was scared, using the phones made me feel like me again, like I was in control of something. Standing in a phone booth outside a gas station in Port Jefferson, I was part of one connected circuit that went all the way down the length of Long Island. I was the human switch. I imagined my voice like the electric fire that came off Green Lantern, my magic power leaking through the telephone wires, flipping switches and opening circuits. My veins were just more wires, or maybe the other way around. My blood circulating like an incantation through the veins in the telephone network, making things happen.

I'd given up on the first number after a week. That day in Port Jefferson, I came onto the second line in the middle of a conversation. I was hungry and my feet hurt, so I wasn't concentrating at first.

". . . but it isn't. The kid was supplying angel dust. Small-time shit."

"The car might belong to John McNamara's kid, but they took the VIN. Can't prove it."

I put my hand over the mouthpiece and retched into the corner of the phone booth. There was nothing inside me, so nothing came out. When I listened again, they'd moved on.

"You sure?"

"Yeah, I'm sure. Connecticut busted a lab. They were bringing it across the Sound. I'm telling you, it's nothing. The McNamara kid was just a pain in the ass. It's a local fix. Close the case."

I didn't even hang up the receiver. I just leaned my forehead against the glass and stood there inhaling the smell of piss and metal. I felt like one of Joan's jellyfish, like the inside of me was just an empty space for swallowing air, trying to use it to push myself away.

When I leaned onto the glass and lit a cigarette I could feel the nicotine burn down through the veins in my arms. I filled that little space with smoke, hoping it would blot out the world outside the glass. When it didn't, I called Beatrice.

"She left, Beatrice."

"Daisy? Why are you not at school?"

"My mother left. She didn't want hope. She didn't want anything."

"I don't know what to say. But you are kind and so intelligent. Make yourself a life now. It's your turn."

"Beatrice, I don't think I can call you anymore. I might get in trouble about the phone calls."

"I've been happy to know you."

"I'm worried about you, though. Can't you leave there? Do you have any money?"

"Silly boy!" she said. "I am an advocate, a lawyer. I'm what you call rolling in money. Not to worry about me."

"You seemed so sad."

"Sometimes, strangers let you be free. You can say whatever you need to. You did a good thing for me."

"My brother's gone, too. I feel like it's my fault."

"But it isn't. I'm sorry to say it, but you're still very young. Go and be happy. Let go of them."

Maybe Joan will never believe me about Beatrice. It doesn't

matter. She was either a miracle or a mirage. Either way, she was part of last year and last year is over.

Across the street from the phone booth was a playground. I looked at the puddle of icy mud at the bottom of the slide and the swing someone had wound up onto the bar. It was frozen there now, sparkling and dripping water in the sun. The whole world had flipped over and gotten tangled up into the sky.

daisy

"COME ON, ARTHUR. I just need to find out what happened to him. You get that, right?"

Me and Arthur were sitting on the Harrises' back steps looking out at the patchy ice. It was freezing, but we wanted to smoke. The quiet lady was sitting on the floating dock with her coat open and her hat on the planks next to her. We'd waved and then all three went back to staring at the ice reflecting the orange-and-purple sunset.

"I get it, but I'm saying maybe you just can't, Daisy. How are you gonna find out?"

"I just want to talk to a couple people. He was dealing with some kids at school."

Arthur blew out a breath and shook his head.

"They might know something."

"Do you have any idea how stupid that sounds, kid?"

"They killed my brother, Arthur."

"First of all, you don't know that for sure. Second, if anybody kills you, it'll ruin my sister's life. So that isn't gonna happen. You hear me?"

"They're gonna come to the house, Arthur. Why didn't they come already?"

"Because they didn't, and that's a good thing. Think about it. What are you gonna get from asking questions?"

He was quiet for a long time then. The sun sank and the ice turned blue.

"What do you want me to do, little McNamara?"

"I don't know. Who else can I tell? Could you come with me?"

"It's dangerous, Daisy. You shouldn't do it, with or without me."

"What if it was Andre? Wouldn't you want to know?"

"Of course. But I wouldn't go stirring some hornet's nest, because that could come back on people I care about, right?"

"I just want to know why. I'm not saying I'm going to do anything."

"You're gonna have to tell someone eventually, Daisy. You can't live alone in that house forever. You're fifteen."

"Sixteen."

"Okay, I'll give you some time. On one condition."

If any of it came out, they'd take me away from Jensen Road. *When* it came out. Because it would. Arthur was giving me some time, but that was all. The only way I wasn't going to get pulled away from Joan was if I ran away myself.

He turned to face me so I had to look him in the eye. "One condition."

"What?"

"Leave Joan out of it. Got it?"

"Yeah, but she won't stop asking questions. You know what she's like."

"Say you got it."

"Okay, I got it."

The quiet lady was walking toward us.

"Hi, Ms. Goldin," Arthur said. "Everything okay?"

She'd been there my whole life, but I'd never heard anybody call her by name before. She pointed at the place where the sun had just disappeared and then back at the floating dock, then she nodded and pointed at the sky again. We looked up at the blue creeping across from the west, washing away the light as it came.

"Mom's fine," Arthur said. "I'll tell her you said hello."

She nodded again, then turned around and walked toward Carter's Bay.

"The quiet lady knows your mom?"

"Sure. They both grew up here."

I had a feeling then, like we were just a place on a turning wheel inside the tides. Me and Joan, Mrs. Harris and the quiet lady and whoever came before them and before them. All playing in the water and coming together and hurting each other and falling away. The ice jerked up and the sky heaved out at me. I put a hand down on the step so I wouldn't tumble down.

"Joan goes to see her, you know."

"Ms. Goldin? She's all right. Just sad."

"You ever think there's something that soaks into us down here? Sometimes I feel like this place is just made out of sadness."

"Don't know why they call you Daisy. You're not exactly a ray of sunshine."

"Anyway, I didn't mean the quiet lady. I meant your mom. Me and Joan went to see her in the city. They had a fight."

"Mom's cool. They'll work it out."

Joan always gave me shit about Arthur. She said I hero-worshipped him. Well, yeah, I did. That's because Arthur is a hero. You'll see.

He handed me a Marlboro and took out a lighter. I pretended I was fine while we blew smoke up into the sky. Andre opened the window and we could hear Boney M. coming from his room. First "Rivers of Babylon" came out, then Andre's arms and his head.

Arthur looked up. "Boney M.? Really?"

"Don't let Gramps see you smoking with Daisy. You'll get the look."

Arthur just raised one hand and waved it without looking up.

"I gotta go in anyway," I said. "See you later, Arthur."

"Remind me what you're not gonna do?"

"Not gonna say anything to Joan."

I got to my feet and stepped on the edge of the ice. I thought about the inside of Joan's dogfish, then I thought about Robbie, about drowning and burning and being out of water with gills.

If he was still alive when the fire started, he would have felt the burning air pressing in, getting heavier and emptier. With the windows rolled up, he would have felt something hungry, sucking all the oxygen from around him. He would have realized, right in that last second, the meaning of time.

I went into my house and I could tell Joan was in the attic. She didn't know it, but by then we were the only two people who were ever in the house. I guess I pretended to myself we had a home together, like I always assumed we would when I was little. Sometimes when she was in the attic I went downstairs and fell asleep listening to the sound of her up there.

I tried reading some Steinbeck, because I was eating and studying and washing the dishes like a perfect teenager. Like maybe if I did everything right, no one would come and take me away.

Then Joan stopped pacing. I knew all her kinds of silence, so I held my breath and listened. She was lost in something up there. When I came up the attic stairs she didn't even hear me. It was February, and the light at five o'clock was orange. It striped in through the window exactly parallel to the attic floor and across to the eaves on the other side. I used to think about the way the sunlight traveled to that window, all the way from space and then through Queens and Nassau to get to us. Joan was sitting in that light now, with a marble notebook on her lap and her eyes full of water. There was a tear on her cheek shining like a red star. I held my breath.

I'd seen Joan nearly drown herself, and break her collarbone falling out of a tree. I'd seen her when we both got beat up in sixth grade for being freaks, when she stepped on a nail in the abandoned house and had to go to the emergency room for a tetanus shot. I'd seen her almost every time her mother drove away. Never once had I seen her with water in her eyes.

It was like all the ice and the rest of everything solid in the world was melting too.

"Joan, what is that?"

She jumped.

"Nothing." She closed the notebook and turned around like she was going to put it away behind her, then didn't. She just shoved it under her drawn-up knees.

"It's not *nothing*. If you don't want to tell me, just say so."

She looked up and I saw myself come into focus in her eyes. Then she turned back to the window, let out a breath, and said to the trees outside, "It's my mother's."

I went and sat down next to her, but not too close. I was afraid she'd close up again. I didn't really deserve the truth from her and I knew it. How many things was I hiding from her? I couldn't even count them at that point.

She was about to tell me something. Something she hadn't told Teresa. Or Mr. Tomaszewski. She was about to tell me. I felt like I was crossing a tightrope back to where we used to be.

"Your mother's what?" I said it with hardly any breath at all, like the connection between us was made of spun sugar or dust and even the force of a whisper might break it apart.

"I don't know. It's like a diary but it's not. It's just a few pages."

"It's freaking you out?"

"She had a brother, Daisy. He was my uncle. I mean, he wasn't, because he died, but he would have been. Nobody told me. My dad knows, right? Remember, she said she talked to him. And Gramps, of course. Gramps had a son, Daisy. Does Arthur know? Why do they all lie to me?"

"Maybe it's too sad for them to talk about."

"That's not a reason. Is that why she won't stay here? I've been thinking about it for months. One of us lives in his room, Daisy. Which one?"

I ran through the Harrises' house in my mind, thinking about the old pictures on all the dressers and the mantel. They must have put all the dead uncle's pictures away.

"Also, she had a friend named Deborah who wanted her to run away."

"Where'd you get the notebook?"

"I found it in my dad's room. Right before the hurricane."

"You've had it all winter."

There was so much more she wasn't saying, but of course I didn't know it then. Even now, I couldn't exactly tell you how it all fit together. The thing is, it didn't fit together. It was the mess that made us. You couldn't measure it or draw a diagram. It was like the difference between the picture of dogfish anatomy and the thing Joan opened up on the dock after the hurricane. Slippery and confusing and full of blood.

"It sounds crazy," she said.

"This is me, Joan. You're allowed to sound crazy."

"I don't want to be crazy; I just want to be a person. Why are everyone's horrible secrets always falling out of the corners onto my fucking head? It isn't fair."

I took a little breath and reached over. She turned her head away, but I didn't pull back. I used one finger to wipe away a tear. It left a streak on her face and salt on my fingertip. I wanted to put it in my mouth but I didn't. *Whatever else happens for the rest of our lives*, I thought, *one time I had Joan's tears on my skin.*

joan

THERE WAS ANOTHER storm before I finally made up my mind to go into the city again. I had to wait two days for the LIRR to start running. When I came up out of the subway at Ninety-Sixth Street, there was still snow drifted on the stairs, but it was raining. I sat on a bench on Central Park West and watched the door until she came out. The rain made dirty slush for two hours while I smoked seven cigarettes. There were trees over me, but they weren't much protection.

Our eyes met before she had time to pretend not to see me. She stepped out the door, crossed between the lights, stood in front of me with an umbrella, and said, "Now what?"

"Fine, thanks. How have you been?"

"You know I love to see you, so stop it. You came all the way here by yourself; I'm just asking why."

"To see you. Do I need a better reason?"

"You look like a drowned rat. Come on, you need soup."

She turned uptown and starting walking so fast I had to skip every third step to keep up with her. The sidewalk was salted ice with rain on top. When we got to 112th Street she plowed around the corner and into a diner. She let the door swing back in my face.

"Why are you wearing Andre's old coat? We bought you a perfectly nice one of your own."

"That coat makes me look like I'm on my way to church every time I go out."

She made me take off the duffle coat and sit in a booth, then asked for two coffees. The white guy behind the counter called her by name, pronounced it right and everything.

"Sit here and get that in you. I need to call the theater and say I'll be late."

She got on the phone in the vestibule and I watched her turn into someone else while she talked. She waved a hand around, making gestures I'd never seen before. When she got back, she ordered soup.

"Please, God, tell me you're not gonna have a baby," she said when the waitress walked away.

I took the notebook out of the bag and put it on the table in front of her.

"Jesus." She laid one hand down on it. "You see what this family is like? Nothing's private. Not even your thoughts."

"Well, not if you write 'em down and leave them in the desk

in a room you don't even live in."

"Stop it. I do live there and you know it. Anyway, it's just a story, Joan. I was just practicing."

"It says about how you met Dad."

"Yes, well, we were different then."

She didn't look at me when she said it. She looked out at the water running off the edge of the sidewalk, over at the streetlight and into the traffic. We could have been strangers, but I wasn't going to let that stop me this time.

"Did you . . . I mean, was he different than other people?"

She shook her head and shrugged, like that wasn't really the right question. "The thing is you're just so grateful. I don't have to tell you what it's like growing up in Highbone. You spend your life trying to blend into whatever is behind you, with some kind of voice-of-God soundtrack telling you no matter how hard you try you'll never be invisible enough. When somebody actually looks at you on purpose, it throws everything out of perspective."

"Would it have been better if you didn't have us?"

She ignored me.

"They only let me go to Brooklyn College because I said I'd study nursing, be a good charitable person and have a pension, too. They were always giving me the 'This house won't take care of itself, Eva' speech."

"I mean, do you think you got derailed? Were you supposed to be somebody else?"

"Me? No. Your father, *he* was supposed to be somebody else. He was doing political science. Arthur Junior happened, and he had to stop everything and be a mechanic working for the same company as his father."

"He's sad. I only noticed it the other day. You broke him."

"I did not. He just rolled over. His books got dusty, and he let other guys run the union. He started hanging around with Howard Earle and talking about baseball."

"I like Howard."

"Howard's fine. He just isn't important." She said it like she was the one who was qualified to make that call. Like God went on vacation and asked her to do the sorting while he was away.

"Your father judged me for hanging on to what we're supposed to be. He blamed me for all the things in me that would have been poetry if I wasn't busy dying of meaninglessness. 'Life is real, Eva.' Like I didn't know that."

"He's not wrong, Mom. You did kind of produce three incontrovertible facts. He's the one dealing with that, so you can hang out and make metaphors in darkened rooms."

"Listen to me, girl. People have to make stories and light them up and get people to sit in the dark and take them in. That's power. If you have a dreaming mind, it's a crime to waste it, especially in this country."

"God, I am so tired of people telling me not to waste my fucking mind."

"Joan, when you use language like that you're inviting people to underestimate you."

"What if I want to waste my mind? What if I just want to take in some facts and let them sit there without moving around and changing all the time?"

"When I go out in the street now I'm aiming for people to look at me, and I do my best not to be grateful. People can think whatever they want, but they'll have to think something because I'll be in the way of whatever they're looking at. That's my job. I give things up for that, yeah. Of course I do. It hurts to do it too."

"First you said you just *wanted* to get away. Now you want to claim it's a holy mission?"

"It's both, honey. Listen to what I'm telling you. Just being who you are is a holy mission if that's how you want to put it. Nothing holier. If your father were brave enough, we could have all moved up here and done it together."

"What did you mean, 'everything is the future'?"

She was quiet for a minute. Remembering, I guess.

"I meant your brother. And mine. When people die and get born, time changes. There's the things that happened before the babies and the things the dead will never see. I don't know how to put it. I wish I did. I've spent enough time in that theater trying."

She called home and told them I was staying with her, then she made me come to the theater. I didn't talk to her about Nick Tomaszewski or what I'd seen that night at Fiddler's Cove. We ended up talking about her life instead of mine, because that's how it is with her. And she's right. What she does is important; I get that now. So I can't even be mad at her for it.

There was some kind of tech rehearsal going on. The theater

was so cold you could see everyone's breath. They were blocking a scene and trying different lights on it. Three actors, a bunch of crew people, and two white ladies in camel-hair coats who were probably deducting the whole thing from their taxes. Behind them, a bare brick wall stretched up past the catwalk into the darkness. The seats were velvet and the balconies had ridiculous cherubs on them.

I sat in the tenth row and tried to put my feelings back together. My mother had a way of landing on your mind and shattering it like a mirror until all you reflected were pieces of her. They didn't even fit together.

So I wasn't paying attention to the stage or the actors, because I was thinking of everything I'd really come to talk about. Whether I should go to Woods Hole, if I could call Nick without making him not like me or getting him in trouble, what I'd seen at Fiddler's Cove and what it meant, and how the hell I could get through the next two years without ever running into Officer Kemp alone again. I was trying to piece together Robbie and Nick and Ray's disappearance and the kind of people who keep human bones in their lockers. How was I going to ask her about any of that? Where would I start?

When I looked up there was just one person on the stage. She was wearing a nightgown and sitting on some wooden stairs under a window.

"I grew up right here on the edge of the harbor," the actress said. "On the edge of town. On the edge of history. There are ghosts leaking out these windows." She pointed up at the window above her. It had a scrim over the inside with a blue light behind it. "The ghosts from the house are calling to the ghosts of boats that threw the ghosts of sailors into the water a hundred years ago. Every day the water tries to reach us, wash us away. Maybe twice a year, it comes as far as the bottom step." She looked down and picked up her feet like they were getting wet. "But there's always a big moon to shush it back."

Jesus, I thought. *It's true.* That house, you can leave it but it just comes with you. That little closed world of tides we live in washes time around in circles. Nothing ever goes away and nothing moves forward. If you grow up there, it shapes your mind. My mother wasn't lying. Wherever she is, she's there with us the whole time, too.

We slept in that big half-abandoned apartment, in one of the dusty bedrooms full of other people's things. She cleared a double bed, made me use cocoa butter, and gave me a nightgown made of gauze and satin ribbon. It was the girliest thing I'd ever worn in my life.

"Why won't you grow your hair, Joan? I can fix it for you."

"I'm not your project."

"I'm trying to be helpful. God knows you spend enough time telling me I don't act like a real mother. Real mothers spend half the night fixing their daughters' hair."

"I like it short."

The traffic on Central Park West sounded like the ocean and there was light all night long. We listened to each other's breathing and tried not to brush up against each other.

"Mom, what happened to Deborah?"

"What do you mean, what happened? I saw her last week when I was home. Her and that damn metal detector."

"The quiet lady is Deborah?"

"She was my best friend, growing up. So don't think I don't understand about Daisy McNamara. I just want you to be prepared for when the world gets between you."

"Is she crazy?"

"I don't know. She didn't used to be quiet. She used to sing like an angel."

"What happened to her?"

"Her sister got married and her parents died, and I guess I left too. She just started crumbling into herself. When I go to see her now, there are just pieces of who she used to be, kind of jumbled up inside her mind."

"Mom! Maybe she needs a doctor? If she's your friend, you should help her. There should be a diagnosis. They could put her on medication."

"You're saying that because you've never been to a psychiatric ward. I wouldn't do that to Deborah just because her feelings are different than other people's."

"All you people and your feelings. Could somebody draw me a map?"

We went quiet again, but her breathing didn't change. She lay with her hands folded on her chest like the corpse at a wake. Maybe if you have a brain like hers it never lets you sleep. If I hadn't been there, she'd have been alone in the single bed down the hall. Eight hours a day, a third of her life, breathing into the dark with no one to hear her.

"Are you ever coming back, Mom? Are things gonna go back to normal?"

"For the record"—her voice was soft and tired—"I wanted to bring you up here with me."

"What?"

"I wanted to move up here with you and Andre. Put you in school."

"You never asked me."

"I wanted to get you away from that house. No matter how much people try to scare 'em off, they won't budge from there. Even your father now, too. They're like barnacles."

"What do you mean, scare them off?"

"You think all those white people in Highbone are happy we live there? Twice your Gram and Gramps had to go to court to keep that house, even though our family have been in it over a hundred years and own it outright. My question is, why? Why do they want to be there?"

"Because it's ours!"

"Well, your life would be better here. That house is like a sickness."

"Where would we live?"

"I don't know. Your father and your grandfather talked me out of it. They think every black kid that grows up in the city turns into a junkie hooker before the end of high school."

"Did you tell them we have junkies in Highbone, too?"

"I could have gotten you into School Without Walls. It would have been so good for you."

I didn't sleep much that night. It took hours to run through all the different possibilities, to split my life off at seventh grade, eighth, ninth, and follow it forward into a time without Daisy or Nick or even Teresa. No tides, no dogfish, no back steps. Empty cathedral subway stations instead. Classes in the Museum of Natural History and anyway that house haunting my dreams, even in Manhattan. Me and my mother together and that house never letting us go.

I fell half asleep and saw picture of the city and all its caverns full of dead things. All its specimens and dissections. Its underground rooms full of bones and switchboards. All the wires and train tracks and connections. When I finally fell all the way asleep I dreamed of phone booths on every corner with Daisy's voice in them.

joan

I GUESS IT was toward the end of winter the day I went up to Daisy's attic window with Thompson's translation of the *Historia animalium*. No one was home and the house was so quiet. I liked reading up there. If I finished the book, I could go over Nick's apartment and tell him.

Things outside were melting. Snow and ice were sliding off the trees, and the whole world smelled like damp laundry. There were piles of slushy snow along the edges of Jensen Road. The quiet lady—Deborah—was climbing between the trees at the edge of Carter's Bay. She had on fisherman's boots and a parka. I could see the orange lining from where I was. I thought, *Why doesn't she zip up?* I thought, *How did my mother leave her?*

The McNamaras' house was so quiet I could hear the kitchen fans at the Narragansett. Suspiciously quiet. I only noticed right then. That seems crazy, looking back, but everybody was distracted. It wasn't just me. There was so much missing, so much empty space that the world was like one of those pictures with the two faces that are really a wine glass. Where the stuff that's not there seems like the stuff that is there.

Where was Daisy? I kept thinking I'd see him coming, but Jensen Road was empty. The wall was throwing a thin shadow toward me, and I could see the melt seeping through it. Every once in a while a car would curve around, heading for Highbone, but none of them carried anything I needed or knew. None of them spilled out Daisy, or Robbie, Ray Velker or Nick Tomaszewski or my mother. None of them stopped to carry me away into whatever my future was supposed to be.

I looked out at the piles of plowed snow. There was pathetic yellow light laid across it, and I knew everything would freeze overnight. Before the sun rose, the water lying on the curve of Jensen Road would turn to glass and we'd be a death trap. Again.

I'm trying to put myself back into the moment just before I opened Mrs. McNamara's bedroom door. Before everything changed shape one more time. There were no towels in the bathroom and she used to keep them in a closet in her room, so I went to get one.

I knocked first, even though I knew there was no one else in the house. There was no light at all, not even a pale edge around the curtains. It took me a while to find the switch; I'd never been in there in the dark before. When my fingers found it and I pushed it up, a man's voice said, "Hello, Daisy. Come on in.

Relax." I turned around and nearly ran away before I realized it was a tape. Daisy had it wired to the switch. When I looked back inside the room I saw the lights.

The bed was shoved to one wall, and the reason it was so dark was that someone—Daisy—had taped the edges of the curtains. There were wires stretching around on boards and tables, and even some on the walls. Some of the boards had light switches embedded in them, regular ones and some dimmers, too. Above the head of Mrs. McNamara's bed, there was a map of North America, made sort of like a blueprint. A satellite picture, maybe. Anyway, it was the biggest single piece of paper I'd ever seen. Where did he get it? Little red and white bulbs were twinkling inside Washington State and Chicago and Idaho. One in Tennessee and one in Utah.

Walking over to it, I tripped over a guitar pedal and a string of dry-cell batteries. When I got up close, I could see the map had more wires and more bulbs, they just weren't lit up.

You're probably thinking, *What the fuck?* Well, so was I. Right now, you know exactly as much as I did when I turned all the way around in a circle in the middle of Rita McNamara's bedroom, trying to understand what I was looking at.

I turned on the light in the bathroom and the mirror came alive. All around it were different colored bulbs and little fans and pinwheels. Something made a sound like whistling. It was complicated and beautiful, and it made me furious. I was so mad I nearly smashed it before I even knew why. I stood looking at myself in the kind of crazy light that happens at the firemen's fair and thought, *He's gonna start a fire. He's gonna overload the circuits.* I thought, *Jesus, who's paying the electric bill*?

Then I stopped looking at the lights and the wires and saw the obvious. Whatever was happening in that bedroom, Rita McNamara wasn't living in it. Right then I was pretty sure Robbie wasn't either. Daisy was alone. Daisy was living in that house all by himself. Things started playing over in my head, taking on different meanings. Someone was there the night of the hurricane, because I heard the door. Was Daisy alone on Christmas Day? Did he know how to cook? Who the hell was washing his clothes?

You ever see a cat trying to touch the cat inside the mirror that's really their own image? I was the opposite, looking from the inside of my life into the inside of his, expecting a reflection. Expecting the other me. What I saw were two completely different landscapes full of mad science and nightmares. Fears and secrets and questions without answers, echoing back at each other in two separate languages.

I was mad because I was scared. Because I'd opened a door in my best friend's house and found out he lived inside Pandora's fucking box and he hadn't even told me.

How long had Daisy been building an electric map of America in the place where his mother was supposed to be?

daisy

TONIGHT, WHEN I stood in Aunt Regina's doorway and watched Joan walk away into the streets of Rockaway, I thought, *I should have told her everything*. The secrets worked their way into our lives and just took us over. I keep telling myself if I hadn't lied to her she wouldn't be walking away, but that probably isn't true. The world is full of hurricanes and riptides and lies. How long would we have been able to hold on to each other anyway?

On the first day of March, we went to Hatchet Mary's because Joan wanted to poke a frozen carp. She knocked on my door at eight on Saturday morning with a rasp and a thermometer and a thermos of coffee. I made her an English muffin and she took it, then I asked her how mad she was, on a scale of one to ten.

"Let's go. I want to be there if the sun melts the ice." I couldn't get another word out of her.

The temperature had dropped the night before, and all the liquid in the world was stopped dead. Every individual hexagon in the chicken wire on the Abbates' front gate was encased in ice. When we ducked under the trees into Hatchet Mary's, all the little branches tinkled against each other. The leaves under our feet cracked and snapped.

"Joan, you have to talk to me. I'm sorry, okay. If anyone finds out, they'll put me in custody."

I expected her to yell at me. I expected her to say, "It's me, Daisy! You don't trust me?" or something. Because really, didn't I? Why hadn't I told her? I'm still trying to figure that out now.

I crunched over the ground in Hatchet Mary's and bent over to read a gravestone through its coating of ice. The cuffs of my jeans were stiff. In a few minutes the heat from my body would melt them and freezing water would drip down into my shoes. I couldn't look at her.

"They don't really know what happens to their brains."

"What?"

"Everything stops, but they don't die."

I turned around and then felt tricked. She just kept digging, asking the world questions.

"Is it like what bears do? Is it like when other fish sleep on the bottom? The temperature of the carp is the same as the water. They freeze completely solid. And then five months later, they just wiggle out and swim away. What the hell?"

"You know what? I don't fucking care, Joan."

I turned away and ducked under the branches. The top pond was frozen like black marble. I climbed up past it and through into the open meadow. The woods stretched along all around, each individual branch coated with ice. There was nothing living in there, no possible movement except mine.

How close did I come to it? To him? I wasn't really looking around. Ever since the day we found out what happened at Hatchet Mary's that winter I've been wondering, did I pass right by it? Was it coated in ice, like the branches and the gravestones? How long had it been there by that point? Would I have even been able to recognize what it was? There must have been footprints and broken branches, a pathway leading to that rolled-up piece of tarp, because everyone said later that Scottie took kids up to see it.

At the time I was so mad at Joan the steamy breath was coming out of my mouth in big, quick puffs. I looked at my feet and stomped through the frozen grass thinking the only other person in there with me was her. We went in that day, digging up fish and fighting with each other like we'd been doing our whole lives. No idea what was lying next to us in the trees.

The weight of the ice had dragged the tall grasses down into clumps and the blades whipped against my legs when I pushed through them. I went back to Joan, because I always will. Of course she was mad at me; I was an asshole. I didn't trust her and she was still worried enough about me to get mad.

I sat down on the wall at the edge of the pond and started talking.

"I was ashamed, okay? Everyone loves you."

That got her attention. She snorted and then turned her head to glare at me.

"Okay, I'm sorry. I know it's fucked-up for you, too. But I mean, there are people who love you who aren't crazy or junkies, or both. Who aren't in jail or unpredictably violent. One day, they'll find out about my family and you'll never be allowed to hang out with me again."

"I'm wondering if we'd hurt the carp if we warmed up the ice."

"I don't know. You're sleeping with a teacher."

"We might hurt it." She went on trying to wear a hole in the ice with the rasp.

"Well, I'm worried about you even if you aren't."

"Shut up now, Daisy. I'm done trying to get the truth from people. I'm going back to fish."

"No, actually. I'm not gonna shut up."

"Stick to talking about yourself then, because I will leave and not come back if you keep passing judgment on me."

I thought that was true. I never doubted it because I didn't trust her completely. I should have.

"Okay, so my mother and Robbie have never been there, really. It's not like anything changed. Except the bills. The bills are kind of intense, but I mean my life isn't really more complicated without them. The thing is, you know a guidance counselor wouldn't see it that way."

My ass had melted the ice and snow underneath it and now it was freezing and wet.

"So you actually think I'd tell a guidance counselor your problems?" She didn't turn around, which was good because she would have seen the smile I couldn't keep off my face when she decided to get into the same conversation as me.

"No! I don't think that. When she left and Robbie was still there, I was scared for you. Robbie got weird. Weirder than usual. And then Ray never came back and . . . I don't know. I didn't want you to be around it."

"And?"

"And then Robbie left, too. I didn't know how to pay for anything, and I was embarrassed, and then I thought people would come and take me away."

"You're not answering the real question. Why didn't you trust me, Daisy?"

"I trust you. I just panicked. Joan, I can't live anywhere else."

I guess we both knew what I really meant. Joan was lifting out of my life and I was clinging on to her like we were on a rooftop at the fall of Saigon. Lying to her and wanting her to be there for me anyway. When I felt myself tumbling into the chaos, I forgot about trust. I wasn't going to let go, even if I pulled her down with me.

"And what the hell is going on in that bedroom?"

"Oh, that's my map and stuff. I started in my room, but then

I moved in there. See, one thing is there's plenty of room at my house now."

"Yeah, clocked the map. What *is it*?"

"It's all the inward operators I've tried and which ones work and where I got to so far. The lights are just for fun. They're on a series circuit. The one in the bathroom mirror is parallel."

"What the fuck is an inward operator, Daisy?"

I explained it again. She kept digging down to her carp. When she got down to the fish, she poked the thermometer into one of the gills and left it there while she made some notes. When we were ready to go, she packed the hole up with snow like she was putting the fish back to sleep.

We walked away from all the dead things sleeping under the ice in Hatchet Mary's, and I felt happier than I had in weeks.

I looked up at the bare branches and thought about spring. I thought about another summer with Joan. The space between us would close, the leaves would come back, and the melted tide would carry our boat out into the Sound. Joan and I would look up and see the same pictures in the sky. I forgot to be scared for a minute and believed everything would fall together again.

Then I remembered Robbie. There were new kinds of emptiness between us now, wounds that would never close up.

daisy

AT THE END of the winter I rode in Arthur's car without Joan for the first time in my life. All the snow was melted, but the trees were still bare. First we just drove up to Head of the Harbor. Arthur swung around the curve with Black Uhuru playing on the tape deck and me rolling a joint on the door of the glove compartment.

"So, what did you think of *The Street*?" He turned the car off and looked at me.

"Bleak, man. Like everything's inevitable. Like America's a big ugly machine, and we're all trapped inside it."

We got out and looked over the edge. In the wind it was still winter. My hands turned red and I could hardly feel them. Arthur had gloves with no fingers.

"Right," he said. "I'm gonna drive you down to the beach.

You can talk to somebody if you want, but be careful. Then you're going to forget it. Seen?"

I looked down past the trees sticking out over the cliff. For a minute I saw Robbie's blackened car sitting on that sand, then falling through the air, burning. The air opened up and the ground was so far away it looked like a map. I had that feeling you get, like I might throw myself off even though I didn't want to.

I pictured Robbie sloping along in his satin jacket, falling asleep in the chair, dropping through the water until the stabbing sunlight no longer reached him. I looked at Arthur and wished he was my brother. I'm sorry, but I did.

"Okay. What if no one tells me anything?"

"Then we're done, Daisy. Then you have to let it go, because you promised you would."

"Would you be able to do that if you were me?"

He put a hand on my shoulder and turned me toward him.

"Let go of this or you let go of my sister. You decide."

I smiled up at him. I don't know why. I guess it had been a long time since anyone touched me at all. I registered that steadying hand and not the words, at first.

"I'm not playing," he said.

I just nodded and then looked back over the cliff. There was nothing in the air and no one on the sand.

We got back in the car and cruised down to Fiddler's Cove in neutral. Patrick Jervis was in Matt McBride's truck. You could just make him out through the steam on the windows. The water was churned up with foam, and smoke was coming out of all three LILCO stacks.

"Go on," Arthur said. "I'll be here."

He kept the engine running and turned the volume down on "Guess Who's Coming to Dinner." Crossing that parking lot was like that dream you have where you're running as fast as you can and not getting anywhere. A whole crowd of people is watching you and you realize you're naked. It isn't funny, it's terrifying. I knocked on the window of Matt's truck with one red knuckle. He rolled it down and a waft of air came out, smelling like cleaning chemicals. He flicked a finger at my forehead.

"What?"

"Patrick said he was looking for my brother."

Patrick laughed out a cloud of smoke. "Yeah, like months ago."

"Just wondering if you've seen him. He, uh—" It occurred to me at the last minute that I didn't want those guys to know my house was empty. "He moved out and my mom is worried."

"Your brother made himself scarce, McNamara," Matt said. "Caused some shit and took off."

"Yeah, maybe look under a rock."

"I just wanted to make sure he's okay. You know, Robbie doesn't take care of himself so good."

They both laughed together then.

"Forget it, man. People have worse things to worry about."

Matt rolled the window up, wiped clear so I could see them

perfectly for a minute. I just stood there thinking in two directions at once, watching them and their chamber pipe disappear as the window misted up again. My brain was putting all the pieces together even though I was asking it not to. There was some circuit of violence connecting everything around us. All the disappearing people were joined up like lights in a series, blinking out one after the other.

Arthur honked his horn and swung the car around. When I got in he didn't say anything or even look at me. He just drove out onto Seaview Road and up the hill to the traffic light. We stopped behind a Cadillac and he finally looked at me.

"You hungry?"

"McDonald's?"

"I don't eat that shit anymore, but I'll drive you through if you want some fries. Coffee'd be a good idea, maybe."

I got both and we headed down Main Street. Arthur pulled over on Baywater Avenue, where we could see down into the park.

Behind the bandstand were three guys I didn't know. Definitely not from school, maybe not from Highbone at all. One of them had something down the leg of his jeans that Arthur said was a shotgun. From where I was sitting I could see him standing like he couldn't bend his knee.

"They'll know," I said.

"Absolutely not." Arthur shook his head. "Seat belt. Time to go."

"Arthur, he's my brother. I need to know."

"No disrespect, kid, but your brother is a liability. You have a brain and you need to start using it."

Arthur was right. In families like mine, you just drift into things. Every time a shiny thing falls into your lap you forget who you wanted to be. And then you drift away. Nothing sticks to us McNamaras, like we have no gravity. You have to concentrate just to stand still.

"He tried to take care of me, Arthur. He did."

"His methodology was a little unsound. Sorry, man. This stops here, right?"

"Okay. Arthur? Can I tell you something else?"

"Only if it's unrelated." He almost smiled then. It was almost like we weren't trying to figure out whether my brother was really dead and if it was his own fault anyway.

"Stuff is going on with Joan."

"Joan just turned sixteen. It'd be kind of weird if stuff wasn't going on with her."

"No, I mean she's pissed off and maybe worried about something, and people are taking advantage of her, Arthur. Maybe you should talk to her?"

"Well, Joan . . . you know. Girl likes to find her own answers. She was always like that. You try to talk to her, she just clams up."

"Yeah, I noticed."

"You want some advice?"

"I guess."

"If you want to do something to help my sister, just hang in there. That's what she needs. And take care of your own shit, so it's doesn't come back on her."

It was dark when we pulled over on Jensen Road. Arthur told me one more time to stay away from people who knew Robbie.

My house was cold, so I went out back and brought an old picnic bench into the garage. After I'd spent an hour smashing it to pieces with a hammer, I felt emptier, but not exactly better. I left the lights off and lit a fire so I could make toast with a barbecue fork and boil some water. I was only using the electricity for important stuff.

After the fire died down, I went up to my mother's room and hit the switch. The mechanical voice welcomed me, and I turned the bathroom lights on, too. Lying on the floor in that multicolored light, I thought, *This. My whole life will always come back to this. These are the years that make people.* Wherever we go from here, I will be the kid who stayed all alone with his toasting fork and his Electric Kool-Aid Bathroom Mirror. The kid with wires for veins and a heart that won't fit in his scrawny chest. The kid who grew up next to Joan.

The next time I saw Patrick and Matt, I knew they were talking about Ray. I can't deny or it or even find an excuse. I didn't care. I didn't pay attention or tell anybody or wonder about the details. I was only thinking about Robbie, which was why I went back without telling Arthur.

Everything smelled wet and dirty when I came into the park

from the bottom of Main Street. I stepped off the path and my sneakers sank into the grass and squelched. The sky behind the pier was pink and there were lights on the boats, people after work, putting back in and checking their tackle. Summer was still far away, but we all felt it coming. I wondered if I'd be grateful when the light came back.

Patrick and Matt were behind the bandstand with some other guy who had a guitar. He was playing "Free Bird" and Matt was singing under his breath. I sat down just outside the circle they made on the grass.

"McNamara!" Patrick said. "Where's your girlfriend?"

"She's not my girlfriend. Smoke?" I pulled a joint out of my cigarette box and waved it.

"Is it the good kind?" They all laughed, and I kept quiet.

A cop cruised by on Baywater Avenue while I lit up and looked out over the water. I could just see his lights over the tops of the bushes. I passed the joint and waited. If I stayed quiet long enough, one of them would say something about Robbie. I was bound to make them think of him and whatever it was they were pissed about. Asking didn't work, and I couldn't do anything obvious. If Arthur knew I was still looking for answers, he'd tell Joan to stay away from me.

"You ever seen a dead person?" Patrick said.

I held the joint out to the guitar guy and thought about pool hopping. Once school ended, Joan wouldn't see Mr. Tomaszewski anymore and we'd have all day to sit in the trees or lie around the abandoned house. All night to row out to the pit, walk barefoot across the sod, and slip into the empty water. I closed my eyes to look at the bright wash of security lights on the back of my lids, smelling the chlorophyll and the bleach.

"Daisy! You retard."

"Huh?"

"I said, have you ever seen a dead person?"

"Uh, nah."

I wanted to say, *Yes. Every night. Every kind of death. Every state of decomposition. There is nothing I haven't imagined.*

He passed me the joint and I saw his hand shaking. "Not even at a funeral?"

"No. Why?"

"Would you? If someone could show you one, would you look? Think you could handle it?"

"Joan would look," I said. "Joan would look inside anything."

I still thought the conversation was hypothetical. It was a little deep for Patrick, but we were all stoned by that point.

"You can't bring a girl."

I guess it was then. That was when I realized they were talking about something real. Physical. Actual and specific. And my brain slammed shut like a metal door. I didn't want any more bodies in my head. I didn't want any more deadly information. I felt like I wasn't attached to the grass. I didn't weigh anything. I couldn't hold on or work my limbs, but I had to leave.

I took a few shallow breaths and said goodbye. When I pushed up onto my feet I fell forward, and they all laughed again. I turned my back on them and walked away through the soggy grass. The sky had gone dark, and most of the boats had disappeared. Someone was rowing toward Carter's Bay, but I only knew that from the sound of the oars. There was a guy lying on the bench at the bottom of Main Street, talking to himself about highways and truck stops. I looked at him, trying to see through into whatever world he lived in. If he'd gone through some door into another reality, I wanted to follow him.

I did learn the truth about Robbie that night, but it wasn't what I was looking for. It wasn't a detail, but it was a fact. There were bodies everywhere and Robbie was just one of them. The whole of Long Island is a graveyard made of rocks and sand, from the body dumps in Queens to the murdered Shinnecocks on the North Fork.

After that night, I knew Ray Velker was lying somewhere in Highbone. That kids were lining up to look at him like he was an exhibit at the Museum of Natural History, and I turned away from that knowledge and shut my eyes. That makes me the same as every other kid in Highbone, just as twisted, just as damaged, just as evil. Doesn't it?

I didn't tell Joan because I didn't want to make words out of it. I didn't want those words in the air between us. All I wanted was nothing. I wanted things to stop happening, people to stop disappearing, the chasm between me and everything else to either close up or kill me.

Sometimes when a hurricane comes, it breaks through Fire Island and tries to clean us away. But we won't let it. If we would just give in to the storm wave, we'd go under, with all our radioactive chemicals and our petty jealousies and our sharp objects. All the toasters and televisions and pathetic longings that count for reality in the suburbs would wash away into the sea. Crabs would eat our flesh but we wouldn't feel them. We'd all be sleeping forever inside the blessed emptiness.

daisy

THAT SATURDAY WE met in our tree and sat in between all the skinny branches full of closed buds. The tree seemed bigger than last time, older and more crooked. Nothing was green or growing yet. The world was still a blank, ready for us to write on it. But all we did was argue.

"I feel like you walked around a corner before me, and when I got there you'd disappeared," I said.

"It just looks like that to you because you don't understand. Girls grow up faster; everybody knows that."

I looked down and saw the crocuses, poking up under the trees. Even after last winter the world was going to resurrect itself, without change or pity.

"So you're grown-up now? You're ready to start playing

house with Mr. Tomaszewski? You're gonna learn to make casseroles and use laundry starch?"

"Nick isn't that kind of person and you know it. You're just pissed off because someone paid attention to me."

"*Nick*. You don't think it's a little creepy that Mr. Tomaszewski put the moves on you the minute you turned sixteen?"

"Come on, Daisy. This conversation is never going anywhere."

It wasn't raining, but everything was wet anyway. The melt was everywhere. The whole world was full of cold water. I looked around at the bare branches, feeling like a clam when Joan breaks open the shell with a screwdriver.

"Don't you realize everything that's going on? Kids are missing and the cops are everywhere. Why did you have to pick now to have an affair with someone twice your age?"

"Your math sucks, Daisy. Nick is nowhere near thirty-two."

"My point is, we're under all kinds of scrutiny here. We've got targets on our backs right now. Someone could pounce on us any minute, some dealer or an FBI agent or someone from the phone company. Any minute, we could be dead."

Or maybe that was just wishful thinking.

"You're tripping."

"Listen Joan, I did. I mean, I did angel dust."

"You what?"

"I didn't mean to."

I told her about Patrick and Ray dosing me that day at Hatchet Mary's. I was just trying to work my way through the lies and get back to her. I thought at least I could clear away the pointless ones. I was drowning in all the things I had to keep knowing, all by myself in secret.

"Jesus, Daisy, how are you so dumb?! If I wasn't around, you'd be dead by now."

"What, you never smoked up with someone in the park you didn't know? Why are you freaking out on me?"

"Because, Daisy, you never protect yourself. You need to learn how to be careful. What if I'm not there one day?"

"Uh, you weren't there then. That's why I'm telling you about it now."

"Yeah, and look what happened! And why the hell did you wait six months to tell me?"

"Five, I think. And I can't really tell you why. It's complicated."

"Don't you think you've lied enough this year, Daisy? I'm supposed to hang around until you need me, but I can't ask questions? Your family deserted you and you didn't think I should know?"

Someone came out to the back of the Narragansett with the garbage. I could see his breath on the air from where we were sitting. People were still moving through the world like nothing had happened. They clocked in and clocked out and rode the bus back and forth to school. People ate dinner and planted bulbs and paid the bills.

"They love me, Joan. You act like they don't, but they do."

"No, I get that. I do. But they took off and left you in the damn house to fend for yourself. *You!* With your hazardous electricity fetish and your fear of laundry soap."

"See why I didn't tell you?"

"Okay, sorry, but Jesus! How am I supposed to jump in and save you like the helpful sidekick from movies if you don't tell me what's going on?"

"You're never gonna be anybody's sidekick, Joan Harris. You'd suck at that."

"Well, that's my career in Hollywood fucked,"

We laughed, but it didn't make anything better.

Once I'd told her about Patrick and the angel dust, I realized I still couldn't tell her why it mattered. It was probably Robbie who sold it to him. Robbie and Ray had both been dealing, and now they were both missing. Well, Ray wasn't exactly missing, was he? Some people knew where he was. And if the guy at Jamaica Bay wasn't Robbie, if Robbie was still around somewhere, I didn't want anyone making the connection. Not even Joan.

"I promised Arthur I wouldn't talk to you about it."

"Arthur? Oh, okay. Sorry, I got confused and thought I was the one that was your friend."

The feeling came back then. The weightlessness and the way people's voices kept fading away from me lately. I was still moving around the same world as everyone else, but I'd become a ghost, a reflection on the air. I moved up and down the staircase and haunted the woods, but I couldn't touch anything. I couldn't move things or make anything happen anymore.

"I'm sorry, Joan. I should have said something."

Any minute I was going to lose my bones and my voice. I'd float up out of our beech tree and turn into smoke over the water. All the truths would come out of me and I'd be repeating them over and over forever, but Joan wouldn't be able to hear me.

joan

I GUESS I stayed mad at Daisy for a while. We did stuff, but I spent a lot of time alone, too.

On a warm Saturday in March I walked all the way to Nick's apartment. I spent most of last year traveling around looking for answers to questions that don't have any. You can dissect a body and find out how it works. That's no help when you're living inside one. People can tell you all about your own glands, but that doesn't help you control them.

I couldn't hang around after school trying to talk to Nick. I had to go to his house before my insides made a complete mess of me. I had a big biology test. I needed to concentrate.

He was leaving when I got there, slinging a bag over his shoulder in the doorway.

"Joan. What's wrong?"

"Nothing. I just wanted to tell you I finished my report."

"You could have told me that at school. Is something the matter?"

I leaned against the door of his car, fumbling in my pockets. I was hoping for a cigarette, but I couldn't remember if I had any or where I'd put them. I couldn't remember anything.

"Nothing's wrong. I—where are you going?"

"To a meeting. Well, let's see it." He put his hand out. Like that was the whole reason I was there. Like we were standing in the biology lab with his table between us.

"I don't have it with me. I was going to talk to you about it, but you're probably late, so—"

"Yeah, I am. That's nothing new, though." He smiled then, and I thought things might rewind. He leaned against the car and I relaxed. Then he said, "Joan, there's a lot happening right now, isn't there?"

"You mean Ray?"

"Did you know him?"

"Not really. He's been around since fifth grade. We went to the same elementary, but he never talked to me."

"The cops are still questioning his teachers. This isn't really a good time for us to hang out. At least until they find him. You get that, right?"

"Yeah. Sorry, I wasn't thinking."

"No need to apologize. We're friends, aren't we?"

"Aristotle was wrong a lot. I mean, he just made stuff up. How is that scientific?"

"He relied on other people. It was harder to get around back then, and there were nowhere near as many books. If someone wrote something about a place far away, people just accepted it. Hence all that medieval crap about griffins and winged elephants and dragons."

"He was wrong about stuff that was right next to him. There's no dogfish that carries a baby attached to the outside of its body. I checked."

"Science is about facts, but it takes imagination, too, doesn't it? Maybe they hadn't worked out the balance yet."

He laughed and touched my shoulder so I'd move out of his way. So he could get in his car and drive to wherever he was going. So I could walk home alone with myself and the whole story could repeat itself over and over in my head. Having emotions is like living in a clothes dryer.

"Maybe we can talk when all this is over, okay?" He looked up at me with his door open. Pretending like he was asking and it was my decision.

For a minute I tried to make excuses, for him and me. Tried to explain it to myself. I wasn't grasping at straws. It wasn't like water slipping through my fingers. It just was. When he pulled away, I sat down on his front step and looked up through the telephone lines at the place where the moon was last time. It was empty. I found my cigarettes right in my top pocket and lit one while I stared at the negative space between the wires.

I was too full of information to even think. Too tired to walk. I was sick of every fact in the world.

* * *

But there were more facts coming. It was like someone had pulled away our shells and left our nerves bare. We were so exposed by then that everything seemed to travel right into us.

We were at Nervous Records the day we heard about Ray Velker's body.

I woke up that Saturday and the tide was so high I could see the water without even getting out of bed. I knew it was really spring then. When I was littler, I used to pretend we lived in a floating house on days like that. I'd sit in bed and imagine that the water came all the way up to the walls of the house, that we got everywhere by boat like people in Venice or the Everglades.

That day I made some coffee and opened my window. I leaned into the trees and breathed smoke out toward Carter's Bay. The air smelled like rot and metal.

It was eight o'clock. I was the only teenager in the universe who voluntarily woke up early on Saturdays. You'd have thought everybody would pat me on the back and tell me what an industrious, responsible kid I was. That never happened, so I stopped using Saturday mornings to do my chores and starting using them for time to be alone.

I still had my mother's notebook in my backpack, and I knew Daisy would be asleep until at least eleven. I put on Andre's duffle coat and my sneakers and climbed the hill. The McNamaras actually kept a spare key under the doormat by the back door. You had to wonder why evolution hadn't taken care of them about three generations back. I opened the back door and made another coffee before I went up to the attic.

When I looked out the attic window the world was full of cross-hatched lines, telephone wires and branches and vapor trails and my mother's geometry notebook. I was full of caffeine, and the whole world was still asleep. I sat there with the notebook open on my lap, reading about Deborah and trying to connect her to that woman who wanders around on our mud. My mother's life was like *Of Mice and Men*, a load of extra drama, bent broken people and people who didn't survive.

At eleven o'clock I went down, got in bed with Daisy, and poked him. He didn't even jump. He just put his head under the blanket and mumbled my name. Then he breathed out a little satisfied sigh, like a baby. I kicked him, but not too hard.

After a while he said, "I need another dry cell."

"Wake up, Daisy. I don't have any kind of batteries."

"I'm awake." He was still under the covers. Well, his head was under but his feet were sticking out. He wore his socks to bed. "I already sold the stereo."

"I figured. Your room stinks. Let's go to Hatchet Mary's and see if the carp woke up."

"No!"

"Why not? If we can catch it, I can take its temperature."

"Because Hatchet Mary's is full of lurking creeps with angel dust, remember? And every time we go there, we fight." He tented the blanket up with his arm but stayed under it. "I'm never going there again."

"We fought one time. And you could just not smoke the angel

dust. You can't not go to Hatchet Mary's. That'll ruin at least twenty-eight percent of our entertainment."

"I have a plan. I need a dry cell and maybe some old vacuum tubes. Can we go to Nervous Records and ask Andre's boss?"

"Your room smells like you keep jocks in the closet. I think your main plan for today should involve laundry."

We took the bus to Huntington and got some cannoli first. Ferravante's in the parking lot behind Main Street has the kind without citron. The entrance to Nervous Records was in an alley off Main Street that had probably been made for people to put garbage in. They had a neon sign that flickered like it was crapped out, but on purpose. Nervous. Get it?

There were bins full of records and cassettes hanging on pegs from the wall, wrapped in enough hard plastic so kids couldn't shove them in their jackets without hurting themselves. The floor was black-and-white tiles, and someone had stenciled a giant solarized picture of Sid Vicious on one wall. When *Sid Sings* came out and Andre put on his version of "My Way," my dad told him he was ridiculous. Even Gramps shook his head and looked out the window so he wouldn't have to deal.

The owner of Nervous Records was white and messy and maybe thirty years old. He thought he was special for being the first one to figure out that everything cool came from England again. He was always calling Andre brother. When we came in that Saturday, there was a kid with a suspiciously large Navy coat on and a guy in the jazz section who looked like maybe he hung out with Mr. Tomaszewski in his spare time. Andre was handing Jimmy, the owner, a brand-new copy of *The Specials*. We waved and went straight over to the tapes on the wall so Andre wouldn't get in trouble for socializing at work. I tried to look like I really wanted to buy the cassette of *Survival* even though Arthur already had it.

Then "A Message to You, Rudy" came through the speakers. It was a nothing moment, but in it something ended for us. Something started, too, I guess, but I still don't know what. I mean, yeah, the music was new last year, but I don't care about that. Andre, in his turtleneck and his black 501 button-flies, I guess maybe he was part of what changed. I realized that day that he was going to be different than the rest of us. He was riding something we couldn't feel yet. Well, maybe my mother could. Maybe that's why she likes him better than me.

Daisy picked up a Joni Mitchell album and waved it at Andre to get him to come over.

"Does your boss sell stereo equipment?"

Andre swept his hand in a circle around the room and looked at Daisy. "No."

"I need to sell some parts and maybe buy some other ones. Do you know where I can?"

I don't know what Daisy really wanted. He'd been to Nervous Records before, and he knew Andre didn't give a shit about his weird electronics. It was all an excuse, but I still don't know for what.

Anyway, freeze that moment. Look at it. It was right before

the final thing fell down into our lives. The one we never asked for and couldn't contain.

"You guys are from over in Highbone, aren't you?" Jimmy shouted over the music.

Andre said yeah and something like, "This is my sister, Joan." Jimmy gave me a look that was a little less creepy than a lot of the looks I get lately. But it wasn't exactly neutral, either.

"What's up with this?" Jimmy held out the Saturday *Newsday*. "Missing Teenager's Body Found in Highbone," the front page said.

Even Andre forgot about work. We all stood around the paper spread out by the cash register. The Specials went on singing, and we read about how Ray Velker had been lying in the woods at Hatchet Mary's for months. People had been going up there to see Ray all winter, getting stoned and staring at him while he disintegrated into the mulch. And it was months before one of them thought maybe they should say something. Finally, a kid tipped off the cops.

I thought about the inside of Ray Velker, open in the woods like some kind of carnival sideshow from a nightmare. I didn't want to picture any of it, the bones or the organs or the way it all worked and fell apart. I didn't want to know.

Jimmy turned the volume down on "Do the Dog" and Andre's face closed over. I knew right then, he was leaving as soon as he could save up enough money or find a free way out. He wouldn't wait for September. We all stood there trying to comprehend people gawking at Ray's dead body like he was a shark strung up at the docks, but Andre just said no. No, I don't have space in my head for that. No, thanks. Daisy and me stood there in Nervous Records, looking at the paper and wishing we could muster up that kind of denial. Well, maybe we already had. Maybe we already weren't telling each other just as much as every other kid in Highbone.

We went back to Ferravante's for coffees and another two cannoli. I climbed up onto one of the high stools and watched the sugar dust fall from Daisy's lips. The world seemed muffled and I couldn't taste anything.

"I love you," Daisy said. "You know, like a friend. I love you."

"I love you too, man." Then I felt bad for being sarcastic. "No, I do."

"I don't want anything to ever happen to you. Sometimes I wake up in the middle of the night with my heart pounding. I can't breathe because I dreamed you were dead."

"We're all gonna die, Daisy. But let's hang out until then."

I was thinking it had been a cold winter. Ray had basically been on ice for almost three months, but still. He must have been pretty far gone by the time they found him. I was picturing his bones with nothing but tatters of sinew clinging to them, his eyes looking at never and nothing and then melting away.

That was before all the details came out. Before we found out what really happened to Ray Velker's eyes.

We went to Radio Shack so Daisy could poke around. The long-haired guy behind the counter looked at us like we were there to steal his dry cell batteries. Did he know? Had he read the paper that day? Did Ray matter in Huntington, or would it just be another gruesome story? How much distance do you need before a dead body doesn't mean anything? I looked out the plate-glass window at the world where Ray Velker's body had lain for months alone in the snow.

Daisy pointed to some vacuum tubes and said, "Inside those it's like outer space. No atmosphere, no air, nothing could live inside here."

"First of all, outer space is way colder. Insanely cold, like your blood would freeze right inside you."

Then I thought of Ray again, with the blood leaking out of him and drying in the freezing air. I didn't think about Robbie. Even after what I'd seen, I still believed he was out there somewhere twitching and messing things up as usual. Except he wasn't, and Daisy knew it. So what was Daisy thinking right then?

"I'm just saying, inside these tubes you might as well not even be on this planet."

"Tetanus could maybe live in there. Tetanus is anaerobic."

"Seriously, Joan. Sometimes you could go with a feeling instead of a fact."

"You know what? I hate Radio Shack. Nothing's alive in here."

I went out front and got out my mom's notebook. I leaned against the plate-glass window and stared at her handwriting, looking for evidence. You don't find the facts in people's words. People use words as camouflage. Ink, though—ink never lies. It tells years later whether your hand shook and where your tears fell and smudged it into puddles. In a way, part of my mother was in that book. Not the words, the tears and the sweat and the skin cells. The breath that dried into the ink. Someday, that notebook will disintegrate too. The paper will crumble and the ink will fade. By that time no one who knows enough to care will still be alive anyway.

Andre came home from work later that night with a copy of *The Specials,* a thin tie, and a long coat from the antique store. Dad gave him a pair of his museum shoes, and he spent the whole night reading the classifieds in a copy of the *Voice.*

daisy

ALL SPRING, WE kept trying. We didn't know what else to do. I sat alone in my mother's room, looking at the picture of her and Robbie on the wall. I had shoved the bed over to the wall and moved most of her stuff into the basement, but I left that picture hanging there. It was taken some dry fall day when everybody was young. The whole thing is blurry and full of sunlight. Behind them there's some scrub pine and a brown mess of dead stuff. The lawn is turning brown, too. I think that picture is in the backyard here, at Aunt Regina's in Rockaway.

My mother is wearing a loose black dress with a cloth rose pinned to it. Her hair is set and she's smiling like a frightened child with one arm around Robbie and the other looking skinny in her lap. When I was little she never went anywhere without her checkered sunglasses hiding her eyes. She made the world talk to her lipstick. I remember the way words came low and breathy out of those red lips. How anyone who talked to her had to rely on that whisper because there was no way into her eyes. In that picture, though, her eyes are naked. Scared, if you look close enough.

One night last spring I looked at that picture and saw how young she was, how she was sitting in the middle of a sudden, terrifying world with babies and sex in it, trying to look happy because that's what you do in pictures. She is showing a row of strong teeth, but the picture is so blurred with light I can never tell about the lipstick. Robbie is wearing a shirt the same red as Mom's cloth rose, and he's moving. He's maybe a year old, doesn't even look like he could walk yet. He's blurred himself into a ghostly smudge, like he's about to fade back to heaven and leave her there.

At least one of the people in the picture was dead, maybe both. I said goodbye to them and went upstairs to the attic. I looked out at Arthur's shadow moving past his window. I watched Mr. Harris park his car and carry his tall, steady presence into the warm house. Looking at their roof, I wished I had one of those infrared cameras that show all the warmth leaking out of doors and roofs and windows. I wished I could lie on the Harrises' roof like a cold-blooded animal, soaking in all the escaping heat.

Instead I went back downstairs and slept under my mother's picture.

In my dreams I saw Robbie in his Charger. I was around him or inside of him, looking out at the sea grass in the Jamaica marshes from behind his shoulder. The sun bleached everything until it was pale and dry and tossing in the breezes. I could feel Robbie all around me. Then there was a bang and all the car windows filled up with a flash of light.

I woke up because Joan was shouting my name. She sounded panicked, and I wondered whether someone else was dead.

"I'm in here!" It came out croaky and I had to shout again. I pushed my grandmother's afghan off me and looked down to see what I was wearing.

Joan threw the door open and hit the light switch.

"Hello, Daisy. Come on in. Relax."

"Jesus fuck!"

"I should really give that thing pathways. It should have called you Joan."

"What were you doing in here? I couldn't find you. This is not the time to go AWOL, McNamara."

"It seemed safer not to sleep in a bedroom."

"This is a bedroom, Daisy!" She looked around at the wires and the blinking lights. Then she seemed to give in. She sat down and lit up a Player's Navy Cut. I wondered where she got it.

"Ashtray?"

I handed her a cream soda can. "This is a cool problem. How could we make the light switch recognize the difference between you and me?"

"I know a cool problem. You're sixteen and no one lives here with you. Your mother fucked off somewhere and you're sleeping on the floor in a nest of live wires. What are you gonna do?"

"I'm fine, Joan. I like living here."

I was so happy that she was yelling at me. It was so much better than when she didn't talk to me at all. Joan is one of those people who gets mad when she really cares.

"Arthur said he already talked to you about your family. What's with that, Daisy?"

"He was helping me. I'm trying to find out what. . . where Robbie is."

"Helping you how?"

"You know, just asking around."

"Asking around who?"

"Just guys in the park. Patrick and people. It's no big deal."

"You *idiot*, Daisy."

"We talked about it and he said not to tell you."

"Hello, remember me? Joan, your best friend. Perfectly capable person who's been getting you out of trouble with a smile since 1972."

"We don't want you to get hurt or get in trouble. Arthur said if I got killed it would ruin your life. If *you* get killed, I'm going with you."

She fell over backward and said, "You really don't get it, do you?"

"Watch out for that casing. There are live wires in there."

She cursed and sat up again.

"How long before you burn this place down, Daisy? I'm tired of being your responsible adult."

"See, you care! It's all fused anyway. Don't worry so much."

Joan looked up at the picture of Mom and Robbie, then over

at my map. It was blinking now that she'd turned the lights on. Then the next thing I knew she put her hands on my shoulders and started shouting.

"You don't get it! You've been my best friend my whole life and you still don't get it!"

"Jeez. Calm down. I can show you the safety."

"Whatever! I don't even care if you burn your house down. Answer me this: you piss off some cops or some dealers, Arthur pisses off some cops or some dealers. What's the difference?"

"I'm underage?"

"Wake up and smell the fucking coffee, McNamara! You're *white* and your dad's friends own the cops. If a dealer kills you, they might actually get in trouble for it."

I knew as soon as she said it. I would have put Arthur in danger. Serious danger, and I didn't even stop to think. He told me he was only doing it for Joan, but I didn't get what that meant, either. Not until later.

"Joan, I didn't . . ."

"Save it. Stay here and try not to electrocute yourself." She threw the door open. "I'll be back in a little while."

I ran up to the attic so I could see her before she disappeared down the Harrises' steps. I looked over at the dormer and pictured that spitting wire writhing over Jensen Road and lighting up the rain. Then I pictured the tear on Joan's cheek, red spark instead of blue. I remembered sitting up there with a cup attached to a long string, trying to talk to Joan across the road. We were maybe nine then.

I checked behind the insulation for Mrs. Harris's notebook, but it was gone. After a while Arthur came out and drove away. For a minute I wanted to throw myself down onto the roof of the car. I might survive, cracked and bloody but alive and clinging on while the force of the curve on Jensen Road tilted me and held me in.

Joan came up her front stairs and all of a sudden I saw how pretty she was. I mean I'd seen her look pretty before, dressed up or floating on someone's pool in the pit, not paying attention. And not pretty too, when we got drunk and threw up or when she was really mad. Right then, though, I realized that some time last year she'd gotten pretty like women are pretty. Like probably most people noticed. Pretty like you couldn't ignore it. Unless you were me.

I heard the front door open and yelled her name.

She came up the stairs and pushed a cookie tin and a pack of cigarettes up onto the floor before her head appeared.

"People can hear you yelling in Commack." She walked under the peak of the roof, where you can stand all the way up. "Gramps made you some cookies. I don't know why."

She pointed at the tin and we both laughed. It was so weird that people were still making cookies in the world we live in now.

"Joan, guys are hitting on you because you're really pretty."

"What, now?"

"Listen. I'm not being weird so don't get mad and tell me to shut up. This year, you got really pretty. I only just noticed."

"Am I supposed to say thank you right now? 'Cause I kinda can't tell."

"No! I'm saying people are hitting on you and I don't think you get why."

She pushed the cookie tin at me with her foot.

"You leave my brother out of your shit, hear me?"

"That's exactly what he said about you."

"Fine. Maybe we're not your own private social workers. Get it together, McNamara."

"I have it together. You guys are the ones freaking out. I'm fine. I have food and I'm doing my homework."

She let out a breath and sat down then, looking fed up and maybe sad.

"All right, Joan. I'll figure something out, okay? But do you get what I'm saying about the other thing? You used to just be you. Now you're somebody people want to get with, even if they don't really care about you."

"Guess what?" She pointed a finger at her own heart. "I live in here. So, you know, I kinda got that already. But thanks."

"Don't you care whether people actually like you for who you are?"

"Not really. What difference does it make to the outcome?"

I looked at her while she looked past me to the window, and I felt like that downed wire in the hurricane. Like whatever kind of energy was bleeding out of me was going nowhere, connecting with nothing, fizzing out in the pouring rain.

Overnight the world warmed up and set all its water free again. In the morning, Joan came up her outside stairs while me and

Arthur were standing around the car.

"Where are you guys going?" she said. "Never mind; it doesn't even matter. I'm coming."

I looked at Arthur, but he just kept his head down, leaning on the car and reading *The Wretched of the Earth*.

"We weren't going anywhere without you. We were only talking."

"Get a grip," Joan said.

Actually it was true, but I guess neither of us believed a word the other one said anymore. Arthur dog-eared his page and looked back and forth between us. That was when the cop pulled up. He stopped in the road and put his flashers on, then he picked me out first.

"These your friends, Mr. McNamara?"

He was the same one who'd been at the bus stop. How did he know my name? What if somebody had called and told them everything? What if he was there about the phones? My knees went soft and I tried to cover it up by leaning back on the car next to Arthur.

"Yes, sir," I said. "We all live here on Jensen Road."

"When was the last time any of you were on Dr. Tukes's land?"

"Sorry, I don't know where that is."

"You do, and you know it. Hatchet Mary's, when were you there last?"

I opened my mouth to say something, but the cop ignored me. He looked at Arthur and Joan like they were the real reason he was there. Especially Joan. The way he looked at her made me feel like that dogfish again, like somebody had cut me open and lifted out my lungs.

"So, which one of you three is coming with me today?"

Nobody said anything. I thought about Patrick Jervis and Ray with his poison weed and about me and Joan having picnics at Hatchet Mary's before all that. I thought about that frozen carp and the moment when it must have moved its tail and broken free. The cop leaned one hand on Arthur's trunk, looking straight in Joan's eyes.

"Ms. Harris?"

Arthur's whole body went stiff, and he lowered his book slowly down. Things were flying between the three of them like switch codes through telephone lines. I could feel them sparking, but I couldn't translate. When a voice came over the cop radio it ripped the air like Joan's scalpel going through fish scales. The cop peeled his eyes off Joan.

The guy on the radio didn't use codes or numbers or cop language like on TV. The voice just said, "You're all gonna want to be there for this. They're bringing him in."

"Don't go too far," the cop said.

He got in his car and turned the siren and the lights on, then sped up around the curve and headed out toward 25A. Wherever he was going, it wasn't Highbone Station. When I looked over at Arthur, he was writing the cop's license plate number down on the flap of his book.

"Change of plan," he said. "I'm gonna take you two to Sag Harbor."

"You're gonna . . . why?" Joan said.

"I gotta see Shirley. Told her I'd talk her through Gramsci, and . . . you know."

Joan rolled her eyes. I tried to see what Arthur was thinking, but he looked away and opened the driver's side door.

"You two can find weird shit on the beach and cut it open, or whatever it is you're into these days. Go get your stuff."

The roads were wet with sun shining on them. Water sprayed up in rainbows from Arthur's wheels, and Joan sat in the middle of the front seat with the map.

"Go to the beach on the east."

"I'm going to Shirley's house. You two can go wherever you want."

She looked at me. "Let's go to the ocean side. There'll be stuff you don't get in Highbone."

The car felt small, and I wanted to open a window. Joan's voice got far away and I thought about the seats bursting into flames. I looked at the road and tried to breathe while I blocked out pieces of my life. I covered up Robbie's burning car and my mother's taillights, the skinny cop and his sticky eyes, Ray Velker's lonely body and the whole of Mr. Tomaszewski's existence.

Then it was just me watching Joan open the glistening guts of something with no consciousness. Me and Arthur and Joan, heading down a road to a beach.

joan

THE DAY THEY arrested Scottie Hall, Arthur took us to Sag Harbor. He went to Shirley's house and we went to Havens Beach. You could walk out around the point there, into more open water where all the life was different. The open ocean was like another planet compared to the beach in Highbone.

On the tide line there were loads of skate egg sacks. Daisy called them mermaid's purses, because he learned to talk from the kind of woman who nicknames her son Daisy. We found some green crab shells and a smelly bluefish, then I rolled up my jeans and went wading. I pulled out a horseshoe crab and Daisy shrieked like . . . Daisy.

"She's early. It's not even April."

"Okay. Joan, you are not going to fucking cut that open."

"Well, I did bring my scalpel." I waved the crab again and

nearly cut myself with the spike.

"Christ! Is it even legal, carrying that blade around? And aren't these things protected?"

"Relax. The scalpel's only three inches, and I'm not going to cut her open. She's alive."

"I can see that! Jesus, it has like four hundred legs."

"Or just ten." The crab was agitated and her legs were waving, but there were only ten. I held her out to Daisy and he backed up. "You should see the blood, though."

"No! I should not. Why am I friends with you?"

"It's blue, because it's made of copper instead of iron."

"Okay, that is kind of cool. Can you put it back now?"

I put her down on the beach so she could go somewhere private to lay her eggs. We went up into the dunes and lay down out of the wind. It was warm in that little hollow, and we took our jackets off. The sun was so blinding the sky didn't even look blue. We put our arms over our eyes and I pushed my wet feet down into the sand.

That day was the first time Officer Kemp had threatened me in front of other people. Did I have a ridiculous fantasy where Nick saved me? Not exactly, but I thought if I was with him other people would keep off me. Hormones, I guess. A lot of stuff that happens in your body isn't rational. It just thinks stuff without you. Not much difference between me and the horseshoe crab, really.

What should I do about Daisy? He just lay there next to me like everything was fine, like he wasn't living off boxed macaroni and cheese and washing his clothes in Palmolive liquid. Maybe I thought about Ray right then, too. Last spring we never really stopped thinking about him. Running away to the Woods Hole summer program was starting to seem like a really good idea.

"Daisy, would you be pissed if I went away for the summer?"

"Yes! Do you think blood conducts electricity? Copper blood would conduct more, I think. Iron isn't such a good conductor."

"And you think I'm the gross one? You are so the mad scientist in this friendship."

"Put us in a bag and shake us up, we'd be Dr. Frankenstein."

"Yeah, we could make creatures that are half squid, half human, half telephone. If we open your attic window we could definitely animate them during a lightning storm. What time is it? We told Arthur we'd meet him at two thirty."

"No idea. Are you still seeing Mr. Tomaszewski?"

"It's complicated, Daisy. I kind of don't know. Have you heard from Robbie?"

"I promised Arthur I wouldn't talk about it."

"Arthur again? Is it Arthur who got beat up with you in fifth grade? Is it Arthur who listens to you go on and on about the telephone network? Is it Arthur who does your biology homework? What the hell does Arthur know about anything? He thinks it's cool that my mother never comes home."

"Arthur helped me, and he's trying to help you. I didn't tell him about Mr. Tomaszewski. I'm keeping your secrets."

"Yes, that's the point. You keep mine and I'm supposed to keep yours. Not Arthur."

"He's trying to protect you."

"Yeah, Arthur's a superhero. I heard you already. You've been telling me since we were nine."

"Robbie's dead, Joan."

So, when I tell you me and Daisy lied to each other, when I tell you that silent chasm between us got too big to jump across, I'm not talking about little shit. I'm talking a hole full of dead bodies and sleazy policemen, naked biology teachers and burned-out cars. I'm talking sex and angel dust and death.

Robbie was dead and I couldn't deny it anymore. Ray Velker, too.

I guess while we were lying there on Havens Beach, they were interrogating Scottie Hall in a gray-painted room in mid-island somewhere. Tape machines rolling and toxic molecules of melted plastic seeping into the coffee from those flimsy cop-station cups. Later, most of what was said in that room wound up in newspapers and magazines. People who had never been to Hatchet Mary's knew how many feet it was from the road to the pond and who owned the land. All those details somehow landed in the space that had opened between me and Daisy, part of what we didn't say, part of why we couldn't really face each other anymore.

I should have hugged him or something, but the minute he said it I lost my stomach. I knew right away that it was me covering up the facts. I had the truth about Robbie all along, and I pretended it didn't mean anything. There was a good chance I saw him die.

Instead of saying that, I said, "So, were you gonna tell me at some point?"

I acted like Daisy was the one with the problem. I'm not proud of it, but it's true. So really, which one of us was the bigger liar?

"I'm telling you now," Daisy said, "even though Arthur said not to."

"You really need to decide whose friend you are, McNamara."

But he'd already decided. We'd both already decided. When Daisy needed rescuing, he went to Arthur, not me. When men started inviting themselves into my body, I didn't go anywhere. Well, I went to my mother. Same thing. If we'd been talking to each other, we would both have known the whole story about Robbie months earlier. We might have even figured things out about Ray.

We got back to the parking lot by the harbor at two o'clock. We ate fried clams and ice cream and sat on the hood of Arthur's car waiting while people stared at us. I looked over at Daisy's skinny little arms and his bewildered eyes and wanted to kill Robbie for dying on him.

"I'm sorry, Daisy. Seriously."

"You didn't like him."

"That's not true." But it was. "I just wished he was a better brother. I'm still sorry it happened."

Arthur came back at three o'clock, when all our cigarettes were gone and we were feeding our crumbs to the gulls. He bounced across the parking lot with that walk of his, his tam on, some book of Marxist theory hanging out of the pocket of his army jacket and a cigarette in his mouth. *Way to blend in,* I thought.

I got between him and the car door.

"I know everything, Arthur. You need to stop treating me like a baby."

"Okay, let's get in the car."

He didn't take the tam off, even on the highway. He thought Daisy's whole family were screw-ups, and he was right, but Arthur has his own way of looking for trouble, too. It's just that Arthur's trouble is always some kind of mission. He gets that from my mom, I guess.

We were on the Northern State Parkway when he started lecturing. The road had dried off, and we were driving into the setting sun. Arthur flipped his visor down and drove sixty miles an hour, straight into the glare.

He talked at us the whole way home, and then we went to Daisy's.

I had a plan. Kind of.

Me and Daisy stood around the McNamaras' kitchen drinking tea and eating crackers with Cheez Whiz. The boy needed someone to teach him to shop before he died of pernicious anemia.

"We have to tell the cops," I said, "and we're not bringing Arthur."

"Why? I mean, why do we have to tell them?"

That was when I explained everything. All of it. Even the cold and the dark in Fiddler's Cove parking lot, the way I felt sitting for hours on the floor of Robbie's car on Meadowlark Road. I told him the facts, and I dug up all the feelings, too. I guess I felt like I owed him.

Daisy washed off our plate and the knife, looking at himself in the window over the sink while his hands moved without him.

"You lied."

"I didn't lie. I just didn't tell you."

"You lied. You told me about Mr. Tomaszewski, but you didn't tell me this? How does that work, Joan?"

"You weren't safe. You don't EVER protect yourself from anything!" I guess I was yelling.

"I wasn't the one that needed protecting. Someone I love did."

"His car was gone. I thought he was alive. And I was afraid of what you'd do."

That wasn't the whole truth. The truth is, I didn't want him to know who Robbie really was. I didn't want him to have to live with that.

"I thought he'd come back, Daisy. I thought if you knew, you'd try to bail him out or something. He tried to get Andre to sell shit for him. He tried to make Teresa into a junkie! He didn't . . ."

"Didn't what?"

"I didn't know how to tell you, okay? And then other stuff started happening. Fast. You were living here alone and you didn't tell me."

"So it's my fault you watched my brother get killed and didn't say anything?"

"I don't know what I watched. I know we have to tell somebody."

"They'll take me away, Joan. Don't you get that?"

I didn't get it. It hadn't even occurred to me. Daisy was the one who watched my life from the attic window. He was the one who stayed scrawny and the same while the rest of the world got way too big and then rotted and bled and tried to terrify me. That was the first time I ever bothered to picture the world without Daisy in it, right there in the McNamaras' kitchen the night they arrested Scottie Hall.

"Joan?"

"Okay but look, this isn't about us. I mean it isn't about you. People died, Daisy. We have to say something. What if they find out later? Or what if we're the only ones who get the connection?"

"What connection?"

"Do the math, Daisy! Robbie was getting people to deal angel dust in school. Patrick was looking for him, and that was after Ray disappeared. Patrick and them knew where Ray was. This is all one thing."

"All one thing, how?"

"Ray was dealing for Robbie. You said so. Patrick too, right? Otherwise why did he keep asking about him? Then suddenly Ray's dead and Robbie tries to steal a stash off some smugglers. They owed somebody, Daisy! We might be the only ones who know why Ray died."

Daisy took a big breath and pulled his skinny arms up into his T-shirt sleeves. He looked at his feet and said, "I saw, Joan."

"Saw what?"

"That cop, this morning."

See? He couldn't even say it.

Half the stuff that was happening to me wasn't even speakable. How was I supposed to tell anyone about it without changing how they saw me? Without getting them killed? Last year the world took all its weird, fucked-up silence and shoved it down our throats. We were choking on it and nightmares were falling down on us out of nowhere and in the middle of all that we were supposed to decide whether to save each other or save ourselves.

"You're not coming in with me," Daisy said, "and you're not telling anyone about what you saw at Fiddler's Cove."

"What I saw at Fiddler's Cove is the whole point!"

"If you try, I'll go get Arthur. I'm gonna go in there and tell them it was my brother in that car in Queens. I'll tell them Ray and Robbie were dealing together. You're going to stay here and wait."

"Fuck you. I'll wait outside the station, but I'm coming."

I went out Daisy's back door and up the hill, but it took him a while to catch up. The reason for that is, he was calling Arthur. I didn't know it at the time. One last lie.

Once we got to the top where we could see the police station parking lot through the trees, we leaned over with our hands on our knees, panting. There was a moon throwing light down through the branches and I could smell the harbor in the breeze.

"I might not come back out," Daisy said.

"Yes, you will. Don't be ridiculous. You're just the grief-stricken relative."

"I'm the grief-stricken relative who's been listening to the cops from pay phones while his dad's in the big house on conspiracy fraud charges. They probably already have a file on me. What if they connect the dots?"

"So it's complicated. They're still not gonna arrest you. You're fifteen."

"I'm sixteen, Joan."

"Shit. Yeah."

We started down the hill, sliding in the leaves and holding on to the young trees to keep from falling.

"They could keep me in there. I'm just saying, if I take more than an hour don't wait for me. I'll meet you at home."

"Shhhh! We're almost there."

"Any of us could disappear any day," he whispered. "You know that, right?"

We sat and slid down the slope into the shadow between the parking lot lights. I could hear "Tangled Up in Blue" coming from the jukebox in Flannagan's and people slamming car doors down Main Street. One of the windows at the back of the cop shop was open, and Officer Kemp's car was parked under it.

Let me tell you about when you live in an incorporated village full of people who spend all day at Junior League meetings and art gallery openings, feeling protected by their own cute little police force. First of all, the cops are useless. They work in an incorporated village because they couldn't pass the physical for the county force. Second of all, they're arrogant. They don't even lock their car doors. One time in ninth grade, they picked up Patrick Jervis and put him in the back seat of a cop car. He was carrying half an ounce and they didn't even search him. He just stuffed it in the crack of the back seat and went back and got it out later that night. No lie.

When I looked at Officer Kemp's car I felt sick and then I felt rage. Daisy though, he opened the car door and looked in.

"What the hell are you doing?"

He took a big breath, then leaned down and ripped the wires out of the back of the radio.

"Hold these for me, will you?"

I just looked at him. "You vandalize police cars now? Who *are* you?"

"Put them in your pocket. Also, I'm hugging you. Deal with it."

And he did. Then he wove his way through the cars and disappeared around the corner of the building.

And I let him go. I smoked two cigarettes and walked around behind Flannagan's to look at the crates of empties and the broken benches rotting in the back lot. After a while I got worried. It might have been about half an hour, but I didn't have a watch.

I thought about all the things I wanted to say. That I should have told him about Robbie. That Nick didn't want to talk to me anymore. I wanted to tell him all about seeing my mother's theater, what she had to say for herself and what she wouldn't say. That I was done trying to figure people out. I wanted to explain why maybe I should go to Woods Hole, why I wanted to spend the summer thinking about nothing but fish.

Then I thought about him, in there standing under the strip lights, trying to tell half the truth and make it sound innocent.

Maybe it was easy. His brother was dead. All he had to do was reach inside himself and strip away whatever it was that had been keeping him from crying and pissing his pants and throwing himself against walls the whole year. Maybe there was another Daisy right under the surface. One he showed Arthur and even the cops, but not me. Because I hadn't even been looking.

I climbed up onto the hood of Officer Kemp's car and tried to reach the open window. I could get my hands on the sill, but I wasn't tall enough to see in. I stretched up and strained my ears for Daisy's voice. We couldn't be more than thirty feet from each other, with just the bricks between us. If only we'd thought to bring two paper cups and some string. I almost laughed. That night when he walked around the corner and into the station, I suddenly knew how much distance there was in the world.

"Hey!"

My lungs stopped moving and my vision blacked out for a minute.

"Nice and slow," Officer Kemp said.

I let go of the windowsill and put my hands in my pockets before I turned around. One pocket was full of wires, and in the other was my scalpel. My fingers closed around the scalpel and I leaned back against the wall.

"They said you were a good girl. I told them they don't make good girls in your kind of family."

When I was climbing down off the car I cut my hand on the scalpel. Bad.

"Just nature, isn't it?" Officer Kemp said.

"My friend is inside. I was worried." I said it like it might actually matter to him.

Officer Kemp took a step forward and I had to lean back against the car. He leaned into my space and smiled while my stomach started to burn and my lungs stopped working. My hand was bleeding inside my pocket, but I didn't let go of the scalpel.

Ever since I was about ten, when me and Daisy clubbed a sea bass so we could dissect it, I swore I'd never cut a living thing again. That night I changed my mind. There were two possibilities in front of me. Either one would ruin my life, why should I choose the one where I got hurt?

My pocket was filling up with blood. The jukebox in Flannagan's went quiet for a minute and then started playing Pat Benatar.

That was when Arthur came tearing down Main Street with the third possibility. He skidded past and his lights swept over the parking lot, throwing Officer Kemp's shadow onto me and then away again. In front of Davis Marine, Arthur slammed in the clutch and downshifted. He hit the brakes, the car spun around, and he zoomed back past us and down toward the harbor.

"Move." Officer Kemp shoved me out of the way and jumped into his car.

I pulled the scalpel out of my pocket and looked at it. Waves of nausea and loose electricity came up through my nerves. I stood there shaking with drops of blood scattering down off my hand, while Arthur disappeared around the corner onto Baywater Avenue with Officer Kemp wailing along behind him.

I sat right down on the asphalt and then stood up again and went into the woods. Once I was in the shadows I turned and looked down into the parking lot lights. Nothing moved and all the sound was far away. I was all alone for what seemed like the first time in years.

For months, people had been trying to rescue me. Nick was trying to make sure I didn't waste my mind. My mother and father were trying to stop Daisy from breaking my heart, and Arthur was trying to keep us both from getting arrested or dead. Right then, he was probably in the process of getting himself killed. The only brother me and Daisy would have left between us would be Andre. Now I knew none of that rescuing was necessary. That night I realized I was perfectly capable of rescuing myself, whatever it took. I still don't want to live with that fact, but I have to.

Up on that hill was the stone ruin where we'd nearly run into Patrick and Matt the summer before. Before we knew who they really were. Before we knew what our world was really like. The ruin is half a dome with a cross-shaped window in it and stone blocks scattered all around. When I was little, I thought it was so old pilgrims must have built it. I guess really it was some nineteenth-century church that we all wrapped in spooky myths and stories. People said a witches' coven met there, that Kieran Johnson and his friends held satanic rituals there. The second one was probably true, but that night it was empty. I stopped next to the cross-shaped piece of moon on the leaves and lit a cigarette.

The world stayed quiet for a while and so did I. There were no sounds from Main Street, no owls or bats or night things crawling through the leaves. No streetlights or fireflies up that high to interrupt the moonlight. I heard the drops of my blood hitting the leaves and thought about Robbie, bleeding on my front porch the summer before. What was the difference between us?

I knew right then that I'd go to Woods Hole, and even UC San Diego if I could get in. If there was a world where I didn't have to choose between those two possibilities, between getting destroyed or destroying someone else, I needed to get to it. I couldn't let anyone stop me, not even Daisy.

After a while I went over the hill and out above the McNamaras' house. I was at the top of Daisy's yard when I heard the siren. I ran through the bushes, thinking the cops still had Daisy and maybe they had Arthur now, too. There were blackberry vines everywhere and I was already scratched all up my arms. The cut on my hand was still bleeding, too. I was wiping blood on my jeans when the wailing and the spinning red light came up through the trees. I could see the new leaves on the maples, looking a weird sickly yellow, and the shadows of light poles striping across the side of Daisy's house.

From the driveway I heard the crash. I swear it was so big I felt it, too. A shock went through the ground under me and I thought the retaining wall would go crashing down onto Jensen Road. The trees and the earth and the houses all tumbling down onto the mud and smashing through the deck behind the Narragansett.

None of that happened. Everything just went quiet. I could smell gasoline and the red light was still spinning in the trees, but all of a sudden there was no sound in the world.

* * *

When I got inside, Daisy wasn't back yet. I was afraid to turn on any lights, so I felt my way to the sink and ran the cold water. The water running into the pain was all I needed to tell where I was cut open. The blood soaked into a paper towel while I got a hurricane candle from the junk drawer in the kitchen and lit it on the hearth. I sat on the bricks with my back to the chimney wall and wondered who was dead this time. All I could do was stay there, hanging over that unknown absence until the next thing happened. I'd just have to wait until whoever was still alive came through Daisy's door to tell me what the next crushing emptiness was going to be.

I don't know how long it was before the phone rang. I almost didn't answer it. After ten rings I picked it up and held it to my ear without saying anything.

"You there, Daisy?" It took me a minute to make sense of the fact that Arthur's voice was coming out of Daisy's phone.

"It's Joan. Where are you? Where's Daisy? There was a car crash. There's cops down on the road. Somebody died again, Arthur."

"Nothing you need to worry about, Joan."

"Why did you do that? You could have died!" I guess I was crying a little.

"It's okay. Dad and Gramps think you're with me. I'm going out to campus. I need to stay away for a while. When you go home, tell them I dropped you off and went to Shirley's."

"Daisy's not back, Arthur. What if they arrested him?"

"After tonight, this needs to stop, Joan."

"What? I didn't do anything!" I felt the pain in my hand and thought about the scalpel. I thought about the other reality, the one where Arthur didn't zoom down Main Street with the third possibility.

"Wake up, Joan! You live in America. The fact that you didn't do anything doesn't matter. You know I like little McNamara, but his family are gangsters. You can't get mixed up with that."

"I can't help it, Arthur. I just am mixed up in it."

"Just this one time, pretend that me being your older brother means you listen to me. Find new friends. Or at least more friends."

"You know what? I don't need you or anybody to tell me what to do. I can take care of myself. You have no idea."

"Okay, take care of yourself. Just stop taking care of Daisy. Stay there till he gets back; say what you need to say."

"He's been living alone for months, Arthur. He didn't even tell me."

"Yeah, I think we need to do something about that, too."

"Where's he gonna go?"

"Somewhere people are responsible. You're kids."

"You can't report him, Arthur! I won't let you. They'll put him in some care home where people lock him in basements and never feed him."

Daisy came through the door right then and started waving his arms at me and mouthing words. I said goodbye and hung up.

"Turn on the light if you want me to read your lips, Daisy."

He hit the lightswitch and then almost fell over. I hadn't realized the front of me was covered in blood.

"Fuck! What happened to you? Sit down!"

"It's okay. I cut my hand on the scalpel."

"Jesus! You lost like a quart of blood, Joan. Let me make you some tea with sugar."

"Where have you been?"

"Did you look down there?" He pointed out to Jensen Road.

"What the hell took you so long, Daisy? I thought they arrested you."

"Joan! Did you look down there? A cop crashed into the wall! There's an ambulance and two county cars down there."

Long story short, that's how they found Officer Kemp. With his front end crushed and burning and his radio ruined. He wasn't dead, but it's been four months now and he still hasn't said anything about Arthur. Maybe he can't remember. Maybe we'll never know. He doesn't work in Highbone anymore.

"Why was Arthur calling? Where is he?"

"He said he's going out to campus. He said he has to stay away for a while. What the hell?"

"You should have seen him, Joan."

"Seen who?"

"Arthur! When I came out onto the steps of the cop shop, he was grinding up Main Street, going about fifty in second gear. I could smell his engine burning from where I was standing. Then he fishtailed around and took off. That cop went wailing after him."

"I did see. I was in the parking lot, remember? What happened to you?"

"They made me wait forever. Then they wrote some stuff down and told me to go home. They seemed like they didn't even care, Joan."

"Do you think they knew already?"

"The county cops have Scottie Hall. I heard them talking about it. They think Scottie killed Ray. They never said Ray's name, but I could tell."

"Scottie? Why?"

"I don't know. Maybe everything you said was right, but they didn't seem interested in Robbie at all. Even if you were right, is that really why? Is there a why for stuff like that?"

There isn't, is there? I mean, you can look through people's stuff and follow them around. You can put together the story of what happened and what happened next. But can you say why someone ended someone else?

The only solid fact that came out of that night was that I could be that person. When it was him or me, I could have put my scalpel into Officer Kemp. Whatever I would have felt later, sick or crazy or glad or just dead inside, wouldn't matter. Arthur saved me, but I could have saved myself. That was the last thing I didn't tell Daisy.

joan

WE WERE UP in the attic the next day when Daisy's aunt Regina pulled into the driveway. In theory, we were studying for the English final.

"You don't have to dissect it, Joan. It's a metaphor. You just kind of feel it."

"You sound like my mother."

"Well, I bet she passed the English final. Just write what you think in the essay part and make sure it has an introduction and a conclusion."

"You know what Mr. Driscoll said? 'Tell 'em what you're gonna say, say it, then tell 'em what you just said.' What is the point of that?"

"Who cares what the point is? We need the English credit. Just go through the motions."

"How can you say that right now? We can't just push everything under the surface. There isn't even any surface anymore. It's all just ripped open."

"Kind of like Coriolanus, then. Why don't you say that in the essay? Bet you'd get an A."

"If I tell you something, don't laugh, okay?"

"Hmmm . . ." Daisy was reading through his notes, color-coding things with his two-ended blue-and-red pen.

"When we were in junior high, I used to wish we could be like everybody else. I used to just want to be into the whole cheerleading and football and making out behind the lacrosse building shit."

"That's not true, Joan. You had a choice and you chose to be friends with me. You obviously weren't that committed to normal."

"I thought we could transform when we got to high school. Don't you ever want to just pretend we live in some dog-food-commercial world where all the lawns are perfect and no one ever dies?"

"No. I have a different utopia."

"What's it like?"

"There are no lawns, and no lawn mowers. This house is just the attic on stilts. No kitchen or living rooms or bedrooms. Our boat is big enough to live in. We spend all summer in the middle of the Sound. There are cuttlefish in North American waters, just so you can look at one up close. Electricity is free. You never die."

He didn't mean "you" like the generic you, like people. He

meant me, personally. The car pulled up while I was still trying to figure out what to say to that. I looked down and there was a lady with piled-up red hair and a pantsuit covered in big flowers. Ten years earlier, she would have been in a magazine. Seemed like she'd been hiding somewhere without magazines and television for about a decade.

"Who the hell is that?"

Daisy looked down and said, "Shit."

The lady put her handbag over one arm and shut the car door. When she opened the McNamaras' front door without knocking, I realized she must be family.

"Hellooooooo . . . ? Anthony Daisy McNamara! Come and give me a kiss."

"Who the hell is that?"

"It Regina. My mother's sister. Why is she here?"

I knew right away. It was Arthur's fault. I found out later it was Gramps who called her, but Arthur is the one who told on us.

NO SPARK
AND NO WAVE

daisy

IT WAS PRETTY much impossible to make phone trips while Aunt Regina was in the house. But I needed to know one more thing. Not for me, for Arthur. I needed to know what had happened to Officer Kemp.

I had to cut school and physically tap into the phone line behind the cop shop. Eighteen months ago, I would have found something like that too terrifying to even contemplate. Right then it was the least I could do. The telephone line went up through the woods so at least no one could see me. I took Aunt Regina's tuna-fish sandwiches in a brown bag, said goodbye at the front door, and then went straight around back and through the woods.

I found out you could be in those woods all day and never run into anyone. I sat on a branch, leaning against the trunk of a maple tree, and read *Stranger in a Strange Land* while I listened to the Highbone Station phone.

Arthur stayed away for three days, with his girlfriend Shirley, I guess. As soon as I saw his car, I told Aunt Regina that Mr. Jensen had invited me over for dinner. She loved Joan's Gramps because he was the one who ratted us out, him and Arthur. Yeah, I know. They meant well.

I went around to Arthur's window and chucked a pebble. The tide was in, and there were only a couple feet of ground for me to stand on. He stuck his head out and held up a finger. After a couple minutes he came out the back door with his tam on, pulling on his flak jacket.

"I get that you're mad at me, Daisy." He handed me a Marlboro and sat down on the bottom step.

"You know what? I'm not."

"I have to watch out for my sister. I like you, though. You're a good kid in a messed-up situation is all."

"I know. I wanted to tell you, Officer Kemp is gonna be okay."

"You don't know that, Little McNamara."

"No, I do. I listened in to their phone."

"Whose phone? What are you messed up in now?"

"The cops, at the station. It doesn't matter. Don't worry. He doesn't remember why he was speeding on Jensen Road. He said he was chasing somebody, but he doesn't remember who."

Arthur's hand was shaking and his eyes were full of water. I realized he'd spent the last week thinking he'd killed somebody. And it was my fault. If not for me, Joan wouldn't have even been there. Joan insisted on following me that night, and I called

Arthur so he'd know. I was trying to keep my promise.

"Seriously, Arthur. The cop's fine, but they don't believe him. They think he was on the take and didn't call in on purpose."

"So, he's not okay, then."

"Why should he be okay, Arthur?"

I didn't say anything more than that, but we were both thinking about Joan.

"I'm sorry about your brother." Arthur put a hand on my shoulder. "For real."

"Yeah, everybody's sorry, but nobody's surprised, right?"

The whole story was coming out, or as much of it as we'd ever know. Aunt Regina was doing loads of paperwork and answering questions in the living room about twice a day. It turned out they did want to know about Robbie. He just wasn't a priority the day they arrested Scottie because he was already dead. Robbie had been trying to be some kind of kingpin, but in his usual messed-up way. He'd been fronting stuff to Scottie, and Scottie had some kids dealing for him at school.

"Daisy, I think it's time someone talked to you straight." Arthur put his cigarette out on the bottom of his shoe and laid the butt on the step next to him.

"I know. I get it. It just took me a while."

"If Joan was your sister, would you want her around all that?"

"She isn't my sister, but that doesn't mean I don't give a shit. I hardly have any memories without her in them. If I'm away from her for too long I feel dizzy and can't figure stuff out."

"Well, you're gonna have to. You both are."

Which is why I went with Aunt Regina and didn't fight. I knew Arthur was right. I'd been a coward my whole life. Letting go of Joan was like crumpling up my whole earth and sky and throwing it all away, but it was my one chance to get it right. To do something for her. Being in a world without her was like learning to breathe water, except I hadn't been practicing as long as Joan, and I didn't want to breathe anymore anyway.

It was Arthur who found a boat to take us out into the Sound with Robbie's ashes. Joan came and Aunt Regina invited Mr. Jensen. The fisherman, Danny Pavlich, said something respectful and then stayed by the engine house to give us our space. The four of us sat on the benches, me across from Joan and her with her head turned away from me, squinting at Connecticut.

It was the Saturday before finals. All our studying was as done as it could be. I don't know about Joan, but my head couldn't hold anything anyway. My whole body was so empty I could hear the whoosh of blood my veins, echoing against my bones. I kept having to ask people to repeat things because I couldn't seem to listen anymore.

When Regina said some words about Robbie, they just tangled up into a ball of sound and fell past me into the water. Then it was my turn. I said something about the way it felt when he put his arm around me, how he was taller and bigger than me, how I could still hear his voice, but it was only in my head, about the day he tried to clean out the empty gutters. I honestly don't remember. People laughed little sad laughs and smiled at me, so it must have been okay.

The wind was blowing onshore, so Aunt Regina didn't open the urn until Danny had taken us out around Head of the Harbor and pointed the boat back toward home. Then she shook it and Robbie's dust came out, ground so fine we must have breathed some in. Most of it went out over the prow, looking like the smoke from a beach fire. A few pieces of Robbie were heavy enough to plink down into the water and sink.

Joan didn't say much and Mr. Jensen didn't either. But I was glad they were there, and I knew they didn't have to be.

When we got back to the floating dock, Danny helped Aunt Regina out first. I got out last. The boat was light and it pitched under me.

"I liked your brother."

Danny said it so quietly no one heard him but me. I looked up into his eyes and they weren't pitying or sad. He was just seeing me, and telling the truth. I memorized that look because I wanted to practice it for the rest of my life.

"I knew him," Danny said. "Before, you know. He was smart, and he liked Doris Bromley. She was in my grade and she never even noticed him." Danny smiled. "He followed her around like a puppy."

"No way." I laughed and it felt good.

"Way," Danny coiled the rope and dropped it on the dock.

Aunt Regina was standing at the end of Main Street, looking

down Jensen Road. I caught the hopeful look before she could hide it. She was waiting, too. We were both expecting my mother to show up any second. She'd bring her lips and her nails and her trench coat, her sparkling copper Chevy and her chiffon scarf. She'd bring everything but her eyes. We'd look into her black glasses and she'd hold her hands out to me, whispering, "best boy." It just seemed impossible, no matter where she was, that she wouldn't feel the moment when we were tossing away the oxidized reduction of her own son.

joan

IT WAS GOOD to have a bunch of stuff that was too intense to tell Nick. The way he slid his eyes away from mine hollowed me out. All that secret information gave me leverage, something to fill me up when he wouldn't look at me. When classes were over and finals started, he invited me to his house again. He even drove me. I felt at least five years older than last time.

"Well, how have things been?" He was opening a carton of shrimp fried rice and two beers we got on the way.

"Things have been intense, actually."

"I know. It's been a terrible year. You don't think stuff like that can happen in your own town, do you? It always seems to happen somewhere else." He was talking about Ray Velker. "But you're okay, and you're going to Woods Hole. I'm really glad."

He sounded like I was a job he'd done right.

"Yeah, maybe."

"Not maybe, Joan. It's done. You need to go."

"Stop talking with your mouth full."

Nick knew how to use chopsticks and I wondered why. I knew too, because Andre had made us all learn, but I used one of Nick's three forks anyway.

"Daisy's aunt is living with him. It sucks because we can't really hang out at his house anymore."

"Daisy? Who's she?"

"Not she; Daisy is my best friend."

"Oh, Anthony. Apparently, he's some kind of engineering genius, according to Mark Nadel. So, you're both geniuses. If you stay friends, you two could win a Nobel Prize one day. You might change the world."

What world? Ours? Or the whole big one everybody's in together? How big does your world have to be before you're allowed to talk about changing it?

The first time, I didn't even think about getting pregnant. There was so much else to worry about. This time I did, but I didn't know how to say anything. I guess that's part of your best friend being a guy, part of what wasn't there between me and Daisy. If Daisy were a girl, we would have run into a bathroom stall, out of breath and whispering about doing it standing up or pulling out early or how Kathy Outhewaite managed to make the quarterback wear a condom. Because even I heard that, from behind the television in the commons. When it came down to it, I said nothing and then lay there being terrified. I stayed terrified for a month.

Nick still had the same three shirts hanging from his coat hook. I looked around at the room, trying to decipher all the presences and absences. I was trying to calculate what had happened in there since January. All right, yeah, whether other girls had been there and what it meant that I was there again.

There were some jeans over the back of the desk chair and the abalone-shell ashtray was clean. There were clean dishes in the drain board, too. Did he do all that?

"I do like you, Joan." It was almost like an answer.

"I don't want to leave Highbone."

"I mean, I'm not an asshole. I like you."

"Woods Hole is really far away."

"But you need to go. You're gonna have a whole life and it's gonna be great. You can do anything."

"That's bullshit." It just came out before I could stop it.

"No, it isn't. You can believe me. I'm older than you."

I wanted to tell him everything, so he would know I wasn't little or quaint or remotely pointless. But they weren't my secrets. I wanted to show him the scar on my hand and tell him I wasn't helpless. I didn't say any of it.

I spent the next month worrying, checking my underwear all the time and imagining I had cramps. Teresa went to Planned Parenthood with me and they put me on the pill. Then I had a splitting headache every single day so I stopped taking them.

Anyway, by that point it didn't matter anymore. I was preparing for nothing because that was pretty much the last time I saw Nick Tomaszewski alone. I didn't get a phone call. No rides home, no invitations, and no sex.

After we scattered Robbie's ashes, I spent two whole days studying for the biology final and didn't call Daisy the whole time. I guess I wanted a good grade to tell them about at the summer program. And Aunt Regina was keeping him pretty close. I was already picturing all the ways I was going to be alone up at Woods Hole. On the beach without Daisy, in bed without Nick, sitting at a breakfast table surrounded by white people. I hadn't told Daisy I was going yet.

It was after finals were over that Andre put his head in my bedroom door and said, "Phone." I had to think for a minute to remember what that meant.

"Joan?" Daisy's voice was buried underneath a lot of hissing.

"Where are you? You sound weird."

"I'm in a phone booth. I need to tell you something."

"A phone booth where? Siberia?"

"Never mind. I . . . um . . . I'm not gonna see you for a while. I left something under the bench."

There were other people, talking on the line.

"I can hardly hear you. Are you okay?"

"Kind of. I'm in Queens."

"You went to Queens for a phone booth to call across the street? You are such a moron."

"No. Joan, I'm staying here for a while. With Regina. Just look in the bench, okay?"

That wasn't how it was supposed to go. I was supposed to leave Daisy, and he was supposed to hang around messing with the phones and mooning out the attic window until I came back and we did eleventh grade.

"I'm going to Woods Hole," I said.

"I know. I'm glad. I have to hang up now, but I left you something cool. Go look."

"Daisy!"

"What?"

"I—don't do anything stupid, okay?"

He had put the stuff inside a Drum tobacco tin then in a ziplock bag, and taped the whole thing under our bench.

There was a battery with a wire and a little red lightbulb attached to it, and a note. The note said, *Call this number Saturday nights at 7:40,* then there was a 718 number. He'd written, *DO IT FROM A PHONE BOOTH* and underlined it twice. On the back of the note it said, *It's an earring. Put the battery in your shirt pocket.*

I went in my room and tried on the earring. The little bulb had a curved wire that went through my ear, and when I clipped the contacts onto the battery, the light blinked. Andre wanted to borrow it right away.

Eugene was back. I ran into him one night at sunset, at the edge of the harbor. I was on my way to the pay phones behind Narragansett.

"You're taller," he said. Then he paused and said, "And prettier."

He smiled and I could tell he didn't mean anything by it. It was like something Gramps would say. I just stood in front of him for a while, breathing that air without menace or meaning.

"Thanks for the scalpel."

"No problem," he said. "Figured you might need it."

When I dialed the number Daisy left me, my dime came back and I got a recording that said "This number is out of service," but I knew Daisy enough to try it again at the right time.

My mother tried to help me pack for Woods Hole. She went through my closets and bought me more ridiculous underwear.

"Lace isn't gonna fix me, you know. I'm kind of beyond that, Mom."

I was sitting on my bed, watching her go around in circles messing up my stuff.

"You're beyond nothing, Joan Harris. And nothing is beyond you."

"Yeah, yeah. Anybody ever tell you people it's bad to put that kind of pressure on a kid? What if I want to just be a nobody?"

"You'll fail at that." She laughed and kept folding stuff backward.

"I still think you're selfish, you know."

"That's because I am," she said. "Well observed. Just be sure you remember to be selfish, too."

I didn't call the number again until I got back from Woods Hole five weeks later. When Daisy answered I realized he must have tried that number every Saturday at seven-forty the whole time I was gone. I called from a phone booth in South Highbone and said, "Daisy?" over the recorded lady's voice. He answered me and we talked over her, going "This number is out of service. This number is out of service," the whole time.

"I'm back," I said.

"How was it?"

"Daisy, this is weird. I can't hear you."

"How WAS it?"

"Good. I might go back next year. What did you do all summer?"

"Beach, mainly."

We couldn't string our responses together between the recorded lady's voice. We ended up exchanging a bunch of conversational sentences that were too short to fit anything into them.

Finally I said, "I'm coming in there, Daisy."

"This number is out of service. This number is out of service."

"That's probably a bad idea."

"Shut up."

daisy

THE ONLY THING left for me to tell is how I learned to breathe again. How I stopped drowning in distance and absence and memories of violence.

If I'd never met Kevin on the train that day in October, I might still be shut in my room, suffocating on my own thoughts. First he came when Anne was visiting him and then he drove over from Bay Ridge alone. He brought a sketchbook just like Andre's and said he wanted to draw my picture.

"I've never seen anyone who looked like you," Kevin said. "I mean, not in person."

I wasn't sure what he meant, but I figured it wasn't a compliment. I sat still for as long as I could but his strange concentration made it hard for me to breathe.

"This beach is so big," I said. "The water goes on forever."

The size of it made me feel weightless and exposed. Like everything was about to turn inside out and swallow me. There was just the blood rushing in my ears and my own ribs trying to suffocate me.

"Can I move?"

Kevin looked up.

"Yeah, sorry."

The wind made me think of that day in Greenport. Of my mother's voice, thinned out through the wires.

"You could talk, you know. I mean while I draw."

"About what?"

"About whatever comes into your head. I'm like a psychoanalyst, but free."

And I did. I talked about all of it. I told this story, from beginning to end. By the end of it, I could breathe.

"You're amazing to draw. You should come up to Hunter."

"Hunter College?"

"It's hard to find models for the summer classes. And it's always hard to find guys. My teacher would be so happy. You'll get ten bucks an hour, and guys get to keep their underwear on."

"Wait. You mean model naked?"

"It's not weird. They're all artists. No one even thinks of you as a person. They're too busy trying to get your proportions right."

He went nuts over the picture Andre took of me in the boat

and asked if he could take it away to show the drawing teacher.

"Hunter is the one with the big computing department, right?" I asked him.

Why could I tell Kevin everything, when I couldn't tell Joan? Because he wasn't her. There was nothing at stake, no one left to lose. When Kevin found me, I thought I was as empty as the beach we were sitting on.

I wasn't, though. Joan was still there. I told you I should have trusted her.

I took the job at Hunter on the condition that Kevin would show me the computer department while I was there. We lied and told his drawing teacher I was eighteen. When you take your clothes off, it's only weird for the first thirty seconds. Everyone is so serious, it starts to feel boring right away. There's lots of time to think, though. And to practice breathing through those moments when the world closes in, when Robbie's body comes back to me, all confused in my mind with Ray's.

I got on a kind of little stage and they put a heater on me, even though it's August. Everyone stood behind their easels with big pads of newsprint paper, concentrating like I was a piece of furniture. First you have to do a bunch of poses that only last ten seconds. Gestures, the teacher called them.

"Do whatever you feel like," he said.

I sat like I was in the attic window, with my head turned toward the Harrises' house. I stood like I was leaning against the retaining wall at the bus stop, even though there was nothing but air at my back. I could hear the slide of pencils and the scratch of charcoal. Images of me were appearing all around the room, hidden from me behind the easels. I sat on the edge of the little stage and stretched my legs out like I was talking to the quiet lady on the floating dock at low tide. I lay down like I was floating on water, and reached my arms out and up, closed my eyes and imagined Joan's hands in mine.

"That's great," the teacher said. "Terrific."

I stood up and wiped my eyes. Then I had to sit still for fifteen minutes at a time. My leg fell asleep for so long it stopped stinging even. I built a whole circuit board in my head. When it was time to stand up, the leg was useless and I almost fell over.

People wait until you're dressed before they talk to you. Mostly, they just smile and say thank you on their way out. A few stopped to ask my name and say they hoped I'd come back. Kevin came over and put a hand on my arm. He smiled into my eyes and asked if I was okay.

"Take me to your computer," I said.

joan

TONIGHT, WHEN I left Daisy at his Aunt Regina's house, I took a picture from the corner, even though it was dark and all I could see was the light glowing in the upstairs window. I have Andre's old Instamatic in my backpack. He's too cool for it now. He saved up and bought a twin-lens reflex that looks like something a newspaper reporter would have had in the thirties.

I don't even know if my picture will come out. Maybe I'll take it to Pathmark and spend a week waiting for an envelope full of nothing.

It doesn't matter though, because I can see it in my head, marked out by the four yellow corners in the viewfinder. Sodium light shining onto the crossroads, angles so perfect you could use them as a T square. The light from Daisy's window, red and blue because he brought the lamp we got in the abandoned house with him to Queens. No map in there, though. No LEDs and hardly any wires. No creepy voice when you come in and hit the light switch. No trees in between me and his window.

Identical houses stretching down those streets in all four directions, all surrounded by nineteen kinds of darkness. I wanted a picture of the world that has Daisy in it now. The power lines are buried. There will never be spitting wires writhing around Rockaway.

When I got there this afternoon and knocked on the door, Aunt Regina opened it looking freaked out. Everyone in their neighborhood is white. She recovered quick, though.

I had the *Newsday* in my backpack with a dry cell battery. Is that paper one of those things people will save? When we're all old, will people have that article describing Ray Velker's death in their scrapbooks? Anyway, I felt like Daisy should have it. Those were my gifts, the only things I could think of: electricity and someone else's death.

"Joan!" Aunt Regina said. "What a journey you must have had."

"Yeah, it was pretty boring. How are you Ms. Carillo?"

"Fine, sweetie. Fine. Daisy will be so happy. Daisy!"

When I saw him at the top of the stairs, he looked three feet taller.

"Come up."

I went past him into his room and then we just stood there, not knowing what to do. It was stifling up there, even with the window open and the sea breeze coming through.

"We can't smoke in here. Shit, sorry. Sit down."

I sat on the bed and he sat on the floor. He was taller, I swear.

"I brought the paper about the trial."

"How was Massachusetts? . . . What trial?"

"I told you on the phone; it was fine. Scottie Hall. Daisy, we walked right past Ray, the day we went to look at the frozen carp. We must have."

"Trust me, I thought about it already. Somebody said they kept him alive for fourteen hours. Jesus Christ, Joan. How the hell did we inhabit the same world as those people?"

So here's the thing about Ray. There was some beef about the angel dust. Robbie gave it to Scottie and Scottie fronted some to Ray. Ray never paid. Guys started hassling Robbie for the money and Robbie started hassling Scottie. So that was why Scottie and them started in on Ray. Then they got really wasted and thought they could offer Ray's pain up to their Prince of Darkness or something. They were into that shit. They cut him a lot without killing him. They took his eyes out with a spoon. They hung him up for a while and, I don't know, chanted weird stuff or something.

They didn't find all that out from Ray's body. I was right; it was mostly bones and a pair of jeans by the time somebody told the cops where it was. We know the story of what they did to him because one of the kids rolled over on Scottie and the other guy. Every bitter detail was in that paper.

Daisy rested the paper down on his knees. "I don't need this in my head," he said.

"Crap, Daisy. I'm sorry."

"How can we put one foot in front of the other, Joan? How are we supposed to think there's an endgame? How are we supposed to manufacture happiness out of this?"

"Facts, I think. You have to just focus on facts."

"These are the facts!" He waved the paper at me.

"No, those are some of the facts. There's other ones. You and me and the laws of gravity and the orbits of the planets and the insides of cuttlefish."

"They had cuttlefish at Woods Hole?"

"Yeah, live ones. In the tanks. I saw one make ink."

"Do you think you're gonna stop calling me?"

"Nah. It's free."

"Not for long. We should probably just pay, actually. I think I got you in enough trouble, and most of the phone fun is over. People are getting busted all over the place."

"What are you gonna do if you can't play with phones? Your brain will atrophy, man."

"I'm saving up for a computer kit. Aunt Regina gives me an actual allowance."

We both laughed. A few months ago Daisy was pawning the stereo so he could buy Cheez Whiz; now he's saving up his allowance to take in to Radio Shack. We could smell stuffed shells baking in the kitchen. Daisy will be okay. Ms. Carillo will actually take care of him and that will drive him nuts, but he'll stay alive until college, which is a definite plus.

We went to the beach so we could smoke. There's a boardwalk

that stretches for miles, and no trees. And real waves, as big as the ones on Cape Cod. First we just rolled up our jeans and buried our feet in the sand.

"Teresa's moving to South Highbone, Daisy. Her parents rented a house."

"That's cool. I like her. The archangel Teresa."

"She always says how beautiful you are. That's the word she uses. Beautiful."

"Yeah, what she means is weird looking. She'll love your documentaries."

"Not everybody at Woods Hole was white, Daisy."

"Oh."

That was it. I guess he didn't know what else to say.

"Listen. It mattered. There was this girl Junie whose parents moved here from Colombia, and a guy named Trevor from Maryland. We sat together in the mornings and all the white kids walked straight past us to sit somewhere else."

"You and Teresa will have to make other friends at school. Girls, I guess."

"So will you." I poked him and gave him a side-eye. Does Daisy even like girls that way? I don't know.

"Seriously, though," Daisy said. "I can come out there sometimes, too."

"The train takes about five million years."

I could feel him breaking. It was like when there's a crack in the ice on the harbor. At first you don't know which direction it's in. You just feel the dread inside you, and then you hear the splintering, louder and louder, coming toward you.

"We could meet in Manhattan?" he said. "By the glass jellyfish."

"Not Manhattan; the aquarium. Actual living jellyfish and it's a deal."

"Yes! We should have thought of that the first time. I didn't think about anything, Joan. I'm sorry."

"Come on. We're going in the water."

"Wearing what?"

"Whatever's under those jeans. Strip, boy."

"Here?"

"What, you do it in front of strangers at Hunter College but not in front of your best friend?"

The sun was setting and there was hardly anyone there. Anyway, I wasn't the one that had to live there, what did I care? I just knew I had to get him in the water. I felt like it would put him back together somehow. So we both stripped down to our underwear. I was wearing a girlie bra my mother bought me.

"Kids taught me how to bodysurf in Cape Cod. You don't try to swim through the breakers. You wait for a wave, then dive under it and come up the other side."

It was cold. We went into the foam and I took Daisy's hand. He didn't shrink back or look away. He was some new kind of Daisy already. We looked into each other's eyes and then into the water.

"Ready." He said it like a statement, not a question.

daisy

I USED TO lie in the attic window, watching the Harrises' house all day and all night. All the rooms in our house would be dark and quiet underneath me, the lights showing the distance in the darkness outside. No one looking up from the road would ever suspect a watcher in that little circle of window. That's how I ended up seeing things I didn't want to see and didn't know how to talk about.

We lived our childhoods in a bowl full of weather that swirled seasons over us while we climbed the edges and grew to match our own gangly limbs. The tension before a summer thunderstorm, the hurricane that tore the world up, the ice underneath us grinding while we ran from a moving crack toward the snow under the trees. We ran around and through the whole thing, getting taller and more ourselves the whole time. Growing to fit the shapes that were already cut out for us and not even knowing it.

Joan told me the names of things, and we took them apart so we could look at the insides and figure out how they worked. Animate and inanimate, radios and piss clams, we wanted to know all of it. When we were nine, we took apart my mother's vacuum and fixed the automatic cord retractor. By the time I started on the lighting in my house, Joan was busy diving all the time. After the sea bass we were too freaked out to kill anything bigger than a clam. We'd put live fish on the mud or in the shallows and watch for a while before we rowed out over the deep and chucked them back in.

We lived under leaves that were first neon and then velvet and later flaming and falling, but I don't remember the branches empty until we sat in them smoking for the first time. At first it was always summer. Our legs were always bare and covered in scrapes and our pockets were full of stones and weathered glass. The scrapes healed into ghostly streaks and then there were more because we never stopped climbing into places we weren't supposed to. We fell out of trees and slid over sharp rocks. We pulled ourselves up on the old floating dock, and the barnacles cut us open. Our blood spiraled down into the water like red smoke.

Did you know that sharks can still smell blood in one part per billion? Or maybe it's one part per million. I can't remember which. I'd have to ask Joan.

joan

WHEN I WAS at Woods Hole, I went to some tide pools on a rocky beach. The waves there made a sound exactly like the hurricane smashing against Daisy's attic window. I lost my breath and had to sit down right there while the memory blotted out the starfish and the anemones. I could feel the heavy air and the pounding over our heads. If I shut my eyes I could hear Daisy, breathing underneath the sound of the waves. For a minute, it was like I could reach through all the time and distance between us, back to our childhood, back to our picture-book world.

If a little kid drew a harbor, it would be a perfect semicircle and always full of water the color of the blue crayon in a box of twelve. There would be boats with perfect white triangles for sails. But our harbor was long and skinny, with twisted fingers branching off into the trees and water that was a different color every day. We lived at the shallow end—no, that is not a metaphor—and down there the harbor was nothing but mud half the time. When the tide was out, we could see the memory of the waves in the shape of little ripples in the mud.

Every twelve hours, the water went out and took a whole world with it, all the bluefish and dogfish and eels. The clams buried themselves and the crabs did their paranoid scuttling, not happy about being in the open. When the water came back, it brought that whole invisible world back with it. That is how we grew up, exposed and then invisible, invisible and then exposed. Every twelve hours, twice a day. I guess living next to that makes you a certain kind of person.

&

WE WAITED ON the beach in Rockaway until we saw our wave coming. It rose up and curled over while we breathed out. Like we were dying or being born, our whole lives flashed between us in those five seconds. The harbor and the dogfish and the curve on Jensen Road. Eugene and the quiet lady and the falling leaves. Climbing in and out of windows and talking to each other through a piece of string. Everything turning around from summer into winter and back again, over and over while we changed and got taller and everyone around us disappeared one by one.

Time unraveled and we imagined Ray on top of the Ferris wheel at the firemen's fair. We imagined him running away with the carnival, driving a painted truck through the tall grass prairie, setting up a Tilt-A-Whirl by a beach where the sun set over the water instead of rising. None of those pictures involved frozen mud or wet leaves or scalpels or spoons. None of them involved Highbone at all. We knew Ray had escaped, but not what it cost to get out. We could almost see our way out from the harbor into the darkness and the blinding light. Then the wave rose over us and we felt the weight of the crashing world.

What was there to balance it? There was us. There was each other and the weight of the love it took to let go. There was trust.

We held each other's hands and closed our eyes so we could see Jensen Road curving past us and around the end of the harbor to Carter's Bay. We saw the two phone booths on the shoulder and the cars parked outside the Narragansett at dinnertime, the summer people on the deck eating lobster and making deals. The street light falling from the wall across the gravel parking lot and glistening out onto the harbor. We saw our boat in the stars and the security lights shining into the dead water of the swimming pools.

We pushed all of that out of our lungs until we were empty. Then we breathed in all the light left on that beach and all the length of Long Island between us.

And we dove.

historical note

THE IMAGINARY ACTION of this novel takes place between the end of summer 1979 and the end of summer 1980. If you've read *Little Wrecks*, this book begins three months after that one ends, in the same town.

Daisy's interactions with the telephone system are based on things done by hundreds of intelligent and slightly naughty young people from the 1950s to the early 1980s. The phone network was essentially a giant computer the size of America that didn't know it was a computer. These were the first hackers. Young people built blue boxes, mapped the system, and exploited its weaknesses. Two of those people were Steve Wozniak and Steve Jobs. To the best of my knowledge, all of Daisy's hacks are realistic and were still possible on Long Island up until the early 1980s. If you want to know more about the practice called phone phreaking, or just want a great story, read Phil Lapsley's book *Exploding the Phone.*

SUNY Old Westbury, where Arthur attends college, was one of several universities set up around the world in the late 1960s that put the principles of the civil rights movement and the feminist movement into practice. These institutions were founded on the belief that education could and should be a force for social change. Professors Charshee McIntyre and Samuel von Winbush, who Arthur mentions, are real-life activists and academics who inspired students at Westbury in the late 1970s and early 1980s. You can see video interviews and photographs from the college's early years at www.oldwestburyoralhistory.org.

For teenagers in the American suburbs, everything in popular music changed during the year in which *How We Learned to Lie* takes place. Though some of the music mentioned here was produced in the mid-1970s, the message didn't really make it to us until the second half of 1979. The difference between the *Little Wrecks* playlist and this one partly reflects that revolution in music that felt so exciting at the time. You can hear what Joan and Daisy's world sounds like on the *How We Learned to Lie* playlist at www.open.spotify.com/user/meredithseven.

acknowledgments

I AM GRATEFUL to my daughter, Maia, for patiently listening to me talk about imaginary people all the time. To MaryLee, first for taking her little sister (me) to the Old Westbury campus with her in the early 1980s and second for sharing her memories and her yearbooks with me while I was writing this novel. Phil Lapsley not only shared his wonderful book, but also generously sent me unpublished research and pointed me toward the work of others. All mistakes and misapprehensions are my own.

Thanks to my friend Danny Reilly who spent an afternoon at Saltram House helping me build this world, and carefully read the full manuscript later. Shamira Meghani, Bryony Randall, Angela Sherlock, and Helen Thomas are amazing friends who listen to me, read my books, and always support me. The rest of my family—Harold, Joan, Jinny, JoAnne, Tom, Steve, Mark, Peggy,

Lisa, Hannah, Matthew, Jason, Shane, and Clayton—read, spread the word, and show up to my readings en masse. I love them all so much.

Thanks to Danielle Zigner and Allison Hellegers for making these books happen. Working with my editor at Harper, Emilia Rhodes, is one of the great privileges of my writing life. I have learned so much from her. Thanks to Jennifer Klonsky, Alice Jerman, Stephanie Hoover, and everyone on the Harper team for taking a risk on me and supporting my books. To Anah Spiers and Maya Myers for their careful and generous readings of this novel, and for picking me up on things. This book is better because of them. To our designers for making covers that get put in the middle of pictures just because they're so beautiful.

Finally, thanks to all the readers, librarians, bookstore staff, and bloggers, known and unknown, who read and shared their thoughts on *Little Wrecks*.